# GIRL EDUCATION
## Challenges, Strategies and Initiatives

# GIRL EDUCATION
## Challenges, Strategies and Initiatives

**Vol. II**

**Deepa Awasthi**

KALPAZ

ISBN: 978-93-5128-177-1

Price: ₹ 880

First Published, 2016

*Published by*

Kalpaz Publications
C-30, Satyawati Nagar,
Delhi – 110052
E-mail: kalpaz@hotmail.com
Ph.: 9212142040

*Printed at:* G. Print Process, Delhi

**Cataloging in Publication Data—DK**
Courtesy: D.K. Agencies (P) Ltd. <docinfo@dkagencies.com>

**Awasthi, Deepa, author.**
Girl education : challenges, strategies and initiatives. Vol-II / Deepa Awasthi.
pages cm
Includes bibliographical references.
ISBN 9789351281771

1. Girls—Education—India. 2. Girls—Education—Government policy—India. I. Title.

LC2322.A93 2016 DDC 370.82 23

# Contents

## *Section – D*

## Girl Education Promotion – Initiatives and Schemes

Acknowledgements

It is my immense pleasure to acknowledge all the learned authors from all over the country who have contributed their valuable articles and research papers written by them with utmost pain, efforts and investment of time. Without their sincere and devoted thinking about the serious issue of "Girl Education" it would have been almost impossible to come up with the desired result. I am also obliged to the distinguished panel of reviewers who invested their precious time and hard work in evaluating the contributions from various authors and further guiding them to make their writings focused, clear and appropriate for this book series. I am also thankful to all my friends, teachers from University of Lucknow and family members who encouraged me from time to time to remain adhered to the mission of publishing a series of book on one of the most discussed and utmost important issue - "Girl Education." Last but not the least, I thank God and all who helped me directly or indirectly at every step and provided me emotional support to compile this edited book series.

—**Deepa Awasthi**
(Editor)

# Authors' Introduction

1. **Deepa Awasthi (Editor*)***
   ***Ph.D - Education, University of Lucknow, UP.***

   (Editor of book series and volume and contributor of article: Coping with Gender Inequality in Education at Secondary and Higher Secondary Level in Context to Rastriya Madhyamic Siksha Abhiyan**)**

Dr Deepa Awasthi, Editor of this edited book series, is a freelance researcher. She is Doctorate in Education and Post Graduate in Education, Sociology and Economics. She has qualified UGC – JRF in Education and Sociology as well and has equal command on both the subjects. She has participated and presented her research papers in more than 45 national and international seminars and conferences. She has also edited a book entitled "*Eve Teasing: A Social Epidemic*." Her publication work also involves five chapters in edited books, three research papers in the form of conference and seminar proceedings and 17 research papers and articles in various journals of national and international repute. Her keen interest areas include the sociological issues related to women and various issues related to the field of Education.

2. **Parvin Sultana**
   ***Assistant Professor, Department of Political Science, Goalpara College, Assam.***

   (Contributor of Article: Education of Muslim Girls: Issues and Challenges)

Parvin Sultana is Assistant Professor in the Department of Political Science in Goalpara College in Assam. She is masters in Political Science from JNU. She did her M. Phil. on North Eastern Council and its role in the development of the region of Northeast. She has been awarded JRF in Political Science. She has presented papers in three national and one international seminars. She writes editorials for newspapers regularly. Around eight research papers and articles written by her have been published in journals and as chapters in edited books. She also writes for online websites on socio-political issues. Her interest areas include gender studies, political economy, Northeast and Muslim politics in India.

**3. Leena**

***M. Phil. Research Scholar, National University of Educational Planning and Administration, New Delhi*** (Contributor of article: Issues and Challenges associated with Girls Education in India: A Critical Analysis)

Leena is an M.Phil Research Scholar at National University of Educational Planning and Administration, New Delhi. She is post - graduate in Human Development and Family Studies. Her fanatical interest involves issues on women and child development. She has attended and presented her research papers and articles in many national and international seminars, workshops and conferences. She has published book reviews, abstracts and articles in different journals. She has actively worked as a volunteer in many social activities.

**4. Raksha Amanna**

***Post Graduate, Department of Social Work, School of Social Work Roshani Nilaya, Mangalore, Karnataka***

(Contributor of article: Hurdles in Girl's Education in India)

Raksha Amanna is a Post Graduate student in the Department of Social Work, School of Social Work Roshani Nilaya, Mangalore. She is specialised in Human Resource Management. She holds a Bachelor of Social Work degree from Mangalore University. She is a passionate artist and a sports person.

**5. Rajendra Baikady**

***Research Scholar, Department of Social Work, School of Social and Behavioural Sciences, Central University of Karnataka, Karnataka***

(Co-contributor of article: Hurdles in Girl's Education in India)

Rajendra Baikady worked as a lecturer in the Department of Social Work/Head of Department of Rural Development at Dr A.V. Baliga Institute of Social Sciences and Rural Management, Udupi. He holds a Masters Degree in Medical and Psychiatric Social Work, Masters Degree in Clinical Psychology, Masters Degree in Mental Health and a Post Graduate Diploma in Counselling and Guidance. a post graduate Diploma in Child Rights and Law, and Criminology and Forensic Science. He was involved in teaching about; Basic Sociological concepts, Social Problems and Services, Social Work with Groups, Social work with communities, Community organisation and Development, Social Welfare Administration, Instrumentation for Social Justice, Persons in difficult circumstances, Communication for Social Work, Non-formal Education, Mental Health Education, and Rural Development. Mr Baikady had also worked as a student welfare officer and Psychiatric counsellor at Dr A.V. Baliga Group of Institutions, Udupi. So far he has published three books in Academics and allied disciplines. Mr Baikady is a member of IASSW, ISPSW, INAAR, IACAM, IACAPAP and NAPSW. Currently Mr Baikady is pursuing his Doctor of Philosophy in Social Work on the topic "Comparing Social Work education in a parliamentary democracy and a communist regime – a study of India and China" at Department of Social Work, School of Social and Behavioural Sciences, Central University of Karnataka.

## 6. Upasna Chhabra

***Assistant Professor SJS International College of Education, Panipat, Haryana***

(Contributor of article: Need and Importance of Women Education)

Author is pursuing Doctorate in Education from Kurukshetra University. At present she is working as Assistant Professor at SJS International College of Education, Dikadla Complex Samalkha, Dist. Panipat. She is Post Graduate in Education (M.Ed.) and Political Science. She is NET in Education. She has attended number of refresher courses, workshops and symposiums. She has presented papers in various national and international seminars. She has published more than five articles and research papers in various journals.

7. **Manjeet Kumari**

***Assistant Professor in Nalwa College of Education, Ujha, Panipat, Haryana***

(Co-contributor of article: Need and Importance of Women Education)

Manjeet Kumari is pursuing Doctorate in Education from Punjab University, Chandigarh. At present she is working as an Assistant Professor in Nalwa College of Education, Ujha, Panipat. She is post graduate in Education (M.Ed.) and Hindi. She has attended several workshops, symposiums. She has presented papers in various national seminars. She has published more than four research papers in various journals.

8. **Fayaz Ahmad Kotay**

***Guest Faculty, Department of History, University of Kashmir, Srinagar, Jammu & Kashmir***

(Contributor of article: Educating Girls, State Paradox and Social Response: A Study of Girls' Education in Princely Kashmir, 1900-1947)

Fayaz Ahmad Kotay is currently working as Guest Faculty in the Department of History, University of Kashmir, Srinagar. He has recently submitted his doctorate thesis to the Department of History, Babasaheb Bhimrao Ambedkar University, Lucknow. The author is mainly interested in history of colonial education in India which covers the issues of educational policies and programmes of colonial government in India. The author often writes on gender and education issues. Moreover author's thrust area is princely India with special reference to Kashmir. He has presented several research papers in national and international seminars and conferences. He has published four research articles in reputed journals.

9. **Fatima Rizvi**

***Research scholar, Department of Social Work, University of Lucknow, UP***

(Contributor of article: Parental attitude towards Muslim girl's education)

Author is a research scholar in Department of Social Work, University of Lucknow, at present pursuing her Ph.D focussing on Impacts of women's work on their families. She is Postgraduate in Social Work and has been awarded UGC - JRF. She has participated and presented her papers in more than 12 national and international seminar and conferences. Her interest areas for research are gender issues, police education and work life balance. Her publication includes two research papers in national/international journals and one chapter in edited book.

### 10. Manvi Manisha Tigga

***Assistant Professor, Jamshedpur Women's College, Jharkhand***

(Contributor of article: Role of Print and Electronic Media in Promoting Girl Education in India)

Author is a voracious reader, a passionate writer and a born story teller. She has completed her Masters in English from the University of Delhi and Masters in Education from Kolhan University. She has worked for 'SRISHTI' publication as a translator for some time, before taking teaching as a profession. Currently, she is working as Assistant Professor in Jamshedpur Women's College. In her copious free time, she enjoys listening to music, reading, writing and putting displaced things in order.

### 11. Md. Nurul Momen

***Associate Professor, Department of Public Administration, University of Rajshahi, Bangladesh***

(Contributor of article: Implication of Capability Approach on the Girls Education - Theory and Reality)

Md. Nurul Momen is Associate Professor at the Department of Public Administration, University of Rajshahi, Bangladesh. He is M. Phil from the University of Bergen (Norway) and Ph.D from Sant Anna School of Advanced Studies (Italy). His main areas of interest include Public Policy and Law, Governance, and Administrative Reforms.

**12. Mst. Marzina Begum**

***Associate Professor, Department of Public Administration, University of Rajshahi, Bangladesh***

(Co-contributor of article: Implication of Capability Approach on the Girls Education: Theory and Reality)

Mst. Marzina Begum is Associate Professor at the Department of Public Administration, University of Rajshahi, Bangladesh. She has a BSS and MSS from the University of Rajshahi (Bangladesh) and Ph.D from the University of Pavia (Italy). Her main areas of interest include Environment Policy and Governance, and Women Development.

**13. Akhilesh Patel**

***Assistant Professor, Sadanand Degree College, Chheolaha, Fatehpur, UP***

(Contributor of article: Promotion of Girls Education in India: Central Government Initiatives)

Akhilesh Patel is presently working as Assistant Professor at Sadanand Degree College, Chheolaha, Fatehpur (UP). He is M.Sc, M.Ed, DPA, NET-JRF and Ph.D in Education from University of Lucknow. He has attended more than 20 seminars and five workshops. He has published 15 research papers in reputed national and international journals. His specialisation is in History of Education, Administration and Management in Education, Methods of Science and Biology Teaching.

**14. Ramesh Chandra Singh**

***Assistant Professor, Hemwati Nandan Bahuguna Garhwal University, Srinagar, UK***

(Contributor of article: Strategies for Girls Education)

Author is pursuing Ph.D. from HNBGU, Srinagar, with five years teaching experience. At present he is working as Assistant Professor at Hemwati Nandan Bahuguna Garhwal University, Srinagar. He is post graduate in Mathematics. His keen interest areas include Measurement and Evaluation and Teacher Education. He has attended and presented papers in various national and international seminar and conferences. He has published more than 15 articles and research papers in various journals.

### 15. Pankaj Pant

***Research Scholar, Department of Education, Hemwati Nandan Bahuguna Garhwal University, Srinagar, UK***

(Co-contributor of article: Strategies for Girls Education)

Pankaj Pant is a research scholar in Department of Education, Hemwati Nandan Bahuguna Garhwal University, Srinagar pursuing his Ph.D. on topic "Academic Achievement of Visually Impaired Children as Related to their Emotional Maturity and Intelligence." He is NET in Education. His keen interest area includes philosophy and special education. His publication includes seven research papers in national and international journals. He has contributed two chapters in edited book. He has attended 14 national/internationals seminars and four workshops.

### 16. Siddartha Lohani

***Research Scholar, Department of Education, Hemwati Nandan Bahuguna Garhwal University, Srinagar, UK***

(Co-contributor of article: Strategies for Girls Education)

Siddharth Lohani is a research scholar in Department of Education, Hemwati Nandan Bahuguna Garhwal University, Srinagar pursuing his Ph.D. on topic "Professionalism among teacher educators in relation to their personality traits and family environment." He is NET JRF in Education. His keen interest area includes educational planning and leadership. His publication includes six research papers in national and international journals. He has contributed two chapters in edited book. He has attended six national/internationals seminars and four workshops.

### 17. Swadhin Shaktiprasad

***Jr. Grade IIS officer, Press Information Bureau, Govt of India.***

(Contributor of article: Government Schemes and Initiatives to Promote Girl Education in India)

Swadhin Shaktiprasad is a professional and researcher in the field of communication and media from Cuttack, Odisha. Currently he is working as a Jr Grade IIS officer in Press Information Bureau, Govt of India. His interest areas are Development Communication, Communication and Culture and Women and Media. His research papers have been published in International journals like IJIMS and American Research Thoughts etc. By passion he is a poet, story teller, theatre artist and an instrumentalist. He is a published writer. His creative publications can be found in many journals, magazines and anthologies. At present he is editing a Science non-fiction. he also has to his credit an international anthology of poetry titled 'Timeless Love', and translation of a famous spiritual book from Odia to English. One of his latest poems has been selected for a prestigious International poetry collection called 'Heavenly Hymns'.

### 18. Natasha Kuldeep

***Research Scholar, Department of Economics, University of Rajasthan, Rajasthan***

(Contributor of article: An Investigation of Gender Inequality and Government Policy Initiatives towards Girl's Education in Rajasthan)

Natasha Kuldeep is a Research Scholar in Department of Economics, University of Rajasthan, Rajasthan, Jaipur. She is pursuing Ph.D. on topic 'Allocation of Public Finance for Rural Sector in India - a State level Study'. She has qualified NET (two times), NET JRF and SET in Economics. Her keen interest area includes Public Finance for Rural Sector in India. She has published three research papers in national and international journals and contributed one chapter in edited book. She has attended one National, two Internationals Conferences and one National workshop.

### 19. Amitaraj Gargey

***Principal, Daleep Walase Arts, Science and Commerce College, Pune, Maharashtra***

(Contributor of article: What Can The International Community do to Ratchet Up Progress On Girls' Education)

Amitaraj Gargey is Doctorate in English, with 18 years teaching experience. At present she is working as Principal at Daleep Walase Arts, Science and Commerce College, Pune. She has earned an M Phil. in Education, a Diploma in German, and a Certificate in Computer Course. Her keen interest involves socio-political development of India and issues related to women and children. She has attended and presented papers in various national and international seminars and conferences and published more than 18 articles and research papers in various journals.

**20. Shashi Bala Kashyap**

***Assistant Professor, SCD Govt. College, Ludhiana, Punjab***

(Co-contributor of article: What Can The International Community Do To Ratchet Up Progress On Girls' Education)

Shashi Bala Kashyap is pursuing Doctorate in Botany, with 14 years teaching experience. At present she is working as Assistant Professor at SCD Govt. College, Ludhiana. She is M. Ed. in Education. She has attended and presented papers in various national and international seminars and conferences and published more than 25 articles and research papers in various journals.

**21. Amit Kashyap**

***Research Associate, Himachal Pradesh University, Shimla, Himachal Pradesh***

(Co-contributor of article: What Can The International Community Do To Ratchet Up Progress On Girls` Education)

Amit Kashyap is Doctorate in Law, with 10 years teaching experience. At present he is working as Research Associate at Himachal Pradesh University, Shimla. He is post graduate Diploma in Journalism and Computers and has also undergone certificate courses in Human Rights and Computers. He is NET JRF in Law. He has attended and presented papers in various national and international seminars and conferences and published more than 40 articles and research papers in various journals.

## 22. Sujata Sinha

***Assistant Professor, Department of Humanities and Applied Science, School of Management Sciences, Lucknow, UP***

(Contributor of article: Importance of Vocational Training for Girls)

Author is an Assistant Professor in the Department of Humanities and Applied Science at School of Management Sciences, Lucknow where she teaches professional communication. She has 14 years of experience as a soft skills trainer and Faculty of Business Communication. She has worked with some prestigious colleges in Lucknow including ICFAI, National College, IISE and Jaipuria Institute. The author is Masters in Modern History and has added Masters and M. Phil in English. Her area of interest is training and placement. In her long career with various institutes at higher education she has published several papers based on her observations of the rapidly changing higher education scenario in India. One of her papers has been previously also included in a book called '*Education and Society*' in 2009.

## 23. Rajni Bala

***Research Scholar, Department of Teacher Education, Central University of Himachal Pradesh***

(Contributor of article: Various Government Schemes to Promote Girl Education in India)

Rajni Bala is a Research Scholar in Department of Teacher Education, Central University of Himachal Pradesh, Dharamshala. She is pursuing her Ph.D. on topic "Anxiety, Attitude and Self-Efficacy in Computer Use: a Study of Teacher Educators and Prospective Teachers." She is twice NET Qualified and M.Sc. in Mathematics. Her five research papers have been published in reputed National/International Journals. She has presented eight research papers in National/International Seminar and Conferences.

# Introduction

Girl Education has been one of the most discussed topics among all global issues during last two centuries because civilised society believes that education is the most powerful instrument to bridge the gender gap existing in our society. Although a lot of efforts have been made in this field but the desired results could not be achieved due to several reasons, out of which social negligence and lack of political will power are the most prominent. A number of scholars have made this issue as part of their study and recommended a number of suggestions, but unfortunately as we move to the implementation part we find unsatisfactory efforts at ground level. When it comes to gender related issues pertaining to education, employment or any other field - Indian society and culture has proved as the most devastating museum where centuries old evil traditions are still preserved as part of everyday life. This book also mentions all the possible strategies which have been put forth till now and about those who can play a decisive role in improving status of girl education in near future if the suggestions are incorporated into our system with true spirit and intention. Mission of resolving the challenges in girl education in India has still many miles to cover.

This edited book series entitled **"Girl Education in India – Still Miles to Cover"** has been divided in to three volumes including six sections, containing 52 chapters. The sections are as follows:

A. Understanding Status of Girl Education in India.

**B. Gender Issues in Education.**

C. Girl Education: Challenges and Strategies.

D. Girl Education Promotion: Initiatives and Schemes.

E. Girl Education: Gateway to Women Empowerment.

F. Linking Girl Education with National Development.

This present volume (Volume II) comprises sections C and D of the book series titled ***Girl Education: Challenges and Strategies*** and ***Girl Education Promotion: Initiatives and Schemes***, these cover vast areas of related fields in total 16 chapters written by eminent scholars.

Section C of this book series ***Girl Education: Challenges and Strategies*** included in this volume deals with the current issues and challenges associated with girl education and the strategies to deal with them. It includes eight chapters.

Section D of this book series ***Girl Education Promotion: Initiatives and Schemes*** includes nine chapters that detail the various schemes and initiatives implemented by central government and state governments to deal with the lacunas and loopholes that exist in our education system and are acting as hindrances to girls' education.

Next part of the introduction details about the summary of every chapter one by one in ascending order with the purpose of providing glimpses and idea of content included in every chapter of this volume.

First chapter of the book titled **"Coping with Gender Inequality in Education at Secondary and Higher Secondary Level in Context to Rastriya Madhyamik Shiksha Abhiyan"** authored by ***Deepa Awasthi*** illuminates the role of Secondary and Higher Secondary education in the life of an individual. She mainly focuses on the types and reasons for existing gender inequities at Secondary and Higher Secondary level in country. She has very well explained the aims, goals, objectives and role of Rastriya Madhyamik Siksha Abhiyan in dealing with the challenges of gender disparity in the field of education step by step. Chapter also studies the intervention programmes and activities taken up by RMSA and their impact to encounter the challenge of gender disparity in education at aforesaid level and factors responsible for the problem. According to the author, since its launch in 2009-10, RMSA has proved to be a mile stone among all the various schemes launched by the Indian government since independence for improving the status of girl education in the country.

In the second chapter of the book titled **"Education of Muslim Girls: Issues and Challenges"** author ***Parvin Sultana*** with the help of reports of various government agencies and committees has focused on the problems associated with the education of Muslim girls in India. According to her the main reasons responsible for backwardness of Muslim community and especially Muslim girls, are: a comparatively low representation of Muslims in parliament and state assemblies, communal violence, low employment ratio in government jobs and low socio-economic status. She also finds that dropout ratio of Muslim girls is much higher than the girls of any other community. She also suggests that lack of good quality girls' schools, scarcity of trained female teachers, conservative thinking of parents, financial constrains and gender discrimination are few important inhibitors which are to be checked on priority basis so as to bring the desired changes in status of girl education. According to her vocational and professional development and computer education can really make the difference and help the Muslim women to stand on their feet firmly with confidence.

In the third chapter of the book **"Issues and Challenges Associated with Girls' Education in India: a Critical Analysis"** author ***Leena*** focuses on the importance of education in life of a women because it not only affects the women's/girl's life but also affects her family life and country's development. She has pointed out at the different types of barriers to girls' education in the context of social, cultural, political and economical factors through literature review. Author also emphasises on the importance of regional differences in attitude of parents towards providing quality education to girls. She also finds that cost of education, attitude and practices in society, scarcity of schools, gender bias in curriculum and social exclusion are the main issues related with the state of girl education in the country. According to her, measures that can improve the status of girl education in India, include: awareness programmes for parents, child care programme for siblings, feeding programme at schools, gender sensitive teaching, training programme for teachers and school management, flexible school timings, flexible approach to school calendar, incentives and scholarship for girl students, employing more and more female teachers especially in rural areas, active involvement of communities and parents, and special programmes for enrolment of socially marginalised communities.

Next chapter of the book titled **"Hurdles in Girl Education in India"** authored by ***Raksha Amanna*** and ***Rajendra Baikady*** focuses on the existing disparity in the status of girl education in rural and urban India. They have tried to point out at the factors responsible for low literacy level of women in the country. They have also explained the various constitutional provisions and schemes to promote girl education. Authors have stressed on the importance of proper funding, effective coordination and control over all viable resources. They have emphasised on the need to legislate on the issue of sending female child compulsorily to school.

In the fifth chapter of the book titled **"Need and Importance of Education"** author ***Upasna Chabra*** and ***Manjeet Kumari*** have explained the meaning of education what should be expected from it. They have also emphasised on the role of education in personality development of individuals. Authors have beautifully explained the historical background of girl education in ancient, medieval and modern India. They have pointed out the need and importance of girl education in social context and linked it with the development of society and country.

In the next chapter titled "**Educating Girls, State Paradox and Social Response: a Study of Girls' Education in Princely Kashmir, 1900-1947"**, author ***Fayaz Ahmad Kotay*** focuses on the status of girl education in princely state of Kashmir from 1900 to 1947, before independence. He argues that in initial years autocratic kings ignored the issue of gender disparity in education. Due to various reasons girls hardly got chance to attend school. In later years, status of girl education was improved to some extent but usually limited only to reading literary, moral and religious books, some arithmetic, needle work and preparing them for their future roles as wives and mothers. He feels that Christian missionaries and women welfare trust are the entities that brought revolution in the field of girl education in Kashmir state inspite of strong opposition from the close minded society. He feels that religious prejudices of Kashmiri people were one of the reasons for the vulnerable condition of girls and that disparity in investment on girl education by government was another main hurdle in the path of girl education. he observes some improvement in later years when government started allocating more funds on girl education.

In the seventh chapter titled **"Parental Attitude towards Muslim Girls Education"**, author ***Fatima Rizvi*** has collected responses from a sample group of parents of girl students through 12 open ended questions and applied qualitative approach to find out the challenges which inhibits the girls from completing their education. According to her, the main barriers to girl education are: security, safety, perception about gender roles and gender stereotyping, mindset about division of labour, early marriages, poverty, increasing cost of education, customary and religious practices, non-Islamic environment at schools, fear of moral corruption, scarcity of well trained teachers - especially female teachers and dissatisfaction among whole community against government policies. Author also accepts that due to small sample size findings cannot be generalised but results can be used to illuminate the relevant issues and fields that affect the promotion of girl education in Muslim community. She also suggests that transforming the attitude of parents is most desirable among all the initiatives.

Eighth chapter of the book titled **"Role of Print and Electronic Media in Promoting Girl Education in India"** authored by ***Manvi Manisha Tigga*** focuses on the important role of print and electronic media in promoting and uplifting status of girl education in India. According to author, deep access to internet in last few years has affected the day to day life of common man especially use of social media through smart phones have brought revolution in field of media communication. She also discusses about the utilisation of internet by the government to disseminate information related to promotion of girl education. Author suggests that government can make better use of Radio and Television to educate people in rural areas especially girls and women who are bound within the four walls of their homes.

Ninth chapter of the book titled **"Implication of Capability Approach on the Girls Education: Theory and Reality"** authored by ***Md. Nurul Momen*** and ***Mst. Marzina Begum*** focuses on the capability approach to girl education evolved by world known economist Amartya Sen and developed by Martha Nussbuan and other political philosophers. Chapter presents theoretical analysis of capability approach and its impact on girl education in context to Bangladesh. According to them when poverty combines with gender inequity, it results in acute malfunctioning of human resource development. They find clear cut link between enrolment of girls in school and reduction in poverty. They have quoted and advocated Amartya Sen for the principles of five freedoms – political freedom, economic facilities, social opportunities, transparency guarantees and perspective security as important for an individual's life. Authors stress that gender inequality still exist in Bangladesh especially in rural areas. They have also argued that religious sentiments also have adverse impact on girl education and address the need of changing mindset of political leadership in context of making serious efforts for improving status of girl education in the country.

In the next chapter of the book **"Promotion of Girls Education in India: Central Government Initiatives"**, author ***Akhilesh Patel*** compares the male to female literacy rate in India since independence for proving that due to the intervention programmes and initiatives taken by central and state government from time to time, the difference between male and female literacy rate has decreased to a considerable extent. He has very well explained the various schemes and programmes started by central government and various state governments for promoting school education (primary to higher secondary level) and higher education. He feels that in recent years steps taken by central government have bridged the gender gap in education to some extent. He further suggests that these initiatives can be more effective by removing the shortcoming and lacunas that manifest their planning and implementation process. He feels that rural areas require much more attention to promote higher education among girls who usually drop out after completing secondary or higher secondary level education.

Eleventh chapter of the book **"Strategies for Girls Education"** authored by ***Ramesh Chandra Singh, Pankaj Pant,*** and ***Siddartha Lohani*** emphasises that Right to Education Act - 2009 passed by Indian parliament reflects the commitment of Government of India towards gender disparity free education in country. The role of government in this regard is based on three principles – creating, enabling and promoting gender equality through legislation and policy reforms; investment in resources; and introducing special measures for empowering the girls to encounter economic crisis. Authors further feel that Constitutional Amendment Act, 1976 was a mile stone in educational reforms through which central government has shared the burden with the state government to educate its citizens. They further support the NGO's playing a decisive role in uplifting the status of girl education in India.

***Swadhin Shaktiprasad*** in twelfth chapter entitled **"Government Schemes and Initiatives to Promote Girl Education in India"** details about the various schemes and initiatives started by government from time to time to promote girl education in the country. He also stresses on the gender sensitisation of teachers and community members as per the norms of National Curriculum Framework (NCF), 2005. He also emphasises on the need of preparing gender sensitive learning material. Author also recommends the development of special models of alternative schools for girls which can be helpful in tackling problems related to girl education especially dealing with the challenge of higher ratio of dropouts from primary to secondary level. He has also made some important suggestions which might help the policy-makers in devising a strategy to bring girls to school.

***Natasha Kuldeep*** in next chapter **"An Investigation of Gender Inequality and Government Policy Initiatives towards Girl's Education in Rajasthan"** focuses on the present status of girl education in context to gender inequality. Through literature review, the chapter studies regarding participation of girls in schooling. Chapter also highlights the effect of gender discrimination and social attitude towards girl education. Author expresses that educating a girl child is much more advantageous as compared to educating boys due to its multitude of positive effects for the development of community and country.

With the help of survey author establishes that gender and economic level of family play an important role in girl education. Author has also mentioned a number of barriers and their solutions as initiated by Government of India and Government of Rajasthan to improve status of girl education the region. Chapter also stresses that due to a number of serious efforts by government and non-government agencies, it has been possible to bring desirable positive changes in girl education in the recent 10 years.

In the next chapter titled **"What the International Community can do to Ratchet up the Progress on Girls' Education"**, authors ***Amitaraj Gargey, Shashi Bala Kashyap and Amit Kashyap*** have focused on the issues which act as inhibitors in girl education. They suggest that per capita income of families have direct impact on status of girl education. According to them communities in which girls have better access to education has better maternal health, reduced infant mortality rates, better nutrition for their children and increased protection against HIV/AIDS etc. They also emphasise on the need of skill development by providing vocational training to girls. Authors suggest that first step towards promoting education among girls is to remove obstacles ensuring easy access to education for them. Chapter also explains that measures such as providing resources to poorest, providing healthy environment, presenting positive role models, opening more schools, appointing more number of quality teachers, investment on their training, use of computers, and effective broadband infrastructure can really make the difference to pave the way forward for girl education.

Fifteenth chapter of the book titled **"Importance of Vocational Training in Girls Education"** author ***Sujata Sinha*** expresses that disparity in field of education still exists in country just like any other field. According to her human capital theory and economic growth theories find a positive correlation between level of education and economic status of country. She suggests that education must be provided to girls to promote entrepreneurship and technological advancement among them. Comparing the work force participation of women in India with other developing countries and workers sex ratio in country, she feels the need of improvement. She further addresses that during the eleventh five year plan, Government of India launched 'National Skill Development Mission' to encounter jobless growth of Indian economy. She has explained the role of vocational training programmes like JSS, STEP, DGET etc in developing and assisting the youth in skill development and getting employment especially in rural areas.

Sixteenth chapter of the book **"Various Government Schemes to Promote Girl Education in India"** authored by ***Rajni Bala*** has emphasised on the historical background of the steps initiated by government from time to time to promote girl education. Author has pointed out the schemes and initiatives being carried out by government in modern days. Chapter successfully explains the various initiatives of the Government of India pertaining to girl education, which include: Mahila Samakhya Programme (1989), Sarva Siksha Abhiyan (2000-2001), Sanskar Bharti Mission for female literacy (2002), National programme for education of girls at elementary level (2003), Kasturba Gandhi Balika Vidyalaya (2004), National scheme of incentives to girls for secondary education (2008), Indira Gandhi scholarship for single girl child for pursuing higher and technical education, Schemes of constructing and running of girls hostel for students of secondary and higher secondary school, Post Doctoral fellowship for women etc.

# (SECTION – C)

# GIRL EDUCATION-CHALLENGES AND STRATEGIES

# Chapter – 1

# Coping with Gender Inequality in Education at Secondary and Higher Secondary Level in Context to Rashtriya Madhyamik Shiksha Abhiyan (RMSA)

—*Deepa Awasthi*

पढ़े चलो, बढ़े चलो

RASHTRIYA MADHYAMIK SHIKSHA ABHIYAN

**Abstract**

*Education means an all round drawing out of the best in child's body, mind and spirit. It is a fundamental mean to bring change in society. Secondary education serves as link between elementary education and higher education and plays very important role in this respect. This stage of education serves to move on higher secondary stage as well as to provide generic competencies that cut across various domains of knowledge as well as skills. Providing secondary education to all, both boys and girls, with focus on quality education assumes greater meaning today. Girls are facing various challenges in attaining secondary education. Due to these barriers girls are not able to complete their secondary educations. In this context starting of Rashtriya Madhyamik Shiksha Abhiyan (RMSA) is very important step. It not only resolves various issues but provide a fair chance of getting secondary education to all without discrimination. This chapter discusses the challenges among adolescent girls in completing secondary education in detail. It also focuses on the framework and goals of RMSA. How RMSA resolves various issues is also discussed in detail.*

**Key Words:** *Competencies, Skills, RMSA, Gender, Discrimination.*

## Introduction

Education means an all round drawing out of the best in child and man-body, mind and spirit. The imperative character of education for individual growth and social development is now accepted by everyone. Investment in the education of its youth considered as most vital by all modern nations. Such an investment understandably acquires top priority in developing countries. Education is a fundamental means to bring any desired change in society, which is an accepted fact throughout the world. Education also brings a reduction in inequalities and functions as a means of improving their status within the family.

## Secondary Education

Secondary education serves as a link between the elementary and higher education, and plays a very important role in this respect. A child's future can depend a lot on the type of education she/he receives at the secondary level. Apart from grounding the roots of education of a child, secondary education can be instrumental in shaping and directing the child to a bright future. This stage of education serves to move on higher secondary stage as well as to provide generic competencies that cut across various domains of knowledge as well as skills.

Secondary education spreads over the ages of 15 and 16, and then to 17 and 18 in the senior secondary grades. These are the years of adolescence, and late adolescence. These are the years of transition; indeed, most crucial years of life. There are steady and fast changes in the body structure transforming to adult form and image of life. At this age, the bodily changes take final shape and stabilise. This is also the stage of emotional transformation and maturity that swings between joy and trauma. Secondary education essentially has to be the education of the adolescence. Experiences in schooling have to be designed to be responsive to the needs of transition and stabilisation. Since large number of students is likely to transit from education to the world of work, it is also the stage of transition to work. Secondary education must foster skills of transition. Though both boys and girls experience transition, there is a special case for girls and it needs special attention. Because of prejudices, taboos and social stigma, phase of transition for girls is more difficult. Also, it will be necessary to develop a gender friendly curriculum.

Providing secondary education to all, both boys and girls, with a focus on quality education assumes greater meaning today, when we consider the emerging challenges in our society. For instance, rising levels of socio-economic aspirations and also the democratic consciousness particularly among marginalised sections of population such as the dalits, tribals, OBCs, religious and linguistic minorities and girls seek space in the secondary education system for greater access, participation and quality.

## Inequalities in Secondary Education Participation

There are several types of inequalities in secondary education which are as following:

- ***Geographic-*** Student's participation in secondary school varies widely across the states of India.
- ***Gender-*** The Gross Attendance Rate and Net Attendance Rate for girls and boys are given in following table which clearly shows that girls lag behind their male counterparts.

**Table: Gross/Net Attendance Rates for Girls and Boys**

| | | Girls | | | Boys | | |
|---|---|---|---|---|---|---|---|
| | *Overall* | *Rural* | *Urban* | *Total* | *Rural* | *Urban* | *Total* |
| **GAR** | 70.2 | 59.1 | 80.9 | 64.3 | 71.2 | 89.1 | 75.3 |
| **NAR** | 41.0 | | | 39.0 | | | 42.2 |

*Source:* National Sample Survey 64th round.

- ***Social and Religious group***- Following table indicates that SC/ST and minority have low GAR and NAR than overall rates.

**Table: Gross/Net Attendance Rates of Social/Religious groups**

| | *Overall* | *ST* | *SC* | *OBC* | *Hindu General* | *Muslim* | *Other religion* |
|---|---|---|---|---|---|---|---|
| **GAR** | 70.2 | 52.5 | 61.0 | 70.5 | 91.0 | 51.0 | 81.9 |
| **NAR** | 41.0 | 27.2 | 34.1 | 41.8 | 56.4 | 27.2 | 46.4 |

*Source:* National Sample Survey 64th round.

- ***Economic status***- The GAR and NAR among the poorest children are about half those amongst richest.

**Table: Gross/Net Attendance Rates by Economic Status**

| *Quintiles* | *Poorest* | *Poorer* | *Middle* | *Richer* | *Richest* | *Total* |
|---|---|---|---|---|---|---|
| **GAR** | 52.9 | 61.8 | 68.1 | 81.0 | 96.3 | 70.2 |
| **NAR** | 31.0 | 35.8 | 38.9 | 46.4 | 59.2 | 41.0 |

*Source*: National Sample Survey 64th round. Quintiles based on household Monthly Per capita Consumption Expenditure (MPCE).

## Challenges in Secondary Education for Girls

Various initiatives have been taken by state and central government to enhance female literacy rate and for universalisation of elementary education. But the situation in secondary education is far different. Rural areas and the backward states have insufficient numbers of secondary schools, distantly located and poorly provisioned. Improper functioning of schools causes students to drop out as, in parental perceptions, the 'costs' are not worth the benefits. Girls are withdrawn from school as soon as they are old enough to be engaged in other domestic or productive activities. Girls are less likely to be sent to school than boys because of a lower value placed on their education by parents, communities and society as a whole. Other reasons include the social practice of seclusion after puberty due to fear of girls being sexually or physically harassed; preparing them for marriage, and so on. There are somewhat different issues in front of adolescent girls in attaining secondary education. Some of them are as follows:

- ***Parent's perception-*** Parent's perception regarding girl child is most important factor in educational attainment of girls. Due to various efforts by government and non-government organisations, girls have performed excellently in elementary education but picture of secondary education is still not very satisfactory. Mainly in rural areas parents do not want to educate their daughters as they assume education has nothing to do with future of girls. According to them girls have to learn household works seriously because it is necessary for an ideal wife and getting education, earning money is the only responsibility of boys.
- ***Patriarchal social setup-*** With few exceptions Indian society is patriarchal in nature. It means male has dominating position in family while female counterpart plays submissive role. In this context male members of family with traditional thinking do not want to empower and educate their girls. They can send their daughters to local primary school to learn basics but they cannot send them to secondary and higher secondary classes to attain some vocational skills.
- ***Economic factors-*** Economic factors play a very important role in education of girls. Till elementary level education is provided free by government. Parents do not feel any financial burden as books, uniform, mid day meal etc. are provided free of cost to students. But in secondary education parents have to bear cost of education by themselves. In case of boys they link cost of education with their future and treat their sons as life insurance policy but in case of girls all equations get reversed. Girls are assumed as 'Paraya Dhan' and any investment in their education is like wastage of money because its benefits would not return to the parents in any form.

- ***Religious factors-*** Religious factors also play a negative role in girls education. So called contractors of religion explains educational development of women as anti-religious deed. They do not want to educate their girls because they do not want them to challenge centuries old traditional patriarchal setup in the name of religion. As adolescence is the age of various physical and emotional changes so attraction among boys and girls is very common phenomenon and it may give rise to inter-religion/inter-caste marriages which is not tolerable by religious orators and society.
- ***Socio-cultural factors-*** Socio-cultural factors make situation of girls more vulnerable. Girls themselves are struggling with many problems and it become worst when they belong to SC/ST or disabled category. From such a long time these sections of society have face a wide range of discrimination. They have to struggle to establish themselves in society and to prove their talent and girls from these sections are facing more vulnerable situation.
- ***Early marriage-*** This is one of the most important hindrance in secondary education of girls. Despite various legal provisions, girls in rural areas become victims of early marriage. This not only acts as barrier in their educational attainment but also hinders their physical, mental and emotional development.
- ***Physical and moral safety of girls-*** Safety issue is another important challenge in front of girls. As adolescence is an age of emotional instability, sometimes girls face such moral dilemmas which make their position vulnerable in their families. Physical safety is other important aspect which affects girl's performance in secondary education. Everyday news-papers are filled with a number of horrible incidents which clearly indicates real picture of society and mentality of some sick people who become danger for girls.
- ***Distance to school-*** Distance is very important factor in attaining secondary education. Generally primary and upper primary schools are situated nearby the homes while secondary schools are situated far away from home of girls. In this

situation parents avoid to send their daughters to these schools as this may be not safe for them. In rural areas, girls have to go very far through lonely routes which ultimately give chances to anti-social elements.

- ***Insufficient number of separate girls' schools-*** Parents in traditional society do not want to send their daughters in co-education school/college. Thus, lack of separate girls colleges is another important barrier in secondary education of girls.
- ***Lack of separate toilets in schools-*** Issue of separate toilet is very important challenge in secondary education. Secondary education deals with adolescence which is the age of puberty. Due to physical and emotional changes girls need privacy. And lack of separate toilets in co-education colleges becomes a strong reason for dropout of girls in secondary education.
- ***Lack of female teachers-*** Lack of female teachers in secondary schools is also an important reason for drop out of girls in secondary education. Adolescent girls feel shy and cannot establish rapport with male teachers while with female teachers they can share their problems freely and feel confident.
- ***Insensitive school environment-*** Insensitive school environment is a strong reason for dropout of girls. Many studies reflect that girls' lack of interest in Science and Mathematics make school environment negative for girls. Male teachers sometimes also humiliate girls on this behalf. Girls have to help their mother in household chores which sometimes negatively affects their educational achievement.
- ***Overcrowded Classroom-*** In government secondary schools classroom are overcrowded. Neither girls receive attention of teachers nor they able to understand subject matter in such atmosphere. This situation becomes worse when schools are with co-education facility because in that case girls have to face hooting and comments of boys which either demoralise them or their parents.
- ***Gender discrimination-*** It is also an important issue in secondary education which becomes challenge for them. Without considering their interest they are forced to study

easier subjects or such subjects who are considered property of girls like, Home science. Boys are considered more intelligent and laborious than girls and subject selection in secondary classes is very much dependent upon this prejudice.

## Rashtriya Madhyamik Shiksha Abhiyan (RMSA)

The Rashtriya Madhyamik Shiksha Abhiyan (RMSA) launched in March, 2009 with the vision of making secondary education of good quality, available, accessible and affordable to all young persons in the age group of 15-16 years. The scheme envisages enhancing the enrolment for classes IX-X by providing a secondary school within a reasonable distance of every habitation, improving quality of education imparted at secondary level through making all secondary schools conform to prescribed norms, removal of gender, socio-economic and disability barriers, universal access to secondary level education by 2017.

### *Goals of RMSA*

- Establishing secondary school within a radius of 5 kms.
- Achieving 75 per cent access by 2012-13 and 100 per cent access by 2017-18.
- Achieving 100 per cent retention by 2020.
  - Providing necessary physical facilities, teaching and non-teaching staff for every secondary school.
  - Improving quality of education imparted at secondary level.
- Eradicate gender differences.
- Remove socio-economic and disability barriers.

### *Physical facilities provided under the RMSA*

- Additional classrooms
- Laboratories
- Libraries
- Toilet blocks
- Drinking water provisions
- Residential hostels for teachers in remote areas.

***Equity interventions provided in RMSA***

- Preference to areas with concentration of SC/ST/Minority for opening of schools.
- Special enrolment drive for weaker section.
- More female teachers in schools.
- Separate toilet blocks for girls.

***Issues, strategies and interventions in RMSA***

An Indian adolescent girl faces a number of challenges in completing her secondary education. These issues are tactfully dealt in RMSA. Various issues, responsible factors and strategies to tackle them can be summarised as below:

| *Issues* | *Factors* | *Broad Strategies* | | *Expected outcomes* |
|---|---|---|---|---|
| | | *General* | *Specific* | |
| **Low enrolment at secondary level.** | Lack of school facilities.<br>Distance factor.<br>Negative attitude of parents and community towards girl's education.<br>Lack of importance of education.<br>Early marriage and sibling care.<br>Gender and caste discrimination.<br>Poor economic conditions.<br>Resettlement of habitations. | ***Community mobilisation-***<br>Awareness generation and sensitisation programmes for mobilising parents.<br>Enrolment drives in critical areas.<br>Counselling for parents and students.<br>Training of SMDC members.<br>Engaging panchayat members. | ***Access***<br>Up gradation of primary schools to secondary schools in SC/ST/Minority concentrated areas on priority basis.<br>Provision of girl's toilets in secondary schools.<br>Provisions of girl's hostels.<br>Provision of transport facility.<br>Empowering girls with self defence techniques.<br>Provision of employable skills at secondary stage to make education attractive.<br>Provision of teachers in language subjects. | Enhancement in enrolment of girls at secondary level. |
| **High Drop-out/Low retention at secondary level** | Distance from habitation<br>Inability to cope with academic rigour. | ***Creating equal learning opportunities:***<br>Conduction of school readiness programme for secondary | ***Educational facilities***<br>Facility of girls' toilet and girls' hostels. | Decrease in drop-out rate and increase in retention rates |

*(Contd...)*

| | | | | |
|---|---|---|---|---|
| **Low enrolment at secondary level.** | Poor performance.<br>Insensitive school environment.<br>Gender and caste discrimination.<br>Adolescent issues and mismanage-ment sexual changes.<br>Lack of female teachers.<br>Poverty and migration.<br>Early marriage.<br>Child labour.<br>Lack of toilet and other facilities in school. | education/foundation course.<br>Learning through open schooling system.<br>Adolescent and life skill education. Counselling.<br>Vocational skills.<br>Special coaching camps for students affected by left wing extremism<br>***Provision of teacher's quarters in case of remote locations.***<br>***Community mobilisation-***<br>***Retention drives***<br>***Attendance monitoring*** | ***Availability of female teachers in schools.***<br>Rationalisation of teachers' deployment.<br>Recruitment/ deployment of tribal language teachers. | |
| **Low learning levels at secondary level** | Poor performance in Science and Mathematics.<br>Biased curriculum.<br>Poor classroom transactions.<br>Poor performance in examination | Improvement of learning levels of students.<br>Revision of curriculum framework/syllabus/ textbooks in as per National Curriculum Framework 2005.<br>Training of teachers on gender issues.<br>Adolescent education and life skill.<br>Vocational skills.<br>Career counselling. | | Improvement of learning levels of girls |

## Conclusion

Secondary education serves as an important link between elementary and higher education. For equal and developed society all its members including girls should be educated properly. Elementary education is of course necessary for all, but it is not sufficient to enable people to lead a standard life free from poverty. There is huge gap in India regarding access to secondary education. Several schemes are launched by government to enhance the students participation at secondary level despite major thrust is received through RMSA, launched in 2009-10. Rashtriya Madhyamik Shiksha Abhiyan projects a proper framework for secondary education. It addresses various issues which act as barrier in girl's education such as lack of female teachers, establishment of new schools, provision of separate toilets etc. Although

RMSA reflects a hope for girls but quality concern is another important aspect to deal with. It is not enough to provide only bookish knowledge to girls but the education must be able to make girls self reliant. It must be ensured that apart from linking elementary to higher education, secondary education must be complete in itself so that if girls would not receive higher or technical education further, they may become self-dependent with their strong base of secondary education.

## References


- Rashtriya Madhyamik Shiksha Abhiyan. www.rmsaindia.org
- Annual Status of Education Report (ASER) 2013. www.asercentre.org
- India: Secondary Education Project Rashtriya Madhyamik Shiksha Abhiyan Equity Action Plan. www.rajrmsa.nic.in
- Kumar J. & Sangeeta. 'Status of women education in India'. *Educationia confab*. Vol. 2 No. 4, April 2013.
- Vineesha, V. & Nath B.K. (2009). 'Quest for quality enhancement in view of Rashtriya Madhyamik Shiksha Abhiyan (RMSA) www.mhrd.gov.in.
- Guidelines for equity and Social inclusion (Dec 2014). www.mhrd.gov.in
- Swati Pathak and Arti Gupta (2013). Status of women in India with particular reference to gap in male female literacy rate in India. *International Journal of Environmental Engineering and Management.* Volume 4, Number 6, pp. 549-552.
- Dalal, R.S. (2015). Access to secondary education through Rashtriya Madhyamik Shiksha Abhiyan in Haryana: An Appraisal. *International Journal in management and Social Science*. Vol. 03, Issue 03 Page 211.
- Rath, A.K. (2008).Girl education in India: Achievements since independence. www.mhrd.gov.inRashtriya Madhyamik Shiksha Abhiyan. www.wikipedia. org
- Sahni, U. (2014). Improving girl's education and status in India with Beti Bachao, Beti Padhao. www.brookings.edu
- Baro, P.K. and Sarania, R. (2014). Employment and educational status: Challenges of women empowerment in India. *Pratidhwani the echo*. Vol. II Issue IV. pp. 55-63.
- Mondal, P. The necessity of women's education in India. www.yourarticlelibrary.com

# Chapter – 2

# Education of Muslim Girls: Issues and Challenges

*—Parvin Sultana*

**Abstract**

*A country's development can be measured by the level of development of its minorities. Empowerment of minorities goes a long way to develop a nation in true sense and educational level continues to be one of the primary indicators of development. Minorities may often feel marginalised in a democratic country as democracy is the rule of majority. Hence a democracy's chief function is to remove these structural obstacles, institutionalise mechanisms to safeguard the interests of the minorities and ensure that the minorities can come at par with other communities. Amongst prominent minority groups, Muslims and mainly Muslim women in India stand out. This community suffers from double marginalisation. This chapter will look at the education of the Muslims in India with special reference to the educational status of Muslim women. This chapter will try to push forth the point that education is crucial as it is the first step to empowerment of a community. It will try to understand the peculiar problems that Muslim women face. Being a part of a religion often seen as patriarchal, education and empowerment becomes doubly difficult for Muslim women.*

***Keywords:*** *Education, Empowerment, Muslim women, Patriarchy, Marginalisation.*

## Introduction

Muslims constitute the largest minority community in India comprising 14 per cent of the population according to 2001 census.

Their presence is visible in every city and union territories. However, this community has been relegated to the lowest socio-economic stratum in post-independence India. In terms of education this community continues to languish as a backward one. Education is both an indicator and an instrument of development and the Muslim community seems to have failed in being the beneficiaries of quality education. Faulty government policies and negative stereotyping of the community along with the orthodoxy of some religious leaders has pushed the community backwards.

## Educational Status of Muslims

India, through Directive Principles of State Policy made a constitutional commitment to provide free and compulsory education to all children up to the age of 14, nearly 65 years ago. In 1993, in a landmark judgment, the Supreme Court of India ruled that the right to education is a fundamental right flowing from the Right to Life in Article 21 of the Constitution. Subsequently, in 2002, education as a fundamental right was endorsed through the 86th amendment to the Constitution. This aimed at ensuring universal literacy. However, despite this commitment education of Muslims continue to be low.

The educational lag among Indian Muslims is documented in various researches and government reports. However, in-depth research continues to be missing.

National Human Development Report 2001 spells out the importance of education. It states: *Education in the present day context is perhaps the single most important means for individuals to improve personal endowments, build capacity levels, overcome constraints and in the process, enlarge their available set of opportunities and choices for a sustained improvement in well being.... Education is not important as means to other ends, but it is an attribute that is valued in itself, by most individuals. More importantly, it is a critical invasive instrument for bringing about social, economic and political inclusion and a durable integration of people, particularly those who are 'excluded' from the mainstream of any society.* (NHDR, 2001:48)

Muslims continue to lag behind in terms of education. The Prime Minister's High Level Committee under Justice Rajinder Sachar points to this deficiency. Few findings are worth mentioning:

*"Muslims are at a double disadvantage with low levels of education combined with low quality of education; their deprivation increases manifold as the level of education rises. In some instances the relative share of Muslims is lower than even the SCs who are victims of a long standing caste system. Such relative deprivation calls for a significant policy shift, in the recognition of the problem and in devising corrective measures, as well as in the allocation of resources."* (Sachar, 2006: 50-51)

Literacy rate amongst Muslims continue to be low and the country could not initiate policies to close the gap between Muslims and other communities. According to the census of 2001, the literacy rate of Muslims is 59.13 per cent. The worse condition in case of education is that of Muslim women. They are marginalised at multiple levels. However, in some states like Jharkhand, Karnataka and Maharashtra, the literacy rate is better pointing to the potential of state level initiatives. Studies show that only 11 out of 100 Muslims take up higher education. This is much lower than national average as well as other religious communities. Higher education points to technical, vocational and professional courses at secondary and post-secondary level. Economist of repute, Amartya Sen advised Muslim clerics to look into core issues of poverty, education and health within the community, instead of skirting them by organising protests against trivial issues like films or writers like Salman Rushdie.

The Indian education system is divided into pre-primary, primary, secondary and higher secondary. Upto the secondary level, all the students are taught a uniform set of subjects. According to Alam (2007), although the Muslim community is represented in primary school in accordance with its percentage share in the population, its representation in the secondary schools is much lower. The number continues to dwindle as one moves upwards the ladder of higher education pointing to a very sparse number in case of research oriented education.

## Causes of Educational Backwardness

Muslims are educationally one of the most backward communities. In terms of rate of progress, the improvement in educational status of Muslims has been the slowest as compared to other socio-religious categories. This has slowed down empowerment of the community as well. A time trend of literacy levels amongst different communities clearly indicates that the Muslims have not been able to respond to the challenge of improving their educational status. Their educational gap *vis-à-vis* other communities has actually increased.

The deprivation of Muslims is clearly indicated in the following statistics:

- The literacy rate among Muslims in 2001 was 59.1 per cent as against the national average of 64.8 per cent.
- Half of the rural Muslim children and one-third of the urban Muslim children are illiterate.
- One in 10 Muslim children is out of school which means the proportion of out of school children is highest in Muslim children.
- The mean time period of schooling of Muslims is the lowest.
- 25 per cent of Muslim children in the age group of 6-14 have never attended school or are drop-outs.
- Muslim children have the lowest rate of completion of elementary education among all communities of India.

Indian Muslims are lagging behind in most socio-economic aspects because of certain problems that the community is facing. Firstly, the Muslim Community does not have far sighted leaders like Sir Syed Ahmed Khan who established the Aligarh Muslim University keeping in mind the educational needs of the community. In present day, education seems to have slipped downwards in terms of priority of the community. With partition, the Muslim elite and middle class moved to Pakistan leaving Indian Muslims under the leadership of the clerics. The clergy became the spokesperson for the community. For them non-interference in Muslim personal law was more important than actual upliftment of the community.

Muslim representation in Indian Parliament is very low. Due to absence of geographical concentration and reserved constituencies. Muslims continue to be too few in the House to initiate policies or influence policy making. Maulana Abul Kalam Azad's famous address to the Muslims of Delhi on October 23, 1947 set a new political trend for Indian Muslims. The occasion demanded leadership for a bruised and bewildered community; the Maulana chose to lace his advice with taunt and reproach, a very different approach from the one he had taken in his presidential address at the Ramgarh session of the Indian National Congress in 1940. His bitterness over the turn of events as he penned down in his book '*India wins freedom*' is understandable. He realised that the community actually got a raw deal post-partition.

Secondly, Indian Muslims suffer from a constant sense of insecurity. Riots, communal violence have become a sad reality of India's life and the majority of the victims of riots in India are Muslims. According to Mr Ram Puniyani, "The data from 1961 to 1992 shows that during these four decades 80 per cent of victims of communal violence has been Muslims." The bloody massacre of Muslims in Gujarat in late February 2002 that led to the death of over 2000 Muslims is a ghastly reminder of an organised violence with tacit support by the ruling authorities.

The political milieu just after the partition was such that it made Muslims feel so demoralised that they could not dare ask the question as to why the doors of defense forces were barred to Muslims under policy directions from Nehru's government after independence. The Muslim civil servants similarly were not to be appointed on sensitive posts and extra caution had to be used for issuing passports to them. The strength of Muslims in the police and state paramilitary forces was deliberately reduced to the extent that in some States including UP and Delhi their representation is very low. The Provincial Armed Constabulary (PAC) of UP - mainly a Hindu paramilitary police force, having only about two per cent Muslims, was alleged to be involved in extra judicial killings in and around Meerut on 22-23 May 1987, by Amnesty International in one of its reports concerning the matter. In 1974, the Commission of Inquiry into Sadar Bazar, Delhi disturbances noted with concern the negligible presence of Muslims which was only 1.3 per cent in the Delhi police force. It is as simple as anything that when a community's physical security is repeatedly endangered it will hardly make any progress in the field of education and economy. The main concern continues to be sustainability.

Thirdly, the Muslim Community suffers from the problem of low income. Although the economic and social situation of Muslims is not the same throughout India, one cannot deny the fact that poverty and lack of genuine financial recourses are hampering socio-educational development of the community at every step. The socio-economic profile that the NSSO estimates paint of the Muslim Indian is a depressing one. In all major socio-economic indicators, the members of India's biggest religious minority are, on the average, worse off than members of the majority community. First, they spend less on items of daily consumption because they apparently earn less. Second, working Muslims are more in casual labour and seasonal occupations. Third, among those with access to land a Muslim household is mostly cultivating smaller plots. Hence, land holdings are not profitably big enough. Fourth, unemployment rates are higher among educated Muslims than others. This overall profile is true of both men and women, in rural and urban India and in all States. It is typical of India's political and social ethos that this fact of gross under representation of a significant religious minority is not allowed to become an issue. Any such discussion would be rather viewed as 'communal' and considered anti-secular and any policy initiative to address this deficit is often dismissed as *'minority appeasement'*.

Fourthly, due to the backdrop of a bloody partition, Muslims were not given political rights through proportional representation. Communal harmony was expected to prevail. Peaceful co-existence between the majority and minority was expected. But the nation saw from time to time how a negative stereotyping have often plagued the community. The community continues to be portrayed in negative terms. The relationship amongst the majority and minority community continues to be tensed. While the community was given social and cultural rights, unlike Scheduled Castes and Scheduled Tribes they were kept out of the ambit of affirmative action.

Apart from these factors, poverty adversely impacts schooling participation amongst Muslims in the same manner as other social groups. Educational opportunities are further limited due to the phenomenon of Ghettoisation especially in communally sensitive areas. Ghettoes are more often than not a picture of neglect manifested in the lack of basic services especially schools. Lack of these facilities in ghettoes translates into little or no access as going outside the boundaries is seen as a threat for young children especially girls.

All these causes have led to a vicious circle of backwardness for the community. Compared to other religious communities like Jain, Buddhist and Christian the literacy rate of Muslims is very poor. According to Census report of 2001, the literacy rate of Jains and Christians were 84 per cent and 69 per cent respectively. These communities don't have the historical disadvantages that Muslims suffer from. As a result, they could take advantage of government policies and develop as a community. The idea of systemic exclusion did not hamper these communities.

## Educational Status of Muslim Women

Muslim girls are among the least educated sections of Indian society. Yet, very little literature is available on this showing the indifference on the part of the community leaders, the agencies of the state and the non-governmental organisations to this particular issue. In their book *Educating Muslim Girls: A Comparison of Five Cities*, Zoya Hasan and Ritu Menon hold a bleak picture of the condition of women's education. Their survey findings point out that as compared to their counterparts from other religions, the enrollment rate of Muslim girls in schools is much low and their drop-out rate is much high.

Educationally Muslim women continue to lag behind their male counterparts. Kept in seclusion for a long time, they are not able to compete with men in terms of education and employment. Studies however reveal that factors such as lack of good quality schools and hostel facilities for girls and poor quality of teachers are responsible for low level of educational attainment of Muslim women. While Muslim women desire for education, hurdles like low access to schools in the vicinity, poverty, financial constraints and discrimination faced at school prevent them from continuing education. Figures show a grim prospect of educational status of Muslim women. As compared to their Hindu (42.2 per cent) and Christian (22.7 per cent) counterparts in urban areas, the level of illiteracy in Muslim women is as high as 59.5 per cent. The enrollment figure of 52.1 per cent for urban Muslim females in school compares poorly to the corresponding figure of 70.7 per cent for Hindu females, which further widens across subsequent age categories to end with 4.7 per cent of Muslim females attending educational institutions compared to 10.2 per cent of Hindu women or 18.2 per cent of Christian women. This trend is all the more alarming when this situation is compared to the advances in Muslim female education in other countries. The situation in India points to a gross failure of government policies to bring meaningful change.

## Empowerment of Muslim Women

Education is the first step towards empowerment. With changing times more and more Muslim women feel encouraged to work towards self sufficiency. They want to come out and take up jobs. The community can become empowered if its members which include women are empowered. There is a need to introduce a comprehensive educational policy that will encourage formal as well as vocational education. Skill development programmes can empower Muslim women and also provide employment. Left outside the ambit of affirmative action, only out of the box thinking can respond to the peculiar needs of Muslim women. The culture of early marriage makes sure very few Muslim women enroll in higher education or research.

## The Way Ahead

The first step to educate women is by eradicating negative stereotypes attached to women's education. The community should work towards ensuring that this does not hamper women's access to education. Education must be geared towards employment generation. Only then Muslim women can be self-sufficient. Muslim women should be provided professional and technical education. They should be imparted computer education. Coaching centres, career counselling and library facilities should be made available to Muslim women.

Education of Muslim girls is not always encouraged. The female literacy rate is an appalling 28.1 per cent. An improvement in the overall literacy rates of Muslims would not just lead to a corresponding increase in Muslim enrollment in universities and professional courses but also ensure more social opportunity for Muslim women. There is a need for Muslim Community leaders as well as the State to take up the issue of educating Muslim girls with the seriousness that it deserves. Given the poor condition of Muslim women's education, there is a special need for the State to take a pro-active role in this regard in order to promote social justice and empowerment of Muslim women and to remove the barriers that systematically reinforce their marginalisation. The only way to ensure that a backward minority community seeped in orthodox patriarchal values can move forward is by giving adequate opportunity to its women to come at par with women of other communities in terms of multiple socio-economic indicators.

## References


- Alam, M. S. (2007). Genesis and Perpetuation of Social disparities in school education in India: An Exploratory Analysis, *Journal of Educational Planning and Administration*, 21(2), 109-123.
- Ansari, M. (2001). Traditional Occupation, Child Labour and Trade Policy: A vicious circle around educational backwardness of Muslims. *Journal of Educational Planning and Administration*, 15(3), 333-353.
- Basant, Rakesh, (2012). Education and Employment among Muslims in India: An Analysis of Patterns and Trends, Working Paper No. 2012-09-03, Indian Institute of Management, Ahmedabad.
- Borker, H. (2011). Contesting Dilemmas: Muslim Identity and Education, A case study of Jamia Nagar, National CRY Research Fellowship, CRY, 2011.
- Nasrin, (2013). "Education of Muslim Women—A Journey from Past to Present", *International Journal of Management and Social Science Research*, 2 (1), 37-40.
- Government of India (2001) Census Report, New Delhi, India.
- Government of India, Ministry of Human Resource Development, (2004), 11th Plan Working Group Report, New Delhi.
- Government of India (2006), Social, Economic and Educational Status of the Muslim Community of India: A Report, GoI, New Delhi.
- Gupta, S. (2012). The Education of Muslims in India, *Research Analysis and Evolution*, 3(35), 2012, 80-81.

- Hasan, Zoya and Menon, R. (2005) *Educating Muslim Girls: A Comparison of Five Cities*. New Delhi: Kali Unlimited.
- Human Rights Today, Vol. III, Nos. 1 and 2, New Delhi 2001.
- Khan, A. (2012). Higher Education and Social Mobility among Muslims and Dalits in India: A Comparative Perspective in the Globalised Times, *Islam and Muslim Societies: A Social Science Journal*, 5(2), 45-52.
- Kotay, Fayaz. (2013). Educational Exclusion of Indian Muslims: Issues and Problems, *European Academic Research*, 1(9), 2843-2866.
- Mainuddin, M. (2010). Understanding Reality: Population Growth, distribution and Educational Status of Indian Muslims, *Asia-Pacific Journal of Social Sciences*, 2, 82-104.
- Murshed, S. M. (1993). "Muslim Factor in India", *The Times of India*, Feb. 16.
- Qasmi, M. Burhanuddin "Education of Muslims in India: Problems and Prospects", Paper presented in Conference on Children, Youth and their Education in a Globalising India, organised by Centre for Post Colonial Education on December 24-25, 2005.
- Sharif, Abusaleh. (2007). "Sachar Committee Report and Pending Promises", *The Hindu*, Nov. 17.
- Shinde, S.V. and Annie John. (2012). "Educational Status of Muslim Women in India", *Review of Research*, 1 (6), 1-4.

# Chapter – 3

# Issues and Challenges Associated with Girls Education in India: a Critical Analysis

—*Leena*

**Abstract**

*The issue of girl education has been receiving the attention of policy-makers, educational planners and administrators yet a large number of girls in India remain deprived of their basic right to education. However, if we see the Millennium Development Goal, goal 3 aims to 'promote gender equality and women empowerment', its target being the elimination of gender disparity at all levels by 2015.There are an assortment of issues related with girl education and also a variety of challenges that the girls are facing for their basic rights. Government has made considerable effort to minimise the challenges and to sort out the issues, in spite of that because of an inefficient and corrupt education delivery system and inadequate citizen participation in the planning and monitoring of educational services the quality of education for girls has been compromised. The present chapter discusses some of the aspects related with girls' education, the problems faced by girls and how these problems are seen by the policy makers. It also studies why government programmes like SSA have not made any difference in the educational status of girls in India. An attempt has been made to critically examine the holistic sphere around the education of a girl child.*

**Key words:** *Girl education, Challenges, Curriculum, School environment.*

## Introduction

***"Education does not mean teaching people to know what they do not know; it means teaching them to behave as they do not behave."***

**—John Ruskin (1819-1900), English critic**

Education is straight forward related to the economic growth. It acts as a mechanism for human resource development in the country. It is a fundamental tool for permeating the barrier of poverty. Women are at the heart of most societies, regardless of whether they are working or not. Mothers are very influential in children's lives. Educating girls is one of the most important investments that any country can make for its own future. Education has a profound effect on girls' and women's ability to claim rights and achieve status in society, such as economic independence and political representation. The following examples demonstrate how education can make an enormous difference to a woman's chances of finding well-paid work, raising a healthy family and preventing the spread of diseases.

Specifically, primary education is the critical enabler required to improve the economic and social scenario in many pockets of the nation. We also need to ensure equal status for the girl children as citizens in their own right. For any country to progress, one-half of its population cannot be denied the right to education. This denial is also a gross violation of many rights enshrined in the Indian Constitution, primary among them being the right to education and the right to equality. Global statistics reveal that 75 per cent of the 130 million children who are out of school are girls. Illiterate girls grow up to be illiterate women. This results in lopsided development as it denies equal opportunities and equal citizenship. We find that South Asia has the widest gender gaps compared to other countries of the world. There prevails many disparities between women and men across the world and they remain persistent in the areas of access to resources, opportunities and in matters of human rights. India is a signatory to many international commitments on women's and girls' development as well as its own national commitments for development and education of girls. The first reference to equal opportunities for education of both girls and boys is made in India's National Policy on Education,

1968. One of the principles of the development of education in the country listed in the 1968 policy was - Equalisation of Educational Opportunity - , in this it was stated that, "The education of girls should receive emphasis, not only on grounds of social justice, but also because it accelerates social transformation." The Indian government's commitment to education is stated in its constitution with an article promising "free and compulsory education for all children until they complete the age of 14" (The World Bank, 1997). The National Policy on Education, which was updated in 1992, and the 1992 Programme of Action both reaffirmed the government's commitment to improve literacy levels by providing special attention to girls and children from scheduled castes and scheduled tribes.

## Rationale of the Study

The Indian government has expressed a strong commitment towards education for all; however, India still has one of the lowest female literacy rates in Asia. In 1991, less than 40 per cent of the 330 million women aged seven and over were literate, which means today there are over 200 million illiterate women in India. This low level of literacy not only has a negative impact on women's lives but also their family's life and their country's economic development. Numerous studies show that illiterate women have high levels of fertility and mortality, poor nutritional status, low earning potential, and little autonomy within the household. A woman's lack of education also has a negative impact on the health and well being of her children. For instance, a recent survey in India found that infant mortality was inversely related to mother's educational level.

## Barriers to Girls' Education

Barriers to girls' education can be categorised as barriers to access, barriers to quality services and barriers to relevant curricula and/or pedagogy. Barriers due to historically embedded chauvinistic stigma attached to the public psyche can be very powerful and subtle social norms. Barriers to girls' education can take differential forms across nations/societies depending upon the socio-economic, religious and cultural contexts. Furthermore, barriers can be perceived as either intrinsic or extrinsic to girls in relation to how they experience educational participation. Also, some barriers can be obvious while others are subtle and tacit. What needs to be acknowledged is that the concept of barriers to girls' education is highly complex; hence for the analysis to be comprehensive, the lived experiential meanings will have to be unpacked through qualitative, phenomenological and hermeneutic inquiry processes. UNICEF (2011) outlines the following generic barriers to educating girls: Household or community level barriers, school level barriers and policy and system level barriers. These are all very important factors but are mostly external and obvious ones. Radical feminists and critical social theorists probe much more deeply into the social contexts of girls and boys – ranging from the closer contexts of household, school or community to more macro and policy contexts of parliament, ministry of education or district education office – and examine the root causes of the barriers to girls' education (Grundy, 1987; Stromquist, 1995). In studying barriers to girls' schooling, the critical perspective seeks an analysis framework to accommodate, among others, questions related to power relations and underlying assumptions of institutional operating processes, as well as of programme or state interventions, use of languages and metaphors. Interventions intended for gender equality, according to Stromquist (1995), often tend to be superficial and illusive. In asserting this point she mentions, as has also been quoted aptly by Heward (1999a, p. 9), that 'women have obtained more symbolic than real victories from their state and have constantly underestimated the ability of education in the reproduction of conventional gender identities' (Stromquist, 1995).

## Issues Related to Education of Girls

In many countries and communities in both the developed and the developing world, parents can take it for granted that their daughters will receive a quality education. Yet, in many other places around the world, providing every child with an education appears to be beyond reach. Five main challenges that make it difficult for girls to access education have been identified. These include the cost of education which calls for ensuring that communities, parents and children be able to afford schooling; poor school environments which calls for ensuring that girls have access to a safe school environment; the weak position of women in society which calls for ensuring that society and parents value the education of girls; conflict which calls for ensuring that children who are excluded due to conflict get access to schooling; and social exclusion which calls for ensuring that girls are not disadvantaged on the basis of caste, ethnicity, religion or disability. These challenges are not exhaustive, but they are recurrent themes in many countries. They constitute additional hurdles that girls need to overcome to benefit from quality education.

- ***Cost of Education***

Educating girls can incur extra direct costs, such as special transport or for safety and 'decency'. Education may actually reduce girls' marriage prospects and raise dowry payments to unaffordable levels. Investing in sons, rather than daughters, is perceived as ensuring higher financial returns for families as boys are more likely to find work and be paid a higher salary. The high cost of education is the biggest deterrent to families who want to educate their daughters; it includes both direct cost of schooling as well as indirect costs. Direct costs include the school fees, clothing and shoes as well as school books and other supplies. When families cannot meet direct costs, children are not enrolled in schools or they drop-out and if a choice has to be made between sending a boy or a girl to school, the boy is usually given precedence. The possible interventions to triumph over this problem are to initiate some incentive programmes such as scholarships exclusively for girls, discounted or free school supplies and micro enterprise programmes. Indirect costs of schooling include opportunity costs. Families cannot afford the loss of income or labour contribution of their children, so their children do not enroll or attend. Traditional division of labour are often disadvantageous to the girls (who are more likely to have to work in the home, care for siblings etc.). The broad strategy used to deal with this barrier is awareness-raising. The possible interventions initiated to overcome this barrier can be Flexible school time tables, Child-care programmes for siblings and children, Reallocation of household task, Mother/parent/caregiver education, School feeding programmes etc.

- ***Attitude and Practices***

It includes the traditional, cultural or religious beliefs, gender stereotypes, lack of knowledge on benefits of education and gender-differentiated child-rearing practices. A finding supports the fact that girl education is not valued or is seen as irrelevant to or in conflict with accepted roles in society. There is limited involvement of parents in schooling and early learning. If we focus on the dimensions of gender, we see early marriage, low status of women, and intractable patriarchal societies often result in lower priority on education of girls, also the content of education reinforces gender stereotypes. "Hidden curriculum" of discrimination is perpetuated. As a strategy, there is a need for Sensitisation and Advocacy of the importance of girls' education and completion of schooling and taking actions to make schools safer and more secure and establishing strengthened links between schools and communities. UNICEF (2011) has listed the possible interventions to overcome this strategy as Media programmes and motivational materials (posters, story books, Meena, Sara, etc.), National Enrollment Days, Culturally appropriate schools, Endorsement of education (particularly girls' education) by religious and other leaders, Gender-awareness training, Micro planning, Better parenting programmes, Village committees, Parent-teacher associations, etc., so as to promote community and parental involvement in girls' education and inclusion programmes (disability, ethnicity, poverty, etc.).

- ***Lack of Adequate Number of Schools***

There is lack of schools close to home. Research findings suggest that it increases the likelihood of non-enrollment or non-attendance and dropping out after enrollment. The issue of safety and security is unanswered. Parents are less likely to allow daughters to attend school if they have to travel long distances. A school environment that may be acceptable to boys may be hostile to girls. The physical and sexual violence against women that is common in many societies is reflected in the school environment in a number of countries. Physical abuse and abduction are a major violation of girls' basic human rights and they also present a major practical constraint in getting to school. Parents for protecting their daughters may decide to keep them at home.

Violence against girls and women has been identified as a key barrier to girls' education in many schools. The broader strategies includes providing support and technical assistance from government and communities to ensure increased access for those children who are hardest to reach. Possible interventions includes school mapping to improve planning and targeting, "Child-seeking" Child Friendly Schools, Infrastructure programmes, Schools closer to home (including through cluster schools, multi-grade or non-formal approaches as a bridging measure) and, Boarding facilities for girls etc. Also the poor quality environment i.e. poor condition of building, overcrowding, lack of water or sanitation are the major school level barriers because of which there is increased likelihood of non-attendance and dropping out, as well as poor achievement in academics. The lack of separate sanitation facilities particularly affects adolescent girls. They are more likely to be called on for service tasks (e.g., cleaning), or be sexually assaulted or harassed. Regarding such issues, the broad strategies include strengthening policies and strategies for Health promotion in schools and advocacy and action for safety and security in schools. The possible interventions include sanitation facilities, separate latrines for girls, rehabilitation as well as mentor programmes (older girls to younger girls).

- ***Curriculum***

Poor quality content of the curriculum such as outdated curriculum, inadequate learning materials and biased or inappropriate content of the book act as a barrier for the girls to attend school. In such conditions the learners are not able to develop to their full potential. There is possibility of non-attendance, dropping out and limited transition from primary to secondary education or from school to work. As a broader strategy, gender sensitive teaching must be promoted and the capacity of teachers and school managements must be built. The possible interventions includes: Training of teachers, especially women; Gender awareness training for teachers, officials, communities, leaders; Training in administration and management; Introduction of new technologies for learning and administration; Provision of quality relevant supplies; Flexible approaches to the school calendar;

Incentives, particularly for female teachers in rural areas; Active involvement of communities and parents in schools.

- ***Tackling Social Exclusion***

Social exclusion is an additional barrier to girls going to school. Certain groups of girls are more likely to be excluded from school on the basis of caste, ethnicity, religion or disability. In Nepal, Dalit girls are almost twice as likely to be excluded from school as higher caste girls. In Malawi, Muslim girls are more likely to be excluded than their non-Muslim counterparts. Disabled children, and among them disabled girls in particular, constitute a significant group that is denied access to education. In a recent World Bank report it is estimated that only about one to five per cent of all disabled children and young people attend schools in developing countries.

- ***Making Schools Work for All Girls***

Skilled staffs with the right knowledge, understandings and experiences are required in order for governments to implement successful plans for girls' education. These staffs need to ensure access of education to girls of all backgrounds - regardless of race, ethnicity, religion or disability. In particular, we should support our partner governments to ensure that there are teachers and education officials who are able to develop policy and curricula, monitor education, and ensure that girls have equal educational opportunities.

## Discussion

Although literacy levels are low yet its levels have improved overtime, there has been progress in improving educational attainment for both the sexes in India over the last several decades. In 1991, only 39 per cent of women and 64 per cent of men were literate (Register General and Census Commissioner - RGCC). By 2001, 65 per cent of women and 82 per cent of men were literate. Thus, there has been a large increase in the proportion of women who are literate in just 20 years. Despite the improvements in literacy, there continues to be a large gap between the literacy levels of men and women. For India, as a whole, the gender gap in literacy has been decreasing since 1981; in some states, however the disparity in literacy between the sexes has been growing. There are dramatic differences in literacy rates by place of residence, with rates in rural areas lagging behind rates in urban areas. While there have, however, been substantial increases in literacy rates in both urban and rural areas, the gap between the two sectors has not narrowed appreciably.

At the turn of the millennium, the international community promised that by 2005, there would be as many girls as boys in school. Later this year, when leaders from around the world came together to take stock of the Millennium Development Goals, there was no escaping the fact that as a nation we have collectively failed to keep this promise. Despite much progress, a child without an education is still much more likely to be a girl than a boy. The implementation of Millenium strategies is a first step to get us back on track and it requires our substantial endeavour in helping more girls to get into school. The situation calls upon us to acknowledge the role of education for lifting nations out of instability and providing a more promising future to their people. Regardless of whether the people live in a wealthy or poor country, nothing has as much impact on a child's future and wellbeing as their mother's level of education (Development, June 2005).

## Conclusion

Research suggests that women with at least a basic education are much less likely to be poor. Providing girls with one extra year of schooling beyond the average can boost their eventual wages by 10 to 20 per cent. An infant born to an educated woman is much more likely to survive until adulthood. In Africa, children of mothers who receive five years of primary education are 40 per cent more likely to live beyond age five. An educated woman is 50 per cent more likely to have her children immunised against childhood diseases. If we had reached the gender parity goal by 2005, more than one million childhood deaths could have been averted.

In India, women have a weak position in society. Within communities girls have to overcome many obstacles before they can realise their right to an education. Before girls can attend school and benefit fully from their education, a number of major social constraints have to be addressed. Girls often have limited control over their futures. Early marriage is a reality for many, where families wish for the social and economic benefits this brings. In Bangladesh and Afghanistan, more than 50 per cent of girls are married by the age of sixteen to eighteen years. Adolescent pregnancy almost always results in girls halting their education. Girls are also more likely to drop-out of school because of their domestic responsibilities, and are often discriminated against in terms of the quality of the schools they are sent to, and the costs parents are willing to pay for their education. Despite the progress being made, gender equality is likely to take generations to achieve.

## References


- Government of India, Census of India 2011.
- N. L. Gupta, 2003, Women's Education Through Ages, Concept Publications Co, New Delhi.
- R. K. Rao, 2001, Women and Education, Kalpaz Publications, Delhi.
- UNICEF report 2011 on girls education worldwide.
- Development, D. F. (June 2015), Girl Education: Towards a better future for all, UK: DFID.
- Velkoff, V. A. (October 1998). Women's Education in India. *International Programme Centre*.

# Chapter – 4

# Hurdles in Girls' Education in India

*—Raksha Amanna and Rajendra Baikady*

**Abstract**

*This chapter focuses on the problems faced by women in Indian education system. Women education ratio compared to the mean is still less and continues to be low in spite of various governmental and non-governmental efforts for its improvement. The aim of this study is to report the major hurdles to women's education; an attempt has also been made to draw the possible solutions to women's needs and for their educational empowerment.*

***Key Words:*** *Education, Efforts, Hurdles, Empowerment.*

## Introduction

In the words of Herbert Spencer, "Education is training for the completeness of life." Education brings perfection to life which means the growth and perfection of personality. It qualifies a person to fulfil certain economic, political and cultural functions and thereby improves the socio-economic status of the people. It also helps to equalise the status of individuals who belong to different social strata. The importance of the role of education in the socio-economic development of a nation has been recognised since long. By increasing knowledge and skill, education transforms human material into human capital. Education plays crucial role in the development of nation by providing the required manpower to the economy. **'Educate women and you educate society',** these words were stated by the Father of our nation - Mahatma Gandhi. Education has radically changed the contour of the lives of Indian women. While the impact of women's education since independence had profound implications for the Indian society as a whole, educated women do not enjoy a status equal with men within the educational system and outside. This situation communicates the binary opposition of feminity and masculinity and its evaluative component of inferior and superior to little girls and boys who grow up interiorising this difference. When they enter schools the same message is conveyed in several ways. Although social change is constant in Indian society. women are expected to be rooted in the past, to be the stable and unchanging element in a rapidly changing world.

## Girl's Education in India

Women education in India has also been a major preoccupation of both the government and civil society as educated women can play a very important role in the development of the country. Education is milestone of women empowerment because it enables them to respond to the challenges. to confront their traditional role and change their life. The status of women in India has gone through enormous changes over the ages and her position has been degraded and she mostly lives her life according to whims and fancies of men. It is a known fact that since the down ages women have been excluded from the educational, political and economic sphere by the male-dominated society. Women constituted about one-half of the global population, but they are placed at various disadvantageous positions due to gender differences and bias. They have been the victims of violence and exploitation by the male-dominated society all over the world. India's constitution guarantees free primary school education for both boys and girls up to the age of 14 years. This goal has been repeatedly reconfirmed, but primary education in India is not universal. Families are more likely not to educate their girls than boys and pull them out of school, either to help out at home of from fear of violence and insecurity. India has the largest population of non-school-going working girls.

## Rural and the Urban Disparity

*"Illiterate people will not keep their freedom"* –

**—Nikki Giovanni**

Universal primary education assumes that all children irrespective of the caste. creed or location would complete primary education of comparable quality within the stipulated time frame. Therefore, all children should have equal opportunities to participate and succeed in primary education. It is also assumed that while moving towards the attainment of these objectives, special care should be taken to ensure that existing disparities do not accentuate. Therefore, more focused attention would be required to provide access and facilitate the retention of girls and children belonging to the deprived and first generation learners' category. Generally, separate goals are specified for the deprived groups which include girls, ethnic minorities, working children, children living under difficult circumstances, children with special needs and those whose continued participation in education is at risk.

The status of women cannot be studied in isolation. She is, after all, a member of smallest social unit - the family and she also goes through a life cycle of her own. She is a creature of birth, growth, maturity, demise, as anyone else. There are occasions when she needs special care, attention, encouragement, consolation and total rest for mind and body.

The rural-urban differences had narrowed down over the period of last thirty years. The rural female literacy had increased more than three and half times than in urban areas, where the increase has slightly been less than two times. There has also been a steady increase in girl's enrollment in elementary levels in the rural areas. The first five year plan (1951-1956) held that women have the same opportunities as men for taking all kinds of work, and this presupposes that they get equal facilities, so that their entry into the professions further enlarges opportunities for education of girls and women. Education has not only helped women to gain knowledge, but also provided them the necessary courage and inner strength to face the challenges of life. Education is a value in itself, as it develops personality as well as the rationality of individuals. Education, broadly perceived as an endless continuance of life-long learning, is essential for human resource development. Women in rural India are greatly in need of improvement in their educational levels, and of practicable suggestions to help improve not only their economic condition but their social status as well. Two-thirds of the population lives in villages with limited exposure to the forces of modernisation and facilities for education, the immensity of the problems of rural women and their mind blogging complexity has discouraged many women leaders from even trying their hand at solving their problems. This calls for the adoption of strategic and concentrated efforts on the part of the volunteers to effect the desired changes.

## Factors Affecting the Low Level of Literacy among the Women

A severe combination of a number of causes is responsible for low level of girls education. These include socio-economic and cultural factors, malnutrition, lack of access to schools, uninspiring school environment and unimaginative curriculum etc. First of all parental attitude towards the girl child is governed by the social and cultural factors and familial roles. Most parents tend to believe that education makes a girl less attentive to household work such as cooking, fuel and fodder collection, fetching of water and sibling care. Parents value a son's education for its effect on his earning potential and on the family status. Household investment decisions also influence gender differences in girl's education. Families prefer to spend money for the education of sons, because the returns to this investment for daughter's education will finally go to her husband's family. That is why female education is neglected and discouraged, particularly in rural areas. Thus, poverty and parental apathy and social attitude towards girl's education are some of the reasons cited for rural girls being kept away from schools. Economic pressures on family for basic survival means an increased burden on rural young girls since young girls have to share the responsibility of the family along with the mother. Their education becomes the first casualty. The common sentiment is that sending a girl to school means losing a worker in the kitchen. When faced with difficult times due to health or economic emergencies, death of bread winner etc., poor families find it difficult to bear the cost of education. So poverty and education are closely interrelated. Sometimes, financial constraints of rural family can be viewed not only from the point of expenditure in terms of fees, text books, note books, uniforms etc. but also from the point of opportunity cost of the school going girl. In a large number of cases, it is sheer hunger and lack of basic nourishment which forces young girls to dropout of schools. They suffer frequent bouts of illness which makes it much harder for them to cope with the physical pressures of attending school and continuing studies. Lack of interest in education has got many dimensions but chief among them is the teacher's behaviour and attitude towards the girl students. In rural areas, the behaviour of male teachers is not always inspiring. Such type of behaviour terrifies the girl students who are much soft hearted than boys and they ultimately discontinue with their studies.

## Constrains

Social constrains push back the girls in the gender specific roles, of doing household work, looking after the siblings, and being treated as inferior to boys. Girls remain deprived of scientific and technological developments which may, at least, save them from the drudgery of hard and hazardous work. The attitude of parents and degraded oral values setup by community and society discourage them from taking any initiative whatsoever, and they are married off at an early age. The reasons for the high rate of illiteracy include the weak community participation and lack of awareness regarding the probable bright future of educated girls. Parents see no relevance of girl education to their immediate needs. They also have inhibitions in sending their daughters to such schools where there are no female teachers, and more so, if it happens to be a co-educational institution. They are afraid of criticism from their own community. The cost of education for their daughters does not bring them immediate gains. Hence, they do not show the desirability of educating their daughters.

Economically also, most parents are not financially sound enough to afford expenditure on the education of their daughters, if they have to spend money on girls they would rather do so in marrying them off. Most of the incentive schemes for girls initiated by the government do not reach the masses. Moreover, the daughters of landless labourers have to perform petty jobs at minimal wages; and in the case of migrant workers, they have to frequently move about with their parents. The villagers are naturally more concerned with their immediate need of earning their bread. Another factor is the fear of parents that once educated, the girl may despise work, especially the manual work they have been doing so far. There are also certain educational constraints that obstruct the way towards developing better self-image in girls. The biases prevailing in the sphere of education are responsible for the situation of non-enrollment and dropout of girls. The rigid school hours due to lack of planning with understanding coupled with the difficulties of the rural children closes doors on girls who 'have' to do household work, whether they attend the school or not.

## Importance of Women Education

Napoleon was once asked, what the great need of France was. He answered, "Nation's progress is impossible without trained and educated mothers. If the women of my country are not educated, about half of the people will be ignorant." A woman has to play three roles in the course of her life. Each of these roles expects some duties from her. It is only with the help of education that she would be able to do them successfully. Women education in India plays a very important role in the overall development of the country. It not only helps in the development of half of the human resources, but in improving the quality of life at home and outside. Educated women not only tend to promote education of their girl children, but also can provide better guidance to all their children. Moreover, educated women can also help in the reduction of infant mortality rate and growth of the population.

## Constitutional Provision for Girl's Education in India

More than four decades ago, the Constitution of India made a bigger commitment. Its Article 45 states: "The state shall endeavour to provide, within a period of 10 years from the commencement of the constitution, free and compulsory education for all children until they complete the age of fourteen years." The National Policy on Education (NPE), 1986 and Programme of Action (POA), 1992 have perceived education as fundamental to all round development of children and stipulates free and compulsory education of satisfactory quality to all children up to 14 years of age before the turn of the century. The NPE aims to fulfil the objective of "Education for All" by providing early childhood care and education, universalising elementary education through formal and non-formal methods, reducing wastage and involving local community in the management of elementary education. The Department of Women and Child Development has been implementing early childhood–

education (ECE) programme since 1987-88. The (ECE) programme seeks to improve the children's communication and cognitive skills as a preparation for entry into primary school as also to release the girl child from task of taking care of siblings.

The major goal of education in the National plan of action for children further strengthens the commitment made in the constitutional provisions and goals of the national policy on Education. It gives priority to universal enrollment, retention, and attainment of minimum levels of learning; reduction of disparities; universalisation of effective access to schooling and expansion of early childhood development activities; and universalisation of elementary education with focus on girl child and disadvantaged groups. After 'Education for All' summit, India has committed to ensure the provision of free and compulsory education of satisfactory quality to all children upto 14 years of age before the twenty first century. The government is now committed to earmark six per cent of the GDP for education. This was marked to be achieved by the year 2000 AD. Fifty per cent of these funds were stipulated for expenditures on primary education. The adolescent girl's scheme aimed at breaking the intergenerational life cycle of nutritional disadvantage and providing a supportive environment for self-development focuses on school drop-out girls in the age group of 11-18 years by addressing their needs of self-development, nutrition, health, education, literacy and skill formation. This scheme attempts to mobilise and enhance the potential of adolescent girls as social animators.

Balika Samridhi Yojana, an integrated scheme to raise the status of the girl child was formally launched by the Prime Minister on October 2, 1997. The specific objectives of the scheme are to change the family and community's attitudes towards the girl child at birth and towards her mother; to improve enrollment and retention of girl children in schools; to postpone the marriage of adolescent girls and to enable girls to pursue higher studies/income generation activities. The other objectives which would be indirectly served are: survival of the girl child; disincentive for female foeticide and infanticide; reduction of girl child labour within and outside the household; reinforcing positive perception of the girl child, changing social attitudes and behavioural practices towards her; raising the over-all status of the girl child; enhancing the self-esteem, and self-confidence of the girl child; correction of the demographic imbalance. Under this scheme, the mothers of girl children born on or after 15 August, 1997 in families below the poverty line were entitled to receive a grant of Rs 500.

The National Policy on Education 1986 (NPE) also reiterated the original issue of providing primary education to all children upto the age of 14. The programme of action (POA) laid emphasis on the twin objective of: (a) enrollment and universal retention of children in schools upto the age of 14 years and (b) improvement in the quality of education.

Indian education commission recommended promotion of female education by giving grants to girl's school on easier terms and appointing female teachers and reducing fees for girls. Gopal Krishna Gokhle moved a bill on compulsory elementary education in 1911 in the imperial legislative council but it was thrown out. In 1917, Vithalbhai Patel got the first law on compulsory primary education in India passed by the Bombay education council. This example was followed by every province of British India and by 1930 almost all provinces had passed a law for primary education - the compulsory education enactment for boys of the age group of 7-12 years and for the girls in the age group of 7-10 years, in 1906.

The passing of the Government of India Act of 1919 and the Government of India Act, 1935 gave more powers to Indian ministers to act independently and education being a provincial subject, a great deal of attention was given to the spread of elementary education and literacy. The leaders of the Indian independence movement were very keen that universal compulsory education of seven years duration should be given to every child in India. It was during the freedom movement that Mahatma Gandhi formulated the scheme of basic education in 1937 which recommended compulsory, universal, seven years education in the mother tongue for all children. This included girls as well. This system of basic education was adopted in all the provinces where the Congress ruled under the Government of India Act, 1935. This goal of compulsory primary education for all children was slightly modified in 1978 where the government stated that 'Every child shall continue to learn, in the age group of six to fourteen years on a full time basis if possible, and on the part time basis if necessary'.

Education was a state subject till 1976 and then was placed in the concurrent list by the 42nd constitutional amendment. Placing education in the concurrent list means a dominant role for the central government viz:

1. To determine the policies, priorities and programmes relating to education.
2. To provide effective leadership to the states.
3. To provide funds for educational development in the states.
4. To take steps for minimising regional imbalances in educational development and for equalisation of educational opportunities in different states.
5. To take steps for promoting national integration through education, and
6. To carry out uniform educational reforms in the country.

Importance of girl education has been recognised by SAARC also. The guiding principles of the SAARC decade plan of action for the girl child are:

1. The Equality of status of girl child will be ensured through special opportunities for her growth and development of her full potential as an individual and as a citizen in her own right.
2. Without prejudice to the integration of the goals for the girl child with the goals for children and development in the 1990s, her situation demands formulation of additional goals and strategies that are sensitive to her specific and multiple needs.
3. The socio-cultural discrimination prevailing against the girl child in South Asia, as revealed by demographic indicators, requires change in social attitudes and behavioural practices in relation to the development of opportunities for her.

## Suggested Strategies

While it is not fair to expect an overnight change in the social situation of women, it is certainly possible to make a dent. If we seriously intend to bring change in the existing pattern of education, we shall have to adopt multipronged strategies. First of all, sensitisation of the community towards girl's education both formal and non-formal is very essential.

The second step will be to evolve such teacher training programmes that will lay emphasis on the personality development of rural children, especially the girls. Special orientation programmes for generating awareness regarding the capacities and capabilities of girls, treating them on par with the boys, giving them equal opportunities in all walks of life, etc. have to be organised for bringing about attitudinal change in society. Elimination of sex bias from curriculum and textbooks, and adequate school resources is another important factor. Free education for all may be an answer to some of the constraints, but if the schools are far from the reach of girls, the distance will become a hurdle for them. Perhaps, providing boarding facilities for girls who come from a distance, and day-care centres for siblings who happen to be the responsibilities of these girls, can be a suitable answer for attracting these girls to schools.

There are several schemes already being run by the Government of India for eradicating illiteracy. Yet what is that that keeps us away from the world of literates? Why have we not succeeded in achieving the goals so far? The first reason is that the education we tend to impart is bookish, and as such of less value to the common people. Hence, we have to be careful enough to develop need-based, skill-based, local material-based and home-based learning programmes for children–a programme of learning that can be related to their economic growth as well. If we can do so, we can certainly reinduct the dropouts into the formal system of education after some time. Special efforts should be made to see that all children have access to schools.

Girl-child education process should be properly funded to enable them have quality access to education. To do this, there should be effective coordination and control of all viable sources of funds earmarked for female education, as without such resources it would be difficult for the education sector to carry out their social and academic responsibilities through schools. The needs and socio-economic concerns of the females should be critically assessed and vigorously pursued by the education sector and schools. This can be done through survey studies using questionnaires, interviews, observations, and through the offices of the guidance and counselling facilitators.

Government should pass legislation compelling parents to send female students to schools because many parents question the intellectual capabilities of females. This can be achieved through sensitisation programmes aimed at parents in order to eliminate the traditional belief of parents that females are the backbone of the local economy to be retained at home. The sensitisation will make them believe that educated females stir greatly the waters of the growth in the society. The education sector should ensure that the management of the education in schools is effectively done. This can be attained by strictly observing the stipulations of the education law as well as the objectives. The management committee should comprise of responsible individuals who see the educational responsibility of students, especially females, as their priority.

Dishonest leadership should be discouraged in schools. This should be done by putting in place adequate checks and balances in the performance of schools, and excesses should be properly controlled. Schools and states that practice gender inequality in educational opportunities should be properly sanctioned and penalised according to the stipulations of the education law.

## Conclusion

Literacy for girls has very far reaching implications both for society as well as the recipient girls. Literacy for girls is a crucial input for developing/preserving human resource development, which in the ultimate analysis is a national asset. Literacy/education equips girls and women to enjoy the fruits of social justice, social culture and of social, political and economic rights. Such are the lofty ideals of girls' literacy and in all respects earnest steps have been taken by the

Union and State governments to realise them in practice. Yet, the ground realities of achieving the goal of Universalisation of education differ from State to State and among the various strata of society. Thus, there exists in India now a dichotomy of 'educationally forward States' and 'educationally backward States'.

## References


- Bakshi, S.R, Bala Kiran, (2000), Child Welfare and Development, Deep and Deep Publications, New Delhi, p. 287.
- Beechal, (2013), Teachers perspective on the causes of high rate of female Drop-out in Chikkun local government area of Kaduna state, Varitas University Language Arts Journal Female Education.
- Bhadra, Mita, (1999), Girl Child in Indian Society, Rawath Publications, Jaipur and New Delhi, pp. 51-57.
- Chanana, Karuna, (2001), 'Interrogating Women's Education' Bounded Visions, Expanding Horizons, Rawath Publications, Jaipur and New Delhi, p. 11.
- Chapman, Robert Jane,(1976), Economic Independence for women the foundations for equal rights. Volume (1), Sage yearbooks in women policy studies, Sage Publications, Berverly 14 Hills/London.
- DC Kumar, Uthpal, Ghosh, Bholu Nath, (2004). Mohith Publications, New Delhi, pp. 337-344.
- Goel, Aruna, (2009), Women Empowerment Myth or Reality, Deep and Deep Publications, New Delhi, pp. 100-101.
- Kumar, Jitendra, Sangeeta, Status of Women Education in India, Uttar Pradesh, India, pp. 168-171.
- Lawani, B.T, Desai Archana, (2012), Participative Development, Centre for Social Research and Development, Pune, Inclusive Education A Strategy to mainstream the Differently, New Delhi, Volume XI, No. 1, p. 1.
- Tripathy, S.N, Pradhan S.P, (2003), Girl Child in India, Discovery Publishing House, New Delhi, p. 53.
- Agarwal, Babitha, (2008), Rural Women in Indian economy, ABD Publishers, Jaipur, pp. 135-143.
- N. Andal, (2002), Women and Indian Society, opinion and constraints, Rawath Publications, Jaipur and New Delhi, pp. 112-117.
- Sarwar High Firoj, (2013), Learning Community, An international Journal of education and social development, Women's role in women education : A case study of nineteenth century's Bengal India, Volume 4, No. 3, New Delhi Publishers, p. 211.

- Seth, Mira, (2001), Women and Development, the Indian Experience, Sage Publications, New Delhi, pp. 116-117.
- Sharma, Rashmi, (2009), 'Women Development' New approaches and innovations, Regal Publications, New Delhi, pp. 113-144.
- Singhe Mohan, (2012), Impact of Education on Decision-making Process of Women in Local Self Governance.

# Chapter – 5

# Need and Importance of Women Education

*—Upasna Chhabra and Manjeet Kumari*

## Abstract

*Women education in India has been a major preoccupation of both the government and civil society, as educated women can play a very important role in the development of the country. Education is milestone of women empowerment because it enables them to respond to the challenges, to confront their traditional role and change their life. Women education is also important as through it women can attain purposeful occupational achievement and satisfaction; a deep self-awareness and understanding can only be attained through effective and functional educational guidance and counselling. This supposition is based on the premise that education has been adjudged to be a viable instrument of change in the positive direction. A nation would find it difficult to stand on its own without an effective, efficient, adequate and functional education for all its citizens (men and women) and which is relevant to their immediate needs, goals and objectives. The brand of education being advocated is that type of education in which is embedded the spirit of self-realisation and all that are needed for the country's overall development like mass literacy and economic empowerment.*

***Key Words:*** *Civil society, Occupational achievement, Self-realisation, Guidance and counselling.*

## Introduction

***"Education of man commences at his birth; before he can speak, before he can understand he is already instructed. Experience is the forerunner of the perfect."***

**—Rousseau**

Education means an all round development and eliciting the best from the body, mind and spirit of the human entity. The imperative character of education for individual growth and social development is now accepted by everyone. Investment in the education of its youth is considered as most vital by all modern nations. Such an investment understandably acquires top priority in developing countries. The end of all education, all training should be aimed towards human development. Main goal of education must be the all round development of humans. The training by which the human expressions are brought under control and become fruitful is called education. Education plays a vital role in giving human beings proper equipment to lead a gracious and harmonious life.

Education is a fundamental means to bring any desired change in society, which is an accepted fact throughout the world. This can be attained only if schools become real centres of learning. Education not only helps in the development of personality of the child but also determines her/his future. Recent psychological research has shown that favourable attitudes towards life develop in the earlier stages of child growth. Education gives solutions for any type of problems. Through education we promote values and good habits and awareness regarding corruption, terrorism and diseases. Education helps to continue communication with known and unknown persons through technology and mass media. Education gives strength to the person. Educated people possess knowledge and ability to discriminate between right and wrong. Education inculcates values in the minds of the students.

## Historical Background

### *Ancient India*

It cannot be clearly stated whether equal rights between men and women prevailed or not during the Vedic period. Available sources show that liberal attitudes and practices pertaining to women did exist. Women were actively involved in religious and social matters. They had some freedom to choose their partner in marriage and a widow was permitted to remarry. As India started taking steps towards civilisation, social discrimination increased. Jainism and Buddhism emerged as potent religious reform movements. According to Buddha, women's spiritual capacities were equal to men's. Buddhism began as a religion that treated women as equal to men in their capacity for personal spiritual development. The universal prejudices against women, who are said to be weak minded, fickle, treacherous and impure are shared by the Jains and expressed in several passages of the canon and in the form of maxims. The high status that women enjoyed during early Vedic period gradually started deteriorating in the late Vedic period. Lineage began to be traced in the male line and sons were the sole heirs to family property. As the economic and social status of sons began to rise, the position of women saw a steep decline. The position of women reached an all-time low during the age of the Dharmashastras. It is during this age that codes of conduct prescribing behaviour norms for women were evolved. This period saw the exclusion of women from both economic and religious sphere. During the period of Dharmashastra, child marriage was encouraged and widow marriage was looked down upon. The birth of girl child was considered as an ill omen and many parents went to the extent of killing the female infants. The practice of Sati became quite wide-spread because of the ill treatment met out to widows.

### *Medieval India*

The system of Purdah which was prevalent among royal families, nobles and merchant prince classes prior to the advent of Muslims spread to other classes also. During the medieval period, practices such as polygamy, sati, child marriage, ill treatment of widows were already prevalent since the *Dharmashastra* age and during this era these practices gained further momentum. The priestly class misinterpreted the sacred texts and created an impression that all these evil practices had religious sanction.

***Modern India***

With the advent of the British, the status of women saw many changes. The East India Company (EIC) was mainly a trading company involved in trade in India. To expand their trade network, they started acquiring territories. As they were a trading company, the question of law and order in the acquired territories posed a great challenge before them. Therefore, the company acquired the rights to make laws related to the various crimes. For dealing with civil matters, most importantly, dealing with matters which involved the personal laws, the EIC consulted Moulavis and Pandits. At that time, the customs were devised and sustained by male members. Women were not even consulted. Women's wrongs formed the theoretical basis for men's rights or more properly male duties towards moderating women's lust. Women were not given equal matrimonial rights to property, rights to remarriage (in case of widows), adoption and divorce rights and many more. This situation was severely criticised by the colonial authorities. In return, Indian cultural nationalism argued in favour of Indian tradition. Therefore, the nineteenth century is often termed as the century of social reform. The criticism angered the people of India and caused a serious threat to the longevity of colonial rule in India. Hence, the Queen's Proclamation of 1859 declared that British authorities will not interfere in religious matters of the people. To bring reforms smoothly in India, legislations transforming the family structure were introduced in Princely States without much opposition. Baroda was the first to introduce divorce provision. The Princely state of Mysore enacted the Infant Marriage Prevention Act of 1894. Keeping pace with these princely states, Malabar part of Madras Presidency and Travancore introduced reforms, but the major drawback was that the Princely States could not stop violation of these laws across their borders.

## Education is a Fundamental Right of All Children

The 93rd constitutional amendment 2001 of 'free and compulsory education for all children as a fundamental right' still remains a ray of hope to millions of children in the age group of 6-14 years. The fundamental right to free education was received with paramount importance by all, but again it is already four years since the amendment and there is no visible development in the field of education and literacy. Parents from backward classes, schedule castes, schedule tribes and other minority communities do not know that the 86th constitutional amendment of India in 2002 has made education of children a fundamental right which cannot be overlooked by them.

## Education for All

Education for All means not only having access to schooling but also having quality education for all children. The SSA programmes of Government of India to provide quality education to children between six and fourteen years has increased the literacy rate of girls and boys (Primary level Sarva Shiksha Abhiyan is completed and Secondary Education Sarva Shiksha Abhiyan is going on). In the past two decades, women's participation in primary, middle and secondary level has increased considerably. The District Primary Education Programme (DPEP) of the Central Government has reduced drop-out rates to less than ten per cent and reduced gender gaps to less than Five per cent. One of the main objectives of the Sarva Shiksha Abhiyan (2001) was to bridge gender gaps in primary and secondary education by 2010. Since after secondary education many girls may not continue, "Extension Education," a policy providing job-related knowledge was introduced for those unable to proceed with formal secondary level education. The National Literacy Mission (NLM) set up in 1988 aimed to mobilise dropouts, introduce mass and functional literacy and involve the community in educating women to the Secondary level.

## Need and Importance of Girls Education

Education is also important for women as well as men. Education is essential for every one because through education only we can be differentiated from the animals as human beings. Education tells us that how can we live in a society; unfortunately it is being hindered due to a lack of women's participation.

Men and women are just like the two wheels of a chariot. They are of equal importance and they should work together in life. One is neither superior nor inferior to another. Unlike ancient times, today in majority of rural areas India women are treated well, but they are cut off from the main stream of social life. The society does not respect them and give them their due position. They have to suffer and work inside the houses. Thus, they are completely dependent on men. In the past women were not allowed to come out of the four walls of their houses. Domestic experience was their only education, but now we are in twenty-first century where men and women have equal rights.

In this century women have the same respect as men. They help each other in every sphere. So education should be given to both men and women. But instead of this there are so many people who do not want to educate their women because they think that women do not need to be educated. These people think that women have to take care of the children, stay at home, clean up the house, and be the self-denying wife and mother and are expected to take care of everyone except their own-selves, for such narrow minded people life of a woman is all about getting married, having children, and being bombarded by unimportant details of domesticity. Such people do not understand that education is very important for women not only for their own-selves but for the whole family because women are the mothers of the future generation. If women are uneducated, the future generations will be uneducated.

In day-to-day life, the real problems are faced first by women and then the same problems are conveyed to men for solution. If the women are educated, they can solve all the problems of their houses by themselves. It is said that educating men is only useful for their own benefit but education of women is useful for the whole family. An educated woman leads to an educated family and an educated family makes a better society.

Without one, the other cannot exist. Education of women can not only give an educated family but education of women can also be helpful in eradicating many social evils such as dowry problem, unemployment problem, etc. Social peace can easily be established. A woman has to play three distinct parts in the course of her life in each of which certain duties are expected of her. The first duty of a woman is to be a good daughter. The second is to be a good wife and the third is to be a good mother. Woman belongs to a weaker section of the society because she suffers from many handicaps due to rigid, outdated social customs and religious practices. But an educated woman cannot be exploited easily. She is aware of her rights and will go any length to defend them.

## Conclusion

Women constitute almost half of the population in the world. But the hegemonic masculine ideology has made them suffer a lot as they were denied equal opportunities in different parts of the world. The rise of feminist ideas has, however, led to the tremendous improvement of women's condition throughout the world in recent times. Access to education has been one of the most pressing demands of these women's rights movements. Women education in India has also been a major preoccupation of both the government and civil society as educated women can play a very important role in the development of the country. India is poised to emerge as one of the most developed nations by 2020, more literate, knowledgeable and economically at the forefront. No doubt, women will play a vital role in contributing to the country's development. Women power is crucial to the economic growth of any country. In India, this is yet to meet the requirements despite reforms. Little has been achieved in the area of women empowerment, but for this to happen, this sector must experience a chain of reforms.

A child's whole future life, to a large extent, depends on the teaching it receives in early childhood and it is needless to say that this first foundation of education cannot be well laid by an ignorant mother. Thus, education will enable women to make their children, husbands and parents truly happy. Consequently, it is very important that women should be educated. On all these grounds girl education is a vital necessity.

## References


- Nair, Janaki. *Women and Law in Colonial India: A Social History*, Delhi (1996), Kali for Women (published in collaboration with the National Law School of India University, Bangalore).
- Mahajan, V.D. *Modern Indian History*, Delhi (2010), S. Chand & Co.
- *Women's Development in India: Problems and Prospects*, (Ed.) Lalneihzov, Delhi (2007), Mittal Publishers.

# Chapter - 6

# Educating Girls, State Paradox and Social Response: A Study of Girls' Education in Princely Kashmir, 1900-1947

***—Fayaz Ahmad Kotay***

**Abstract**

*The present chapter attempts to assess the development of girl's education in Kashmir formerly princely state of British India. Princely India had been most backward in most of the development indicators although there are a few exceptions. Kashmir, which was under the autocratic rule of Dogra Maharajas, was the most backward among all princely states and education was no exception. Initially the Dogra Rajas utterly ignored the education of girls. The vacuum was filled by the Christian Missionaries. The chapter will mainly focus on the educational policy and the attitude of the Dogra State towards the development of girl's education in the Kashmir state. The nature of girls' schools was confined to reading of literary and moral books, some arithmetic, needle work, household work etc. So by education women were tied more securely to the home to domestic tasks by realigning the patriarchal domesticity. Moreover, religious and moral education was part and parcel of curriculum of girl's schools, since they were supposed to be of better character and discipline oriented than the boys. First part of the chapter will discuss the governments' laissez faire policy and the role of Local Advisory Committees in the dissemination of education among girls.*

*Second part will elaborate the shift in the government policy, although some reforms were brought, but government showed an ambivalent policy towards it, and invested less in girls' education compared to boys' alongside ignoring higher and technical education all together. Third part will look into the role of private agencies especially Christian missionaries and Women Welfare Trust. Notwithstanding the government and non-government educational ventures development of girl's education has not been able to follow a progressive pattern.*

***Key Words:*** *Princely Kashmir, Advisory Committees, Christian Missionaries, Literacy Rate, Dogra State.*

## Introduction

Education has been a great source of empowerment for disadvantaged sections. In case of women, education should have been of immense priority. But to our disappointment as per 2011 Census female literacy in India is only 65.46 per cent (male literacy is 82.14 per cent), which is one of the lowest in the world. Today, female education may be widely advocated as a fundamental right and a matter of social justice and equality, but it is still regarded as 'consumption' and welfare expenditure, if not as a burden (Gyatri, 2014, 90). However, female education occupies a special place in the history of modern India, and its development is marked with controversies, debates and immense struggles (Bandyopadhyay, 2004, 281-84). In British India, the agencies for the spread of education lay with three groups—the British rulers, Christian Missionaries and Indian male reformers. The colonial state's limited commitment to the project of female education, and its dependence on private funding, shaped the contours of institutional education in India.

In this chapter we will discuss the development of girls' education in princely Kashmir, which was indirectly ruled by the British Government of India. Since the state was ruled by autocratic Dogra rulers, there was no preference for the social or economic development of the people. Maharaja Gulab Singh, the founder of the Jammu and Kashmir state, spent most of his time in consolidating his territories. He did little for the field of education. Maharaja Ranbir Singh, who succeeded Gulab Singh, was the first one to take interest in education

(Rasool, 1986, 173-74). The system of education that prevailed during his tenure continued to be dictated by indigenous functional concerns, although Ranbir Singh encouraged religious education through a study of classical languages—Persian, Arabic and Sanskrit. However, keeping in tune with the religious tenor of his rule, Ranbir Singh's ultimate aim was to spread classical Hindu learning among his Dogra subjects. Education as envisaged by Ranbir Singh was to be the sole preserve of the ruling class and religious elite (Zutshi, 2003, 172).

Akin to pre-colonial systems of education in India and pre-national educational systems in Europe, indigenous Kashmiri education in the early nineteenth century was firmly rooted in diverse traditions of communities, localities, castes and religious traditions. The indigenous schools of Kashmir have always been connected to the mosques, where the boys are taught to read Arabic so that they may be able to recite the Quran, but not necessarily to understand it. Similarly, the Brahmans have their schools, where Sanskrit was taught so that the boys may be able to read the sacred Hindu books (Biscoe, 2006, 184). In the traditional institution there was little scope for girl's education. Education in modern sense in Kashmir was only initiated by Christian missionaries during 1880s. Later on, the State Council also brought some measures for the improvement of education (Kapur, 2009, 119).

The traditional patriarchal definition of women solely as housewives or mothers meant an early pre-pubertal marriage for girls, an immediate post-pubertal consummation of marriage, and early and frequent child-bearing. In this definition there was no space for education; and even if it was imparted for a few years in childhood, it was only rudimentary "informal, religious and practical" so as to enable them to fulfil their domestic roles. Kashmiri women like other South-Asian counterparts were so secluded that they were totally ignorant of their own needs, so much so that they did not even have an identity and remained mere shadows of their men folk. The studies on the development of girls' education are very negligible. Therefore, the present chapter explores the government's policy *vis-á-vis* girls education, moreover it analysis the public response towards the education of girls.

## Initial Government Policy and Role of Local Advisory Committees

There was no definite policy of government so far as the female education is concerned. Keeping into consideration the very fact that even the advanced provinces and states of India were very backward in the education of females, it was but natural that the condition in this rather backward state was very discouraging.

The people were highly conservative about *Purdah* system and the problem of girls' education was a sensitive social question. Towards the close of nineteenth century Church Missionary Society of London established a girls' school in Srinagar, which was closed due to the indifferent approach of local people, however, it was reopened later. Taking into consideration the people's attitude and the mode of their thinking, State Council adopted a very cautious policy and did not take any step towards the opening of schools for the education of girls. It favoured helping private efforts and a grant of Rs 1000 was sanctioned in 1901 for Kanya Pathshala at Jammu (Administrative Report, 1904).

It was in 1904, that State Council for the first time provided funds for establishing two girls' schools at Srinagar, one for Hindus and the other for Muslims, to be managed by separate Advisory Committees of the leading men of the two communities under the guidance of educational authorities. In the year 1905, the number of girls' schools were two and one was an aided middle school. The total number of students on the roll was 369, showing an increase of 51 over the figures of the preceding year. During the year the total expenditure on female education was Rs 2,540 (Administrative Report, 1905).

Regarding the female education Narian Das, the Education member stated, "My policy to such schools has been to let them be managed by private individuals acting under the advice and control of a local committee consisting of the leading residents of the place both official and unofficial. There is no need of official interference in the internal management of these schools, all which is necessary on the part of the inspecting officers of the educational department is to satisfy them that the aid granted by the state is being properly utilised and for purposes which have been duly approved by the Minister of Education.

If interference beyond this limit is allowed there is fear that the schools will collapse. The subject is very delicate one and need careful and sympathetic handling. We have to overcome many prejudices in imparting education to girls and where the people are so jealous of interference on the part of outsiders, it becomes us to be careful as to how we adopt any steps which instead of fostering a desire on the part of the people to impart education to their girls are calculated to engender suspicion and thus retard the progress of female education" (Old English Records, 1906).

The State Council expressed satisfaction with the small results in the beginning but also opined that when the desire for female education shall have become general throughout the country and gained in intensity, there would be time enough to think of enforcing stricter rules of supervision and controlling the inner working of schools receiving grants from the state in this respect. However, advancement of female education was consistently receiving the attention of State Council. The result was that the number of girl's schools increased, two of which were middle schools. The management of these schools rested with locals committees to a certain extent. These committees worked well and tried their best to popularise these institutions. Their efforts proved fruitful as even people with most orthodox ideas had commenced to recognise the advantages of female education and were sending their children to school (Om 1986, 56).

In 1916, Mr H. Sharp, suggested a number of reforms for girls' education. Regarding the girls' education Sharp report recommended an organised attempt to open primary girls' schools at those places in Srinagar where boys high or middle schools existed. Secondly, it was suggested that a small capitation grant to be given to the girls so as to induce them to accompany their small brothers to school. Besides, the Maharaja was asked to seek the services of Christian Mission Ladies and other private agencies (Sharp, 1916).

According to the Census reports of 1921, on an average there was one literate female to over fifteen literate males. The proportion of literate women to the total female population aged five and over, was three per thousand. Jammu district was on top in female education with nine literate female out of every thousand, which was the highest proportion among the districts of the state. In Kashmir Valley, 999 out of every 1,000 females were illiterate. Following table demonstrates the education of different communities, with respect of gender, in whole Jammu and Kashmir State, Christians were the leading community and Buddhists and Muslims were most backward communities with respect to education (Census of India, 1921).

**Table 1: Literates per mile of Different Religious Communities of Kashmir in1921**

| *Religion* | *Total* | *Males* | *Females* |
|---|---|---|---|
| **Hindu** | 115 | 189 | 25 |
| **Sikh** | 116 | 189 | 34 |
| **Jain** | 412 | 612 | 129 |
| **Buddhist** | 3 | 69 | 2 |
| **Muslim** | 12 | 20 | 1 |
| **Christian** | 280 | 275 | 286 |

*Source: Census of India, 1921, Vol. XXII, Kashmir Part-I.*

## Shift in Government Policy

Maharaja Hari Singh, the successor of Pratap Singh, who brought a number of reforms in education system of Kashmir, brought changes in girls' education too. The first reform which Hari Singh introduced was the creation of a separate department for the girls' education. Till then girls' schools were an adjunct of the Education Department primarily meant for boys. Now the department was bifurcated and girls' education was kept under the control of a Chief Inspectress (Bazaz, 1959, 229). The policy of giving Advisory Committees maximum powers for maintaining the girls' education with minimum government supervision was abolished.

From the year 1928, the Advisory Committees for middle schools in the cities of Srinagar and Jammu were abolished. Similarly after a year their control on primary schools in the cities of Jammu and Srinagar was also eliminated. Although government appreciated the role of Advisory Committees which had done very useful work in the past, but it was found that the Department had now outgrown the need for them, and they were a cause of considerable friction (Administrative Report, 1929-30). With a view to efficiently control the middle and primary schools at the headquarters and to train the old teachers, on newer lines, the Inspectresses were required to pay frequent visits to such schools at Jammu and Srinagar. To facilitate their work in this connection a conveyance allowance of Rs 15 per month for the Inspectresses was sanctioned.

**Table 2: Number of Girls' Institutions in the Year 1929-30**

| *Institutions* | *Number* | |
|---|---|---|
| | *Year 1928-29* | *Year 1929-30* |
| High Schools | 2 | 2 |
| Govt. Anglo-Vernacular Middle Schools | 2 | 3 |
| Govt. Vernacular Middle Schools | 2 | 6 |
| Aided Middle Schools | 6 | 6 |
| Aided Primary Schools | 14 | 14 |
| Govt. Primary Schools | 79 | 97 |
| Maktabs and Pathshalas | 8 | 8 |
| **Total** | **113** | **136** |

*Source*: Estimated from Annual Administrative Report of Education Dep., Jammu and Kashmir, 1929-30.

The foregoing statement shows that there was an increase of 23 institutions over the previous year. Moreover, it can be said that the private agencies were also playing their role in the development of girls' education. As far as the Maktabs and Pathshalas, Finance Department questioned the value of such institutions in consequence of the general advance in education and increase in the number of primary and other schools. But the report of Education Department made it clear that, "Although it is undoubtedly true that Maktabs and Pathshalas represent very primitive type of school, yet in remote villages, where the opening of a school is not justified at present, they are much better than no school at all and they prepare the way for subsequent opening of schools" (Administrative Report, 1930).

## Educational Reorganisation Committee (1939) and Girls' Education

In 1939, a committee known as Educational Reorganisation Committee was appointed by Maharaja Hari Singh. Its aim was to give a new orientation to educational setup and to reorganise existing educational system in the state, and to make recommendations for fostering a more vital touch with the needs of the people and the ideas of the good life (Educational Reorganisation Committee, 1939).

As regards the girls' education, Committee considered very carefully the position and problems of the education of girls in the state in consultation with S. W. Shaw, the then officiating Chief Inspectress of Girls' Schools who had been specially co-opted on the Committee, for this purpose.

The Educational Reorganisation Committee heartily endorsed the view expressed by the Hartog Committee (Ghosh 2013, 157) that in all schemes of future expansion, priority must be given to the question of girls education and this recommendation appears to be particularly applicable to this state where unfortunately 99.5 per cent of the women were illiterate. The members of the Education Reorganisation Committee made it clear that, "It is obvious that no education can be effective or successful, so long as practically all the mothers continue to be illiterate and consequently unappreciative of the advantages of education. Nor can we expect education to become an instrument for raising their cultural status of the homes and permeating into the life of the people, so long as it continues to ignore the problem of the education of girls" (Educational Reorganisation Committee, 1939, 71).

### Recommendations of the Committee

In the direction of the promotion of girls' education the Committee recommended that increased facilities should be provided to women teachers. The Committee found that only 16 teachers were trained every year in the junior vernacular class in both the provinces. This number was entirely inadequate to meet the needs of the situation, particularly because a majority of the teachers in service had very poor academic qualifications and it has been represented that in their case it seemed doubtful whether they possessed even the bare minimum of literacy.

Committee, therefore, recommended that 20 primary schools and four middle schools should be opened every year in each province. Committee was aware that even this provision was far too meagre to cope with the immense problem of the illiteracy of women in the State. As a further strategy of attracting a large number of girls to schools, who were reluctant or unable to join them without scholarship, Committee was of the opinion that it was necessary to increase the provision made for the award of scholarships to girl students and that it should also be permissible for the department to transfer scholarships from one school to another, in order to extend the benefit of these scholarships as much as possible and to avoid the lapse of funds which was occurring on account of the inadmissibility of such transfers.

Committee recommended that the number of Inspecting offices should be increased, and as a necessary measure of immediate relief, one more Inspectress should be appointed for each province. In order to minimise the wastage and check the lapse into illiteracy, Committee recommended that financial provision should be made for the distribution of free books in the fourth and fifth standard of the primary school so as to retain a much larger number of girls in the upper classes of the schools. Educational Reorganisation Committee recommended that the Education Department should undertake a careful scrutiny of the existing syllabus and courses for girls' schools and overhaul them with the object of making them more suitable and congenial for the present interests and the future occupations and responsibility of the girls.

After examining the recommendations of the Committee government accepted them but not all of them were implemented. A number of half-hearted steps were taken during the decade of 1940s. Mention may be made of the opening of a number of primary and middle schools. The number of primary schools rose to 270 and the number of middle schools was raised to 47 in 1945 (Administrative Report of Education Department, 1945). Three high schools were established in different parts of the State during this period. As far as the teachers training is concerned no systematic steps were taken to train the female teachers. Although a refresher course for the female teachers was held at Srinagar during the year 1939, which was attended by 30 teachers (Administrative Report of Education Department, 1945).

No major change was brought in the curriculum, in fact, science subjects were not introduced even up to 1947. The work of inspection and supervision was still handicapped on account of insufficiency of inspection staff but two new posts of Inspectresses were sanctioned in the year 1940. The building infrastructure problem also remained there. Only one girl's institution was housed in a government building while all the others were accommodated in unsatisfactory buildings.

There was no representation of girls in higher education up to 1932; it was in 1932 when a Pandit lady named Vimla Kaul got enrolled in Sri Pratap College (Bamzai, 2007, 359). In 1940, there were about 40 women who were enrolled in higher education. In 1947, only six Muslim women were studying in colleges (Seru, 1973, 269), this shows the dismal representation of women in higher education. It is true that the society was averse to co-education especially at the higher stage of education. Many parents were not in favour of co-education they did not send their daughters to Boys Colleges for the fear of public opinion (Khan, 2006, 181). The State knowing the conservative nature of Kashmiri society did not try to open a women's college. Therefore, the non-existence of women's college deterred women's higher education to a great extent.

## Expenditure on Girls' Education

Government from the very inception was not kind to female education in the matters of finance. It was not able to construct a single building for the female institutions. The other aspects of the female education received least attention of government. Although government claimed that society was not responsive to the new education for their girls, but during the decade of 1930s a number of factors have transformed Kashmiri society. Thus, their perception was changing fast, but as far as the budget for education is concerned government maintained the gender discrimination policies even in 1930s and 1940s.

Gender disparity can be seen in the distribution of educational budget among the boys and girls in the following figure.

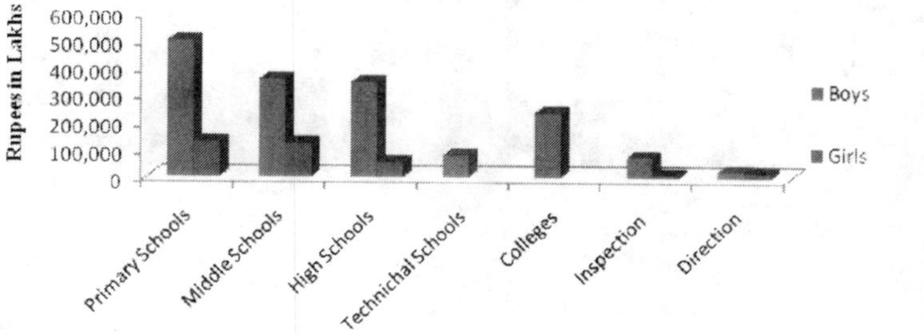


*Source:* Estimated from the Annual Administrative Reports of Education Department Jammu and Kashmir

***Fig. 6.1: Distribution of Education Budget of Boys and Girls Education in 1937-38.***

Above figure indicates the glaring discrepancy in the distribution of educational budget so far as the two genders are concerned. In the primary education there is huge difference–for the boy's education an amount of Rs 5,01,088 was allotted, while for girls' primary education only Rs 1,29,499 was granted. Same disparity can be seen in the middle schools. In the high school education, the difference is even more than middle and primary education. Since there was no representation of girls in the technical and college education thus no amount was allotted for these items. In the inspection and direction aspects there is little disparity.

The disproportional educational budget consequently widened the gap between the number of boys and girls on rolls. As is shown in the following figure, the number of boys in 1927 were 47,201 and rose to 82,303 in 1937. While the number of girls in 1927 was 4,763 which rose to 15,426, although their number had increased, but gap between the two widened as the time passed.

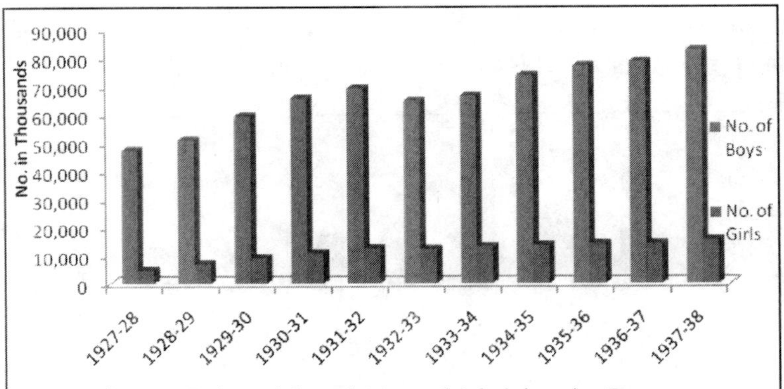


*Source:* Estimated from the Annual Administrative Reports of Education Department Jammu and Kashmir

***Fig. 6.2: Increase in the number of Boys and Girls from the Year 1927-28 to 1937-38.***

## Role of Private Agencies

Private agencies, particularly Christian Missionaries, played a leading role in the development of girls' education in Kashmir. Like in the case of boys' education, it was no other than Christian Missionaries who started the experiment of girl's education. It was somewhere between 1893 and 1895 that a girl's school was opened in Fateh Kadal, Srinagar by the Church of England Zenana Missionary Society. The opening of girl's school shocked the people of Srinagar. The people thought that the missionaries aimed at polluting the minds of young girls with impure ideas. This school continued until the first prize day, some European lady visitors were invited to the school by the lady superintendent, thinking it would be an encouragement to the girls and their parents. But on the appearance of the English lady visitors, some mischief mongers in the street shouted out that the European had come to kidnap the girls. This episode resulted in the closure of the first girl's school for some time. A few weeks later the school was re-opened and surprisingly the school registered an increase in the number of girls (Biscoe, 2006, 245).

This phenomenal success emboldened the Christian missionaries to open another girls' school which was attached to the boy's school at Fateh Kadal, Srinagar. The Christian missionaries through brave spirit and inexhaustible patience removed one impediment after another that was placed in their path and ultimately came out with flying colours in the struggle. Missionaries made people to understand the importance of female education. Among the heroic personalities that made girl education acceptable in Srinagar were Miss Churchill Taylor, Miss Robinson, Miss Fitze, and Miss Mallinson. The story of struggle of foreign missionaries against male arrogance and distrust forms a glorious chapter in Kashmir's history of cultural renaissance (Bazaz, 1959, 213).

When Miss Fitze started a girl's school in 1912, the majority of the girls attending her school were Muslims. In her yearly school report, Miss Fitze remarked: "Our chief trouble is that Hindu girls were taken away from us early on account of its being considered improper for them to go out after the age of 12, until they are married. I have lost a number of promising ones in this way and consequently, Hindus on the rolls were 35, while Muslims run up to 40." (Khan, 2007, 168). In the beginning Miss Fitze faced a strong opposition from various quarters but by 1914 opposition seemed to have calmed down when the number of girls schools rose to three in the city. By 1916, the girls were seen to be coming in greater numbers than ever before and mothers were actually eager about their learning.

In 1918, the school was raised to middle standard and it received a grant of Rs 700 from the state. Missionary Girls School underwent a dramatic transformation during the period of Miss Mallinson as principal (1922-1961). It was Miss Mallinson who was instrumental in bringing about enough educational and cultural advancement among the women of Kashmir. Under her inspiring leadership the school became a hub of cultural activities. She introduced swimming, dancing, drill, picnics, camping and mountaineering in the school. It was thrilling to see the girls moving about freely and enjoying fresh air during the picnic and camping time. Besides teaching English, Urdu, Persian, General Knowledge, Mathematics and Nature study were also taught. Miss Mallinson dedicated her life for the empowerment of Kashmiri women; she generated respect for mothers and daughters, infused self-respect and confidence into them. The missionaries left no stone unturned in attracting girls to their school.

Besides Christian Missionaries who created milestones in the growth and development of girls' education in Kashmir, the role of Women's Welfare Trust is worth mentioning. It was established in Sep. 1926 in Srinagar, the founder members of the Trust were: Mrs Margaret E. Cousins, Mrs L. D. Van Gheel Gildemeester, Professor S.K. Toshikhani, Shri Shridhar Kaul Dullo and Shri Aftab Kaul Nizamat (Bazaz, 1959, 222).

The Trust began its work by starting a primary school for girls. In 1929, the Trust opened a primary school for Muslim girls. By 1933, the Trust was running six primary schools, three middle schools and one high school, with the total enrollment of 575 students. The Trust started primary education in the mother tongue and *Mullahs* were appointed to teach Arabic while *Pandits* were appointed to teach Hindi. As the number of schools increased the Trust appointed a supervisor of schools to supervise the teaching and the organisation of Trust schools, P.N. Bazaz was the first supervisor.

A fully fledged high school for girls was opened by the Trust in 1934 for both Hindu and Muslim girls. The trust started ventures in adult education of women as early as in 1930 (Rasool, 1986, 82).

Social reformers of both Hindu and Muslim communities' also popularised female education, but their efforts were limited to their respective communities (Khan, 2007). Notwithstanding the government and private efforts, female literacy did not increase as much as compared to that of males. From the forthcoming figure it can be inferred that male education although low made significant progress, moreover it can be deduced that from the decade of 1930s female education also made some relative progress.

**Table 3: Literacy rate of Jammu and Kashmir from 1901-1941**

| *Census Year* | *Per cent Males* | *Per cent Females* |
|---|---|---|
| 1901 | 2.40 | o.11 |
| 1911 | 2.67 | 0.13 |
| 1921 | 2.79 | 0.33 |
| 1931 | 5.92 | 0.53 |
| 1941 | 7.17 | 2.31 |

*Source:* Census Reports of India Jammu and Kashmir Part.

## Conclusion

The development of girls' education in Kashmir faced a number of problems due to indifferent attitude of the government and conservative attitude of the society. The state and representatives of the community seemed more concerned with the religious education of females rather than the efficacy of education being imparted to them. Until 1928, management of the government girl's schools was left largely to advisory committees and private managing bodies composed of leading members of religious communities, the schools themselves were connected to particular communities. State was apprehensive that communities would perceive State's interference in women's education as an attack on their religious sensibilities. Religious prejudice of the people of Kashmir and their prejudice against education, especially of females, were cited as a reason for placing of the education of girls in the hands of advisory committees. However, these committees remained in the charge of the education department which supervised over the general working of the schools as per the rules sanctioned by the Education Minister for the purpose. This gave State sanction to overtly religious policies recommended by the advisory committees, such as closing Muslim girls' schools on Fridays instead of Sundays for the reason that women were supposed to be more religious and moral.

The curriculum introduced in the girl's school was aimed to inculcate the concept of home-industry among the students. Subjects like needle work, household work, tailoring, sweeping, reading of literary and religious books, besides some arithmetic was taught. Thus, through education women were tied more securely to domestic tasks by realigning patriarchal domesticity. There was a great deal of wastage in girls' educational schools due to the fact that a large majority of girls did not carry on their education to even the fifth class – a time by which they may be reasonably expected to achieve permanent literacy. Although Hari Singh brought the control of girls' education under the newly carved girls' education department, he seems to be ambivalent when girls were excluded from the Compulsory Education Act of 1930. Moreover, girls were totally excluded from higher and technical education due to the absence of these institutions for them. The State's expenditure on education of girls was far less as compared to boys' education. Thus, literacy rate of girls' remained low throughout the period concerned. The legacy of princely Kashmir is still persisting, as there is big gap between male and female literacy, according to Census 2011 there is a gap of about 20 per cent among the two genders in Jammu and Kashmir.

## References


- Annual Administrative reports of Jammu and Kashmir (1904, 1905, 1930, 1945).
- Annual Administrative reports of Girl Education Department (1929-1943).
- Bandhopadhyay, S. (2004). *From Plassey to Partition: A History of Modern India.* New Delhi: Orient Longman.
- Bamzai, P. N. K. (2007). *Socio Economic History of Kashmir, Shrinagar: Gulshan Books.*
- Bajaj, P. N. (1959). *Daughter of Vitasta: A History of Kashmiri women from early times to present.* New Delhi: Pumposh Publication.
- Biscoe, T. (2006). *Kashmir in Sunlight and Shade.* Srinagar: Ali Mohammad and Sons.
- Census of India, 1901, 1911, 1921,1931, 1941.
- Gayathri, R. Silent Voices: Women Perception about Self Education in Late Ninteenth Century India in P. V. Rao (ed.) (2014). *New Perspective in the History of Indian Education.* New Delhi: Orient Black Swan.
- Ghosh, S. C. (2013). *The History of Education in Modern India 1757 – 2012.* (4th Ed.) New Delhi: Orient Black Swan.
- Kapur, M. L. (2009). *Kashmir Sold and Snatched, Srinagar:* Jay Kay Publishers.
- Old English Records, F. No. 237/1906, Jammu and Kashmir State Archive.
- Khan, G. H. (2006). *Freedom Movement in Kashmir 1931 – 1940,* Shrinagar: Gulshan Books.
- Khan, M. I. (2007). *History of Srinagar (1846-1947): A Study of Socioeconomic Changes.* (3rd Ed.) Shrinagar: Gulshan Books.
- Om, H. (1986). *Muslims of Jammu and Kashmir: Astudy of spread of Education and Consciousness, 1857-1925.* New Delhi: Archive Publishers and Distributors.
- Panikkar, K. M. (2008). *Gulab Singh (1792-1858), Founder of Kashmir.* Shrinagar: City Book Centre.
- Rasool, G. and Meenakshi Chopra (1986). *Education in Jammu and Kashmir: Issues and Documents,* Jammu: Jay Kay Publishers.
- Reports of the Educational Reorganisation Committee (1939). Srinagar: His Highness Government of Jammu and Kashmir, Kashmir Mercantile Press.

- Seru, S. L. (1973). *History and Growth of Education in Jammu and Kashmir: 1872-1973*. Srinagar: Ali Mohammad and Sons.
- Sharp, H. (1916). *A Note on the Education of State of Jammu and Kashmir*, Calcutta: Superintendent Press.
- Zutshi, C. (2003). *Languages of Belonging: Islam, Regional Identity and the Making of Kashmir*. Delhi: Permanent Black.

# Chapter - 7

# Parental Attitude Towards Muslim Girl's Education

—*Fatima Rizvi*

**Abstract**

*Usually it is found that girls and women coming from a Muslim background lag behind in the educational sphere. Parent's attitude towards their children's education is affected adversely by their low socio-economic status. Since the Muslims constitute the disadvantaged population with reference to education, it is expected that the attitude of parents of Muslim children will be unfavourable towards education. However, the present study aims to examine the kind of attitude of Muslim parents towards their daughter's education. The study adopted a qualitative approach and used focus group interviews with a convenient and purposive sample size of 12 parents. Based on the findings of the study which clearly shows that parent attitude towards girl-child education is challenging as parents mostly prefer to train the boys than girls. Government also on the other side has not participated fully, especially for necessary instructions on Muslim girl education.*

***Key Words:*** *Muslim, Parents, Attitude, Education.*

## Introduction

Islam is one of the most revolutionary faiths, which transformed the lives of women of Arabia who were earlier leading a life of degradation and were victims of female infanticide. The Prophet termed woman as the 'Queen of the House' and a delicate crystal while the

Quran has said, "——**And women shall have rights similar to rights against them, according to what is equitable.**" Education has always been important to Muslim community. The common picture of a Muslim woman is the stereotype of a woman hidden behind a veil, a voiceless, silent figure, bereft of rights. It is a picture familiar to all of us, in large part because this is invariably how the media portrays women in Islam. Very contrary to this picture, Islam has actually worked much to protect human rights, especially women's, with integrity, strength, strategic genius, beauty and divinity, and to honour humanity by freeing it from the chains of prejudice, manipulations, personal and social injustice.

But still Muslim women face restrictions in accessing education that differ greatly from one region to another. For example, in Afghanistan there is a denial of adequate education for young girls and women. Repression of women is still prevalent in rural areas, where girls are forced into early marriage and denied basic education. Numerous schools for girls have been burned down and some girls have even been poisoned to death for daring to go to school. Unfortunately, 80 per cent of Afghan women are illiterate and only 30 per cent of girls have access to education. This is a sharp contrast to some universities in the United Arab Emirates that have a female population approaching 80 per cent.

Religion acts as an important cultural factor, which reinforces the traditional perception of women as subordinate to males. The unequal position of women in the family is determined and reinforced by the dictates of the organised religion.

Parents' positive attitude towards child's education is important in determining school attendance and academic achievement of the child. The attitude of the parents signifies the supporting nature of family in their children's education. The parental attitude can be negative or positive. The negative attitude of the parents regarding education and schooling can prevent their children from getting education. Less parental support in school work, low level of motivation can result into poor self-esteem of children. Positive attitude of the parents can be beneficial to their children in many cases and can be reflected in the improvement in class performance, creating of interest among children to learn, and higher achievement scores in reading and writing.

## Methodology

This study is based on primary data. The study has been designed to explore the perceptions of girl's parents on dropout causes in primary level focusing on the socio-psycho analysis. Following is an outline of the methods of study that was adopted during this study. The researcher conducted her study in Malihabad block of district Lucknow, Uttar Pradesh. Parents were selected through purposive sampling method under which convenient sampling was used. Reason for selecting was feasibility for researcher to access the site and to collect data. For this chapter, data were drawn from 12 in-depth interviews. Of the twelve parents who participated in the interviews, there were eight males and four females. Researcher selected in-depth interview because in-depth interviews are used when seeking information on individual, personal experiences from people about a specific issue or topic and to capture people's individual voices and stories. It is important for gaining a detailed insight into the research issue from the perspective of the study participants.

Parents were encouraged to illustrate the causes of dropout reasons of their daughter through specific examples. Parents described their perspective on girl's primary education. They were frequently asked additional follow-up questions to clarify their feelings and their points of view towards the issues addressed. The clarifications for conflicting or unclear answers were sought during the interviews. Extensive handwritten notes were taken, which were transcribed at the earliest possible time after the interviews.

## Data Analysis

The researcher used in vivo analysis while making notes and themes. The interviews were reciprocal, both researcher and research subjects were engaged in the dialogue. Therefore, duration of interviews and the number of questions varied from one participant to the other. Interviews were audio-recorded, with the permission of interviewees, each interview was assigned a code, and notes were taken during the interviews. For the very purpose of phenomenological analysis researchers transcribed key words, phrases and statements to consolidate the emerging themes. The systematic procedure of transforming the data through interpretations was followed.

## Thematic Analysis

Thematic analysis was used as the method for analysing the qualitative data. We identified various themes from analysing the data and counted the frequency of each theme in the participant's answers to the open-ended questions.

## 1. Socialisation and its Impact on Girl's Education

The perceived ideal roles and characteristics of women and girls influence how girls and boys are socialised in the home, community and school. Since girls and women in general are considered physically weaker and less capable than men, they are often over protected and supervised to keep them away from what is considered threatening to their safety including physical, sexual, mental and emotional safety.

*'I know, education is the need of hour and my daughter went to school and studied till 10$^{th}$ but inter college is too far from our village. Either she will have to go alone or I will have to accompany her to school which is not possible on daily basis. So now she has dropped studies.'*

*'Time has changed now. Any place has not remained safe for girl's not even schools. Don't you read newspaper? Girl's molestation by their male teacher is reported frequently. We are poor people we just have to earn respect in society, if this will be lost then what will we do?'*

*'There is no separate girl's school in our village and her father doesn't like girls to study along with boys. He says that girls get spoilt if we send them in co-education. Boys abduct girls to marry them. Many girls have run away with boys in our village. We can't take that risk at all'.*

*'School is far from our home and the road is isolated. Many incidents have been heard in the past so I don't want her to go alone. I just want my daughter to be safe whether educated or uneducated.'*

Some parents were reported to be reluctant to send their daughters to school because of the belief that education and school could be a corrupting influence. There was the view that in co-educational schools, as most primary schools are, girls' morals would be corrupted because of the amount of time they would spend with boys. There was also fear for the physical and sexual safety of girls in school due to cases of physical and sexual harassment and abuse from peers and teachers in the school. Where schools are situated long distances away, parents also worried about their daughters' safety while travelling to and from school. This harassment has also been proved through research to have a negative effect on girls' attitudes towards school and their ability to focus on and perform well in their academic activities.

## 2. Influences of Perceived Gender Roles on Girl's Education

According to many of the parents in the study, it is expected that in adulthood girls will only take on the roles of wives and mothers. As a result many parents do not enrol their daughters in school or withdraw them before completion. Many parents have the attitude that educating girls is a waste of time and money, because they will eventually be married off and their education would therefore only benefit their husbands and the families they marry into. Money spent on the girl's education is hence considered a loss to the girl's family.

Some statements made by parents during interview clearly point to the negative attitudes that many parents in general have towards educating girls. For example, the following statements were all made by parents who participated in interview:

*'This is the age when she should learn household chores which will help her in her future. What's the use of wasting time on education, I have seen my female relative in city who is highly educated and doing a good job but she still has to do the household chores. When at last women have to do the all household work then it will be foolish to take extra work on our shoulders'.*

*'Nature has assigned household responsibilities to women and outdoor duties to men. This is a perfect work distribution system. Why do we need to change this? Girls are fit for doing the household chores then why are they being prompted to behave like boys? They should be happy within boundaries where they are safe and secure'.*

*'I am managing my house since twelve years but I don't feel any difficulty even though I did not go to school too.'*

Girls are expected to take up the roles of wives and mothers in adulthood and their socialisation at home, in the community and school is geared towards providing them with experiences that will prepare them to carry out these roles effectively. These expectations determine the division of labour within the household, with girls being assigned the home making household chores like food preparation, cooking, cleaning, fetching firewood and water, washing clothes and, caring for younger siblings. In addition to this in some areas girls are also expected to participate in farming activities.

## 3. Traditional Practices that Affect Girls' Participation in Education

In Muslim community, there is the practice of marrying girls at a very young age. The practice of early marriage often therefore leads to the end of a girls' formal education. In most cases, the girls have little say in the matter of whether or who they want to marry.

'See I explain you whole thing. Normally Muslim girls get married after reaching puberty which is based on Islamic values. If anyone does not gets his daughter married at the right time still she would be sitting at home doing nothing. So it's better to get them married as they will be adjusted well in their future families.'

*'I want to marry my daughter as soon as possible. You know, in Islam there is no provision for dowry but nowadays people demand money and other things without any hesitation. This demand depends on girl's age and beauty. She is young now so we will not have to give big amount in dowry.'*

For many parents schooling means delaying their plans for their daughter's marriage and parents fear that their girl would become a spinster by the time she finished her school. This mentality is also a big hurdle in the way of Muslim girl's education.

## 4. Poverty and its Effect on Girls' Participation in Education

It was noted that, enrollment levels were low due to their inability to meet the costs of education. Another issue that further aggravated this situation is the fact that, especially in the Muslim community, families tend to have a fairly large number of children. The cumulative effect of the finances required for education often proves to be too much for many families.

*'I have five daughters and two sons; I go for work early in the morning. It's not that we don't want our daughters to study but you tell me if I send all my children to school then who will take care of smaller ones?'.*

*'Boys are the breadwinners since ever; they should be given better facilities to prepare them for their future. I don't have money to send both of them so I send only my son to school'.*

*'What's the use of wasting money on girl's education? We should keep that money saved for their marriage concerns.'*

In Muslim faith, the use of artificial contraceptives is forbidden, resulting in families having large numbers of children. The large family size was said to be the result of traditional attitudes, an example of which is the view that many children is a source of free labour and a source of security during parents' old age.

## 5. Perceived Image of Modern Education

Hesitation and misconception about modern education were also the noted reasons for withdrawal of girls from education. Many of the parents said that after having higher education, people forget their roots, customs and religion. Specifically girls abandon hijab, talk to males without any hesitation. It's a matter of shame. Girls and boys are told to stay away from non-maharam, i.e. those who are unlawful to marry according to Qur'an. Modern schools are offering co-education which is also against Islamic customs. Schools mainly have Non-Islamic environment and do not allow Muslim girls to wear Islamic costumes.

*'My daughter wears hijab as it is compulsory in Islam. If I send my daughter to school she will have to take off this hijab in class room, and male teachers and peons are all around there. I don't want to go against my religion for just giving her education'.*

*'My daughter is eight only and she is learning Quran, which is all what we should give our children. Schools are giving more and more western education to children which leave bad impact on our children.'*

*'Modern schools are spoiling our children specially girls. They organise dance and singing programmes frequently, watching this, our children will also insist to do that. These sorts of things are prohibited in Islam. I don't understand whether they are there for teaching children or make them singer or dancer.'*

*'They learn the things in schools which we never appreciate. Take a small example, my fourteen years old now started liking nail paint because all her friends do. But she can't offer Namaz while wearing nail paint so I strictly told her not to do so.'*

## 6. Perceived Irrelevance of the Government Schools

More Indian children are in schools than ever before but the quality of government schools has sunk to spectacularly low levels. Some parents also complained about the way that children were taught in schools and felt that the teachers lacked the qualifications and motivation to do a good job. They felt that many of the teachers were poorly trained, had little of the knowledge necessary and most were too inexperienced to carry out effective teaching.

*'Everybody knows the conditions of the government run primary schools. Teachers are always busy in doing some sort of non-teaching activity like: election duties, polio booth organising, register maintaining or building constructions. They do everything apart from teaching. I don't want to send my children in those schools and I do not have money to pay fees for private schools.'*

*'They are opening more and more primary schools but not even a single school provides good education.'*

*'Ask any government school teacher that whether his/her own child is studying in government schools. No, because they don't want to spoil their child' future, they send their child in good private school using money which they earn for teaching our children but which they actually don't.'*

## 7. Dissatisfaction with the Government Policies

The Muslim representation among the government jobs and welfare programmes is much low, for this reason many parents feel that there was no immediate need for their children to be in school and considered time spent in school as time wasted, which could be put to better use on domestic chores.

*'I am very disappointed with the government. Nobody cares for our development, they just use us as vote bank. The boys who have completed their graduation and post graduation are not getting any jobs and are compelled to do aari zarzodi (embroidery work), then what about girls. We get them educated but at last they won't be getting any job according to their education then what's the use of wasting their precious years on education when they can get married, have babies and establish their own families?'*

*'We heard that government main concern is to provide education to all, they spend a lot on distributing dress, scholarships and books in schools but the quality of education is still very poor. Why don't they understand schools are for studies not for having food and all? If they enhance the quality of education then the literacy rate will automatically increase'.*

## Limitations of the Study

The study had its flaws as well. The first limitation of the study is the small sample size, which weakens the chances of generalising the findings beyond the sample that was involved. Due to the small sample used, results can only illuminate the issue, but cannot be generalised widely although they could possibly be generalised to girls in similar circumstances. For example, it could be argued that the results could be generalised to those attending the same schools and hailing from the same socio-economic background.

## Conclusion

The findings suggest that parents under the influence of their religion or socio-cultural factors can find education a threat for women's upbringing and thus might avoid taking any risk of their daughters learning things contrary to family values at school. The study concluded that there is a strong need for significant others, especially parents and teachers, to help girls by deconstructing the gender-role stereotypes or perceptions of roles society considers appropriate for girls. In addition, it was discovered that government participation is still inadequate to facilitate change in the area.

On these bases, the researcher recommends the urgent intervention of government to implement the laws governing Muslim girl-child education to enhance and change the negligence of Muslim girl-child education as provisioned in national policy and provide equal access to education. This study indicated that government should set up girls' school/college where both Muslim and non-Muslim girls can acquire knowledge and should launch promotional programmes targeting Muslim girls. The school must allow Muslim girls to wear their own costumes i.e. Islamic dresses. Similarly, government must provide special scholarship to Muslim girl students in order to attract them towards education. In the policy level it should provide reservation quota to both Muslim male and female teachers so that Muslim girls could feel sense of belongingness. The new curriculum must accommodate knowledge from both Qur'an and Hadith as it has been done with the Hindu and Buddhist texts.

## References


- Census. (2001c). Census of India 2001. New Delhi: Registrar General of India, Directorate of Census Operations and Government of India.
- Department of Education: National Policy on Education 1986, Revised Programme of Action 1992, Ministry of Human Resource Development, Government of India, New Delhi.
- Sacher Report Social, Economic and Educational Status of the Muslim Community of India Prime Minister's High Level Committee Cabinet Secretariat Government of India, November, 2006.
- Saukath, A. Muslim Women Emerging Identity, Rawat Publication, Jaipur, 1997.

# Chapter-8

# Role of Print and Electronic Media in Promoting Girl Education in India

*—Manvi Manisha Tigga*

**Abstract**

*The battle for girl education has been a long one. Historically, children have been accorded little, if any, status in society. Deprived of rights and perceived as the property of their parents or guardians, children could be treated any way their guardians or parents thought fit. In India, the thought of parents changed with the change of rulers or kings that is with the advent of the British. Firstly, in the medieval period, in India, education was influenced mostly by foreign invasions. These invasions resulted in the decline of female literacy. The Muslims rule also discouraged girl education. Girls were treated as objects and inferior human beings, relying heavily on male members. Since then, girl and education were antonyms and would have continued to be so if print as well as electronic media had not helped to push the cause of girl education not only forward but to the doorstep of every Indian. Media, has undoubtedly and undisputedly changed the mind-set of the people, broken the shackles of gender discrimination and promoted girl education. It became the unheard voice of millions of girls who were uneducated for the simple reason that they were girls. As media evolved from print to internet, it continuously promoted girl education. The unveiling of orthodox and demeaning outlook of people towards girls took place. With the support of media, education, the fundamental right of every child, till afore only in pen and paper, had a tryst with reality.*

**Key words:** *Girl Education, Female Literacy Rate, Media.*

## Introduction

The term "Media", is the plural of "Medium." It is derived from the Latin term "*medius*" meaning "Middle." It refers to anything that carries information between a source and a receiver. Its purpose is to facilitate communication and learning. Communication channels through which news, entertainment, education, data, or promotional messages are disseminated is Media. Media includes every broadcasting medium such as newspaper, magazines, TV, radio, billboards, telephone, fax, and internet. Information is power and those who control the media empires have great power and a great responsibility to use that power positively.

According to Berkowitz and Rawlings (1963), "Electronic Media" can be defined as those communication means that are based on electronic or electromechanical means of production and is most often distinguished from print media. The main electronic sources used by general public normally include radio, television, sound recordings, video recordings and internet. It indicates the primary means of communicating with large groups of people. There are four basic functions of electronic media which generally include to inform, entertain, educate and, the most important, to influence public opinion. Berkowitz and Rawlings further argued that twentieth century is heavily dominated by communication technology. The means of mass communication grew in succession as the century unfolded. These means of communication extensively promoted girl education. It lends voice to millions of girls who were deprived of an opportunity to go to school. Assuredly, the government made policies and provided with funds but it was the widespread popularity of Media due to which girl education was promoted.

## Role of Print Media

The British rule brought print media to India. Along with it, it brought a fresh outlook that perceived girls as individuals and the spreading realisation among the masses regarding the importance of girl education. It opened a whole new perspective on the treatment of girl child. Articles written by Rabindra Nath Tagore, Raja Ram Mohan Roy and other visionaries opened the mind of the Indian masses.

Though, the press was not the most important means of communication in a country like India because of its large illiterate population, yet because of the existing power structure which was dominated by the educated people, the written records carried much value. Hence, it had the capability to influence the attitudes of both ordinary readers and policy-makers on a large scale. The significance of printed media initiated from India's struggle for independence. The Press was one of the most important weapons used by the great leaders of national movement against the British government.

Since independence, print media has brought to the notice of the public various schemes and policies for girl education. Books, journals and articles are published time and again, promoting girl education. The initiatives taken by successive Indian governments like the National Committee on Women's Education (1958) to address the difficulties that hindered the progress of girl's education and its recommendations for making girls' education at par with the boys, was able to be communicated to large number of people through the media and this made the people aware of the steps taken towards girl education. In this way print media has been successful in educating the masses to acknowledge the necessity of girl education. The power of words has narrowed the difference between girl and boy child and subsequently, the education books, once the proprietary of boy child has become the weapon of girl child. This spark of girl education was rekindled by print media. Print media was limited to people who could read so girl education was limited to the upper class who knew the value of educating the girl child. Gradually, girl education became the trend and middle class began to send their girl child for education.

The mention of names of Annie Besant, Sarojini Naidu, Subadhra Kumari Chauhan, Joan of Arc, Jhansi ki Rani, Barkha Dutt, Kiran Bedi, in the newspapers and journals spread the message that girls are no less than boys. When television was still a luxury for the middle class family, which comprises of majority of Indians, magazines and newspapers printed the rare accomplishments of women like Sushmita Sen, Aishwarya Rai etc. and tried to eradicate the taboos and norms around girls. The various educational schemes for the girl child published in newspapers, journals reached the doorsteps of the masses and unveiled the evils of orthodox customs, rituals, female foeticide and other evils against women. People who thought girl education to be a waste came to know that it is the right of a child to be educated irrespective of being a girl or boy and it is the duty of parents to educate the child. Parents must fulfil this duty without any greed; it's an investment towards humanity and society. Print media not only educated the masses about the schemes of girl education, it also opened the doors for new employment opportunities for them.

**Gujarat CM's girl child education fund gets Rs22 cr in donations**

**Thursday, 8 October 2009 - 8:59am IST | Place: Gandhinagar**

In the past 3 years, it has been used to provide aid to more than 33,000 girls.

Chief minister Narendra Modi's initiative for educating girls seems to be paying off. His personal and constant efforts record reveals that funds amounting to more than Rs22.38 crore have been collected in the past six and a half years by CM's Girl Child Education Fund (Kanya Kelavani Nidhi). Moreover, during the same period, Rs9.59 crore were used for girl child education in the state, and in the past three years the fund has been used to provide assistance to a total of 33,410 girls. www.guruprasad.net

*Source*: http://guruprasad.net

Prime Minister Narendra Modi releasing the special postage stamps while launching the nation-wide campaign of Beti Bachao–Beti Padhao Abhiyan in Panipat, Haryana, on January 22, 2015, urging the people to take an oath to fight female foeticide, celebrate the birth of a girl and educate them, was extensively covered by media. Such campaigns would have been lost had it not been for the media which continuously and consistently has taken up the cause of girl education.

## Role of Electronic Media

In the contemporary age, electronic media is increasingly being used to reach the masses. It has been able to give voice to various causes, especially the cause of girl education. In fact, it has proved to be a useful medium to promote girl education. If one has to ask what is today's most powerful vehicle in moulding of beliefs, attitudes, values and lifestyles, one would say it is electronic media. By becoming more gender aware in content and language, media presents a clearer and more accurate picture of the roles and responsibilities of both men and women in the society. The need for mass media to cover the entire population is widely admitted. Print media, through words, has been able to propel the bourgeoisie towards educating their girls'. In the present information period, we have noticed printing technology against a revolution in communication technology. Communication satellites, cable networks, computer systems, and their usages and ideas have become a central feature of modern life. Whereas electronic media, through words as well as actions, has been able to reach the masses even in far flung areas, pushing the cause of girl education forward. The popularity of Media can be ascertained from the fact that India's 230 million Television viewers now exceed its 203.6 million newspaper readers.

### 1. *Radio*

Radio came to India according to an agreement of **23 July 1927**. The private Indian Broadcasting Company LTD (IBC) was then authorised to operate two radio stations; the Mumbai station began on **23 July 1927**, and the Calcutta station followed on **26 August 1927**.

UNICEF developed the Meena Communication Initiative (MCI) as a mass communication project aimed at changing perceptions and behaviour that hamper the survival, protection and development of girls in South Asia. Meena is widely recognised and appreciated in most South Asian countries, and is a successful advocacy and teaching tool for girls' and children's rights. The Meena figure has achieved remarkable popularity as she tackles the key issues affecting children, and the threats to the rights of millions of girls in South Asia.

All Radio Stations broadcast programmes for rural women as well as urban women at the timings convenient for listening by the respective target groups. The programme directed to women listeners cover subjects related to socio-economic development of women, health and family welfare, food and nutrition, scientific home management, women entrepreneurship, education, including adult education, gender issues etc. These programmes also aim at creating wide social awareness about rights and privileges of women through the propagation of legal literacy. All India Radio strives, through its programmes, to seek to raise the social consciousness of the country with regard to attitude towards women. Different traditional folk forms are used to communicate specially with the rural women audience.

Besides the issue of women forming the main part of the women's programmes, the problems in general faced by women and the need for change in social attitude towards women also forms an integral part of the general broadcast. Special programmes as well as general audience programmes are being broadcast that focus on the issue of the required change in social attitude and behavioural practices towards women.

## 2. *Television*

Television programmes around the twentieth century increasingly started showing women oriented serials. Majority of the masses watched and followed these serials closely which helped in promoting girl education. Talk shows held by women and daily advertisements show casing women helped in changing the mindset of the people. The change in mindset of the people led to more attendance of girls in schools. The myth of men or boys being the sole caretakers of parents in their old age was debunked. In the late seventies when women organisations kicked off movements, media invariably played an important role in spreading information and ideas about the status of women in society and the need to improve it. The crucial role of media for transmitting the development information was well perceived in Seventh Five Year Plan (1985-99) when a separate Chapter on 'Communication, Information and Broadcasting' was included in the planned document. The mass media had been highlighted as, 'A vehicle of education and extension to narrow the information gap between different target groups like youth, women, children and weaker sections'.

With the proliferation of 'women's genres' soap operas, melodramas, women's magazines and so on women emerged as powerful identity. The mass media set the agenda for public opinion by selecting themes, items and points of views that tended to break the shackles of patriarchal culture. A research was enhanced during Satellite Industrial Television Experiment (SITE), results of the study revealed that those women who viewed Television gained more than men in areas like family planning, health and nutrition. Another significant finding of the study was that illiterate women, more than literate women gained knowledge from Television viewing in the same areas thereby indicating that literacy was no barrier for learning from Television.

Thus, social media has played an important role in spreading awareness, promoting alternative-empowered images of women, breaking down stereotypes and shaping mindsets. The entering of women in the labour markets is at its peak, there is increase in the number of educated women, and heightened awareness of their mobilisation to fight against injustice and discrimination. The role of women in the family has undergone significant changes; from educated housewives they are now educated working wives. Woman have acquired a respectable place in society. Today's women are increasingly conscious of the change in the civil society and magazines especially on women's issues spread awareness as they carry a lot of information on social issues and personal family issues. Now, being aware women have taken upon to themselves to educate their girl child. Radio, television, newspaper, magazines and films have played a vital role in spreading information, propagating concepts, educating and enlightening, strengthening national integration, creating national identity etc.

A series of world conferences related to women have strengthened social economic and political magnitude of gender equality through empowerment of women, nationally and internationally. The two calculated objectives of Beijing Platform of Action concerning women and media that aim to promote women empowerment are to increase women empowerment in decision-making through media and other technologies of mass communication and promotion of non-stereotyped portrayal of women in media. Had it not been for electronic media Malala Yousafzai would not have been a household name. The wide coverage given by media to the girl who stood against the Taliban and got shot in the head brought a new light to the cause of girl education. Malala's voice in favour of girl education led her to be honoured by the Nobel Prize for peace. Her determination and story will go down in history because of media. There are other similar stories in the form of books, journals, television which time and again reminds one and all of the value of educating girl children.

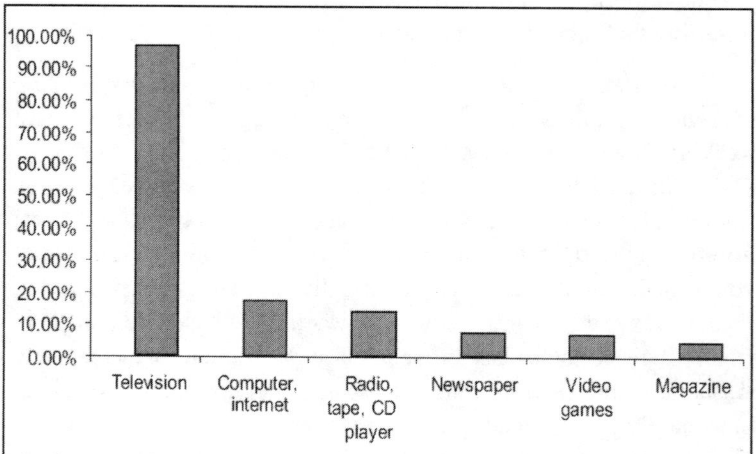


*Source*: http://bni-india.com

Survey conducted in the year 1999, around 99 per cent of people preferred to watch television.

***Fig. 8.1: Per cent Media Usage Distribution.***

### 3. *Internet*

In India the web is now established as a mass market media channel. The main changes in internet access have happened in the last five years and the internet has become an essential part of office life and also plays a key role in many homes. The number of people with internet access continues to rise. More people spend more time online in India every year, and the digital tools and sites they use play an ever-growing role in their lives. The following statistics reveals the growing importance of the internet:

- 2 per cent - Number of rural Indians using the internet.
- 25 per cent - Growth in Indian internet users in India over the past 12 months.
- 59 per cent - Number of Indians who only access the internet via mobile devices.

According to new research, with two-thirds of the country's web users accessing social media daily, Social Media has now become part of everyday life for a majority of online Indians. According to a study on social media usage by The Nielsen Company conducted in collaboration with Absolute Data, nearly 30 million Indians who are online are members of social networking sites and about two-thirds of them spend time on these social networking sites daily.

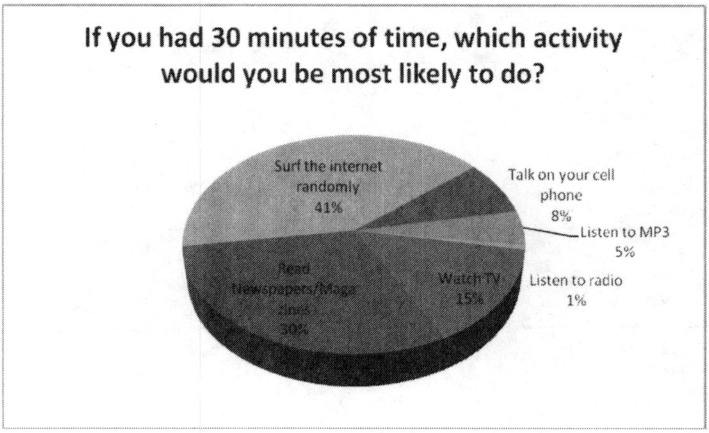


*Fig. 8.2: Media Preference Mapping.*

*Source:* http://business-networking-india.com

In a survey conducted in the year 2010 by Niraj. R. Shah, it was found that 41 per cent of Gen X (between ages of 36-45 years and **30 per cent Gen Y** (age group of 26-35 years) surfed the internet randomly, if they had 30 minutes of time. A startling **33 per cent** were on the net to **research prospects**, while a whopping **27 per cent** were interested in **networking**. Internet has gained momentum due to social networking sites. These networking sites help in linking the world together. Networking sites often share information and advertisement on girl education.

Internet has helped in spreading awareness regarding girl education. In case someone is desirous of donating money for the cause of girl education, then all the questions on the knowhow of donation can be found on the internet. Various plans and policies made by the government and the current status of girl education can be found with the click of a button. The social media in twentieth century is enabling the sheltered and isolated women curbed by old societal norms to know their rights and revolt against inequality. The present decade is a decisive time for Indian society as the nation is facing gender imbalance, the consequences of which is unravelling glaringly and is threatening the whole civilisation. To build a sustainable future, the minds of the society need to be nurtured in a desirable manner.

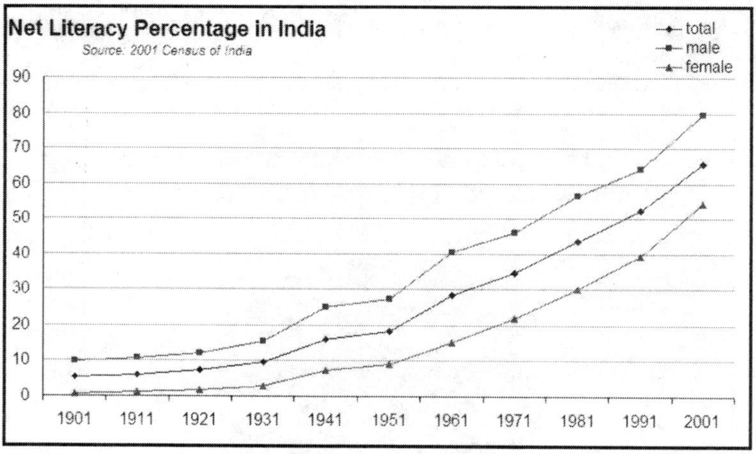


*Source:* http://commons.wikimedia.org

*Fig. 8.3*

## Conclusion

The increase in literacy rate from the year 1901 to 2001 has been possible because of the widespread impact of media (both print and electronic) on the Indian masses. If more girls are educated they are more likely to marry late, more likely to have less children, more likely to have healthier children and more likely to be able to send them to school. It will be a win-win situation for one and all.

On 5th September 2014, the Prime Minister of India Narendra Modi, in response to a question on girls' education said, "There is an old saying that if a boy studies, only one person learns but if we educate a girl, two families learn along with it. Women's education plays an important role in the nation's development. Why else do you think I have made girls' toilets a priority for my government? So that they stay back in school and learn. I have given much thought to this programme and its results will be seen soon", the PM said. Assuredly, a nation can progress only when its communities progress, communities can progress only when men and women simultaneously progress. To bring about progress, media has played and is still playing a fearless and significant role.

## References


- Government of India, Census of India 2001.
- Survey conducted by Niraj. R. Shah, 2010.
- Mahajan, V. D. (1988). History of Medieval India, S. Chand and Co, New Delhi.
- Avasthi, A.P. (2011). Indian Government and Politics, Lakshmi Narayan Agarwal Publications Co, Agra.
- http://commons.wikimedia.org/wiki/File:India Literacy Rate 1901-2001.jpg
- http://business-networking-india.comhttp://bni-india.com
- http://guruprasad.net

# (Section – D)

# Girl Education Promotion – Initiatives and Schemes

# Chapter – 9

# Implication of Capability Approach on the Girls Education: Theory and Reality

***—Md Nurul Momen and Mst. Marzina Begum***

## Abstract

*Capability approach offers a radical generalisation of the conventional approach to welfare economics. Many researchers are now exploring its implications in the different areas of social arrangements. Until now capability approach has been highly influential in the development literature. The capabilities approach was developed by Amartya Sen and was later expanded by Martha Nussbaum and others political philosophers. The approach emerged as a response to the theoretical difficulties of the conventional approach to welfare economics. However, Anand observed (2005) that welfare economics works by identifying optimal allocations of inputs and outputs, whereas individuals are often concerned with their rights, which form legitimate claims independent of the outcomes to which they might lead.*

*This chapter aims to present a theoretical analysis of the capability approach and its implication on the girls' education in the context of Bangladesh. However, we intend to focus on the main conceptual ideas of the capability approach, as developed by Amartya Sen and Martha Nussbaum, and in the later part we intend to measure the idea of capability approach with the current situation of girls' education and causes of potential low girl education in Bangladesh which lead to poverty. In this chapter the terms: female, girls and women have been interchangeably used.*

**Key Word:** *Bangladesh, Capability, Education, Girls, Amartya Sen, Martha Nussbaum.*

## Theorising Capability Approach

The capability approach is a framework for the evaluation and assessment of individual well-being and social arrangements. As we have already said that it is used in a wide range of academic fields, for example, most prominently in development studies, welfare economics, social policy and political philosophy.

The capability approach has provided a theoretical base of the human development paradigm (Fukuda-Parr, 2003, cited by Robeyns, 2005). The chapter explores the question as to how does capability approach work to evaluate people's well-being, for example, inequality, poverty, the well-being of an individual or the average well-being of the members of a group. As observed by Robeyns (2005), it can be used as a framework within which to design and evaluate policies, ranging from welfare state design in affluent societies, to development policies by governments and non-governmental organisations in developing countries.

In the academic field, the approach is being discussed in philosophical terms and empirical studies as well. Therefore, it is important to note that the capability approach is not a theory that can explain poverty, inequality or well-being; rather we do believe that it provides a framework within which to conceptualise and evaluate such phenomena.

Sen's (1999) capability approach was developed in conjunction with the political philosopher, Martha Nussbaum. To them, the central idea is that what people can do (capabilities) as opposed to what they actually do (functioning) should be the focus of conceptualisation and evaluation. Individual behaviours can be overly typical, for instance, a person might have luxurious opportunities to live in society but yet she may maintain her life in a miserable way. So, the choice context does matter in the evaluation of behaviour, for example, a person may not be eating food because she is fasting, whereas, this behaviour can be seen in a different way by another person who actually cannot find anything to eat (Anand, 2005). The above examples are not relevant to the capabilities approach, although these have been highlighted by Sen and Nussbaum as one of the motives for emphasising how a person can behave.

Martha Nussbaum (2000) presented *capabilities* approach by describing three kinds. First, there are '*basic capabilities*' which include sight, the ability to taste and all other capabilities a normal human possesses by birth. The second category she termed as *internal capabilities*, which require maturation such as the realisation of one's sexuality. She calls the third set of capabilities as *combined capabilities*, the attainment of which requires not only maturation but also an appropriate external environment, for example, physically attending school.

## Development and Gender Equality

Developing countries including Bangladesh still present gender inequality in different spheres of life such as access to health and education, employment opportunity, and political participation, though situation of gender inequality has been slightly improving in Bangladesh. In 2013, Bangladesh was ranked 142 out of 187 countries on the Human Development Index and 115 out of 149 countries surveyed on the Gender Inequality Index (UNDP, nd).

According to different empirical research, it is observed that gender inequality is strongly correlated with poverty. To us, when poverty combines with gender inequality on education, the result will be more acute malfunction of human resource development. It has been empirically proved that schooling helps to increase production in agriculture; for example, farmers will have access to the necessary inputs needed to increase production when they are knowledgeable by means of education. There is no doubt that the income of the self-employed are higher for educated than for uneducated. As observed by Oxaal (1997) that increasing the percentage of schooling girls brings beneficial effects for their own development, for their own health, and as a consequence that of their families also. The findings clearly indicate that there is a link between high percentage of enrollment of education among girls and reduction of poverty, although there is effect of macro and micro-level poverty on levels of education (Oxaal, 1997).

In the category of *medium human development* countries, the adult literacy rate is 83.3 per cent for men and 67.3 per cent for women. On the other hand, in the *low human development countries*, the rate is 57.2 per cent for males and 35.8 per cent for females. Percentages of school enrollment in the *medium development countries* is 60 per cent for females as against 68 per cent for males. In the *low human development countries*, it is 33 per cent for females as against, 44 per cent for males. In terms of real Gross Domestic Product per capita, women control $2220 and men control $4414 in the *medium development countries* and the comparative values in the *low human development countries* are $ 691 for women as against $1277 for men (Nussbaum, 2000). Given the statistics, it can be concluded that countries with low per capita incomes tend to have low school enrollment ratios.

Bangladesh is one of the densely populated countries in the world. Its population is larger than Russia, but it is also an extremely poor country where the GDP per capita income was $957.82 in 2013. It is estimated that 4.9 million children in Bangladesh aged 5 to 15 are engaged in child labour. The situation of child labour makes it difficult to break the vicious cycle of poverty that contributes to one of the lowest adult literacy rates in the South Asia. With a dropout rate by grade five of about 50 per cent, the challenge is not just admitting girls in schools rather it is keeping them in classes.

## Gender Equity and Access

There is no doubt that education contributes to economic development in a society. Elaborately, it has been established that education is crucial for improving the lives of people living in poverty. Furthermore, we do believe that education helps to alleviate poverty by improving labour productivity and rendering other social benefits. Education is, therefore, a vital social and economic development goal of any nation.

If a girl is barred from going to school, her combined capability of attending school will not come into realisation. This situation is prevalent in the case of girls in Bangladesh, especially those living in the rural areas. The fact is that rural girls in Bangladesh have the internal capability of attending school, but they do not always possess the combined capability to attend school. Further, it is seen among rural girls in Bangladesh that girls not only face social obstacles, but also financial challenges that prevent them from realising the combined capability to attend school.

Amartya Sen (1999) points out five basic freedoms that are not only important for their inherent value, but also for their instrumental value. Sen (1999) argued by saying that freedoms contribute to the well-being of individuals. Furthermore, freedom not only functions to improve the lives of humans but an entire country. To him, the five freedoms include: *political freedoms, economic facilities, social opportunities, transparency guarantees, and protective security*. Sen (1999), furthermore, discusses his ideas by illustrating that these five freedoms are important for three reasons: their *direct importance, instrumental value, and their constructive role*. First of all, direct importance refers to the intrinsic value of freedom to an individual. To him, the instrumental value is perhaps one of the most important aspects of freedom. As Sen (1999) argues, "*freedoms and rights may also be very effective in contributing to economic progress*", so, it can be said that freedoms are not only important, but they are also vital to the process of development as they create avenues for economic and political progress. Lastly, according to Sen (1999), the constructive role of freedoms gives meaning to and defines an individual's life.

## How Gender Discrimination an Education Works in Bangladesh?

If a social science researcher intends to measure well-being of a girl in Bangladesh, according to Sen (1999), the proper strategy would be an examination of the five freedoms mentioned earlier. It is important to measure to what extent these freedoms of each rural girl in Bangladesh are being fulfilled? When it comes to reality, by not receiving an education, girls in Bangladesh cannot properly enjoy many of the listed freedoms. Without the ability to read or write promoting basic rights among girls gets difficult. Therefore, it can be assumed that girls cannot enjoy freedoms without being educated. We think that if girls attain higher levels of education, girls are more likely to occupy higher paying jobs. As a consequence, this will allow girls to fully support themselves and their families as well. But the fact is that many rural girls in Bangladesh do not complete even primary schooling, therefore, their chances of financially supporting themselves and their families are highly minimal.

The inferiority of girls is deeply rooted in Bangladesh and it is worse in rural society. This discrimination starts from birth and even persists throughout their whole span of life. Many rural families still keep their girls away from schooling because they don't believe a girl needs education. Therefore, many girls are getting married at very early ages and thus eliminating any chance to explore their potentialities. The scenario is that in rural Bangladesh girls kept themselves only for household activities, which eventually lead to the worsening of the problems of accessing social opportunities in society. From the above points, it can be concluded that education itself is a social opportunity and a status symbol for every individual. Without education girls cannot understand the violation of their basic rights.

Rural girls in Bangladesh may not enjoy freedom because of their lack of education, as education brings a wealth of knowledge and a lot of opportunities in social life. Without education, girls in rural Bangladesh find themselves in unpleasant circumstances. For example, in the event of sudden demise of husband, a woman may find herself vulnerable if she does not have education. No education will mean nil job opportunities. Thus, girls' current level of education makes them difficult to possess any such freedoms in rural Bangladesh. Sen's tools of evaluating girl's freedom suggest that in rural Bangladesh girls' well-being is very minimal.

Sen (1999) demonstrates that freedoms contribute to individual well-being and development and his view has been supported by other political philosophers as well. We also support Sen's argument. On the other hand, as an opposing way, Nussbaum elaborated the idea how a lack of freedoms and education can be unfavourable in the realisation of long-term opportunities and achievement for females. To her, individual development is the by product of education and these freedoms. However, rural girls in Bangladesh face choices what Nussbaum terms as 'adaptive preferences'. To her, 'adaptive preferences' are the set of choices that individuals make based upon socialisation and the dominant factors within the environment. For example, one may believe that it is indeed the choice of a girl to marry at a young age and leave her education. In fact, it may be the case that a girl in rural Bangladesh is simply raised by believing that she has no place in a school and that home is her only place. A girl is meant to occupy certain roles at home, but not to get education as a student. Thus, education takes a back seat due to the beliefs in which many girls in rural Bangladesh are brought up.

Girls may make decisions in certain ways. Their decision might be influenced by socialisation and other potential factors within the environment. A girl may *choose* to marry at a young age while she has the option to marry or not to marry. But in rural Bangladesh it may be the case that she never has the opportunity of such an option. Instead, the way in which she is brought up and her lack of options ultimately influences her decision as opposed to her positive future. Nussbaum pointed out that such preferences extend to all stages of life, for example, child bearing, voicing political opinions, and even making a public appearance (Nussbaum, 2000).

## Is Access to Girls Supportive in Bangladesh?

*"No country has ever emerged from poverty without giving priority to education and if education is the escape door from poverty, then girls' education is the key to that door"*, so said UNICEF Executive Director, Carol Bellamy. When it comes to the practice of girl education in Bangladesh, in the urban areas gender equality in terms of education has been somewhat achieved in primary school enrollments. In the urban areas, in many places, girls have higher enrollment ratios than boys. This does not mean, however, that access to primary education is equal for girls across the country. However, many empirical studies on school enrollment in Bangladesh have shown that girls have been targeted for primary school enrollments in rural areas. But still girls' attendance rates are considerably lower than the boys. As stated earlier,

girls are often kept at home to take care of household activities. Therefore, this situation causes girls to be at an immediate disadvantage in the education process. The same holds true although to a lesser degree in urban areas, the problem is worse for girls of poor families (Kalene Ardt, *et. al,* 2005).

The gender inequality in education in rural Bangladesh indicates a sense of something happening wrong in the process. Therefore, there is a need for urgent solution. Now the pertinent question is what the gender gap implicates within the same environment, since two groups of students are not producing the same results. Therefore, there must be some potential factors within the environment that leads to females being outperformed by males. Potential factors, physical environment and all other things being equal, certain forces must exist to create such a disparity between male and female in education sector. Because males are attending school for much longer, so, there is reason to believe that females could also perform like their male counterparts if they also do so.

Given the context, the possibility of improvement exists within the environment. We think changing improvement for the females' education in Bangladesh must be sought. Solutions should make females' education not only the means to a solution but ends as well. As ends, females have the ability to improve their basic rights by being provided the opportunity to receive a better education. As means, females serve as the pathway to development, as explained by Sen.

Sen (1999) argued on development in his book *Development as Freedom*. He pointed out that *"Development can be seen as a process of expanding the real freedoms that people enjoy."* In the case of women, Sen (1999) viewed that development is a byproduct of not just women being recipients of increased freedom; rather women's roles should be as *'agents'*. Furthermore, he referred the agency is rooted in female education which increase their economic activity and overall empowerment. Summing up, what Sen (1999) asserts is that education is an intrinsic freedom which all individuals must attain. Not only does it make the case for personal development, for example, personal well-being, scholarly growth, etc., but Sen (1999) also pointed out at the practical aspects attainable through education. Elaborating the notion he basically promoted that educated people are economically and politically empowered and thus contribute to the improvement of their own lives as well as the development of their countries.

Many political philosophers have identified obstacles that females face in the education process, especially in developing countries like Bangladesh. For example, Nussbaum (2000) argued that religion poses obstacles to female education and there is a huge difficulty in addressing religious sentiment that is much evident in society. Keeping the religious obstacles in mind, Martha Nussbaum's goal is to stress the importance of understanding the context while advocating any changes on female education in society. Nussbaum also acknowledges that allowing for the free exercise of religion and being aware of social and cultural context are extremely important in progressive movements. Nussbaum (2000) observes, "*When we tell people that they cannot define the ultimate meaning of life in their own way-even if we are sure we are right, and that their way is not a very good way-we do not show full respect for them as persons.*" In this specific context, women should serve as agents in their own empowerment process.

We have already pointed out that women in rural Bangladesh have lack of access to fundamental rights of a normal human life. They are less well nourished than men, less healthy, and more vulnerable to physical violence and sexual abuse. They are less likely to be literate than men and further still women are less likely to have professional or technical education. Furthermore, if women intend to enter the workplace, they face greater obstacles such as workplace bullying, sex discrimination and so on. Similar obstacles often impede their effective participation in political life as well.

In many nations, women are not considered full equals under the law. Therefore, they do not have the same property rights as men. Furthermore, a woman does not have the same rights in many issues, for example, for making a contract, the same rights of association, mobility, religious liberty, etc. (Nussbaum, 2000). However, in the developing countries including Bangladesh women have full responsibility for household activities and child care. Therefore, they lack opportunities for the cultivation of their cognitive development and interaction with outside domain. All these factors take toll on their psychological development. Apart from that, women have fewer opportunities than men to live free from fear. From the above discussions, it can be concluded that in the developing countries including Bangladesh women still lack essential supports for leading lives that are fully human. This lack of support is frequently caused to them due to their being women, even though they live in a constitutional democracy like Bangladesh. In summing up, it can be said that all these practices, unequal social and political circumstances render especially the rural women unequal human capabilities.

Hence, recognising the seriousness of lack of education for rural girls in Bangladesh is important. The argument here is that it is necessary to improve the level of attainment of education among girls which might lead to the possibility of further development in society.

## Bangladesh–Is There any Hope?

Basic rights such as education are produced at the lowest per capita for the 150 million of people living in 155,000 sq.km (55,000 Sq. Mile) areas. However, the political leadership is still living in their traditional mindsets. Political leaders are acting in such a way as if they are still fighting against the Pakistani military rulers. However, Bangladesh got independence from Pakistan through a nine months long bloody struggle in December, 1971.

Furthermore, the ruling party in Bangladesh is used to address their daily lecture to the poverty stricken population so as to present themselves as honest and dedicated to their daily work, but in reality, these politicians are now destroying public resources for their own private gain through many corrupt means (see the reports from Berlin Based Transparency International which publishes Bangladesh Chapter every year). Apart from that, ruling party politicians always provoke government servants and ordinary citizens to raise their voice against their opponent political parties who may come into power in future. On the other hand, the opposition always is agitating to overthrow ruling party as well. These are the common scenarios in the political arena of Bangladesh.

Despite lack of commitment of the political leadership in Bangladesh, much progress has been made regarding girls enrollment in education in rural Bangladesh. In the recent days, Bangladesh has witnessed an increase in girls' access to primary education, especially by those who live in rural areas. Furthermore, to support the cause of girls' secondary education, the Government of Bangladesh has already introduced public policies, for example, free education at the secondary level. These policies have been introduced in 2005. It is our hope that within a certain time period these policies will produce better results for women in the primary and secondary education sector, which in turn may produce more women in the employment sector leading to more empowered women in the society.

## Conclusion

In the last decade, there has been an enormous interest in the capability approach among researchers and policy-makers as well. Many have read something about the approach and want to know more about it and its implication on different social arrangements. However, the interdisciplinary nature of the capability approach has led to development literature that is scattered over a wide range of books and journals, which has created the need for a new article to justify its implication in different social settings. Through this chapter we tried to analyse capability approach and its implication over education that is directly involved both in poverty eradication and comprehensive development in Bangladesh. Summing up, all activities whatsoever undertaken to eradicate poverty in order to achieve development, may go in vain if there is no education among women in Bangladesh because they are the half of the total population.

## References


- Anand, P. (2005). "*Capabilities and Health*" Journal Medical Ethics, No. 31: pp. 299–303.
- Kalene, Ardt et. al. (2005). "*Report on Primary Education in Bangladesh: Challenges and Successes*" Bangladesh Bureau of Education Information and Statistics (BANBEIS), Bangladesh Ministry of Women and Children Affairs (MWCA), the Third Summit on South Asian Development, hosted by South Asian Society for Regional Cooperation (SAARC) May 19, 2005.

- Nussbaum, Martha (2000). "*Women's Capabilities and Social Justice*" Journal of Human Development, Vol. 1, No. 2, ISSN 1464-9888 Print/ ISSN1469-9516, online/00/020219-29. 2000, United Nations Development Programme.
- Oxaal, Zoë (June, 1997). "*Education and Poverty: A Gender Analysis, Report prepared for the Gender Equality Unit*" Swedish International Development Cooperation Agency (SIDA), Report No 53, © Institute of Development Studies, ISBN 1-85864-346-5.
- Robeyns, Ingrid (March, 2005). "*The Capability Approach: a Theoretical Survey*" Ingrid Robeyns is a research fellow at the Department of Political Science and at the Amsterdam School of Social Sciences Research, University of Amsterdam Journal of Human Development, Vol. 6, No. 1.
- Sen, Amartya (1999). "*Development as Freedom*" Anchor Books: New York. pp. xi-298.
- UNDP (nd). "*Human Development Report*" Available at- www./hdr.undp. org/ (Last accessed on 30 January, 2015).
- Helping Bangladeshi Girls, Go Further, Available at www.worldbank.org (Last accessed on 10 January, 2015).
- Investment in Girls' Education key against Poverty" Available at- www.afrol.com (Last accessed on 21 August, 2014).

# Chapter – 10

# Promotion of Girls' Education in India: Central Government Initiatives

*—Akhilesh Patel*

**Abstract**

*The importance of education has increased manifold in the era of knowledge, based society. The progress of the nation can be achieved only through educating the human beings and developing them into valuable resources. The avenues of education should be freely and equally available to all sections and strata of the society. The women and men should have equal access to quality education. The government interventions for education have borne fruits and the literacy rate has increased substantially and the gender gap in education is also declining steadily. But, still there is a lot to do in order to bring education of men and women on equal platforms. This chapter takes a stock of ongoing Central Government schemes for bridging the gender gap in education and puts forward some valuable suggestions to make these schemes more effective.*

***Keywords:*** *Girl education, Higher Education, School Education, Gender Gap.*

## Introduction

Education is an effective tool for empowering the human being. This becomes more important when the case is for women empowerment. Due to various social, economic, historical, political, religious and cultural reasons women education in India has not got due recognition and importance. The literacy rate among women is significantly lower than that of men. Women are not accorded equal position in comparison to men in most of the sections of the society. In our country, according to Census-2011 the female literacy rate and male literacy rate is 65.46 and 82.14 respectively. There is gender gap of 16.68 in literacy rate. The Table 1 gives a glimpse of literacy rate after independence and gender gap in literacy rate.

**Table 1: Literacy Rate in India: 1951-2011**

| *Census Year* | *Average* | *Males* | *Females* | *Male-Female gap in literacy rate* |
|---|---|---|---|---|
| 1951 | 18.33 | 21.16 | 8.86 | 18.30 |
| 1961 | 28.3 | 40.4 | 15.35 | 25.05 |
| 1971 | 34.45 | 45.96 | 21.97 | 23.98 |
| 1981 | 43.57 | 56.38 | 29.76 | 26.62 |
| 1991 | 52.21 | 64.13 | 39.29 | 24.84 |
| 2001 | 64.83 | 75.26 | 53.67 | 21.59 |
| 2011 | 74.04 | 82.14 | 65.46 | 16.68 |

*Source:* Census of India.

The table reveals that female literacy has always been lower than male literacy rate in India. The positive aspect is that literacy rate is increasing steadily after independence. A trend of decline in gender gap in literacy is visible after 1981. The government interventions and efforts of various organisation of the society have made this possible.

The very first education policy of independent India, National Policy on Eduaction-1968 recognised the importance of girl education and accordingly recommended, "*The education of girls should receive emphasis, not only on ground of social justice, but also because it accelerates social transformation.*" This recommendation provided impetus to governments' initiatives for promoting girl education. The Education Commission observed in its report, "*The role of women outside the homes has become an important feature of the social and economic life of the country and in the years to come, this will assume large proportions affecting a majority of women. It will, therefore, be necessary to pay adequate attention to the problems of training and employment of women."* The National Policy on Education-1986, which was framed in the light of recommendations of this commission, also emphasised the importance of education for women empowerment. NPE-1986 recommended, *"Education will be used as an agent of basic change in the status of women."* Accordingly women education was given importance by all successive governments of Centre and States.

To promote active participation of the Central Government, Education was made a subject of Concurrent List in 1976 by the 42nd Constitutional Amendment Act. Earlier education was a subject of State List of VII Schedule of the Constitution of India and it was primarily the duty of States to provide facilities of education to its people.

The Government of India as well as State Governments have come up with many schemes covering one or the other level of education viz. elementary, secondary and higher education. In this chapter focus is on the ongoing schemes launched by Government of India.

## Schemes for School Education (Primary to Higher Secondary Level)

School education covers the formal education from pre-primary upto 12th standard. This includes elementary education and secondary education. The various schemes of Central Government covering school education are discussed in following paragraphs.

## National Programme for Education of Girls at Elementary Level

For bridging gender gap in elementary education, Government of India launched this scheme. The scheme addresses the needs of girls who are 'in' as well 'out' of school in educationally backward blocks. The scheme put responsibility on teachers to recognise vulnerable girls and pay special attention to bring them out of the vulnerability and preventing their dropout from school. The scheme promotes inclusiveness of girls in education system and promotes quality of girls' education.

## Rashtriya Madhyamik Shiksha Abhiyan

Rashtriya Madhyamik Shiksha Abhiyan was launched by Government of India in 2009 to increase access and quality of secondary education with due importance to equity. The scheme aims for universal access to secondary education by 2017 and hundred per cent retention by 2020. Though scheme is for both boys and girls but some special provisions have been included for girls in the scheme–

- Separate toilets for girls
- Bridge course for older girls
- Recruitment of 50 per cent women teachers
- Gender sensitive teaching-learning material including textbooks
- Gender sensitive pedagogy

## Setting up Girls Hostels in Secondary and Senior Secondary Schools

This scheme was launched with the objective to improve access to and retain the girl child in secondary and higher secondary classes (IX-XII). The scheme envisages the construction of a hostel of the capacity of accommodation of 100 girls in each of about 3500 educationally backward blocks. The scheme reserves 50 per cent seats for girls of SC, ST, OBC and minority communities. The girl students in the age group of 14-18 years are eligible and are covered under the scheme. The girls who pass out from KGBVs are given preference in admission in hostels.

## National Scheme of Incentive to Girls for Secondary Education (NSIGSE)

This centrally sponsored scheme was launched in May 2008 with the objective to reduce dropouts and to promote the enrollment of girls belonging mainly to SC and ST communities in secondary schools. Under this scheme a sum of Rs 3000 is deposited in the name of the unmarried eligible girls as a fixed deposit. The beneficiary can withdraw it along with interest on attaining 18 years of age and passing X class examination. During the period from 1st January, 2013 to

31st March, 2014 an amount of 99.02 crores have been sanctioned covering 3,30,076 girl students.

## Kasturba Gandhi Balika Vidyalaya

Kasturba Gandhi Balika Vidyalayas (KGBVs) are residential upper primary schools for girls of Scheduled Castes, Scheduled Tribes, Other Backward Classes and the minority communities. These schools are set up in areas of scattered habitation where schools are at great distance and are a challenge to the security of girls. KGBVs reach out to–

(i) Adolescent girls who are unable to go to regular schools.

(ii) Out of school girls in the 10+ age group who are unable to complete primary school.

(iii) Younger girls of migratory population in difficult areas of scattered habitations where schools are at great distance.

There is reservation of 75 per cent seats for girls of SC, ST, OBC and minority communities and rest 25 per cent seats are reserved for girls of families below poverty line. Till 2013-14, 3609 KGBVs have been sanctioned in the country, their present total enrollment being 3,47,725 girls.

## Educational Development of Women in Kendriya Vidyalaya

In order to promote girl education, Central Government has exempted all girls of tuition fee up to class XII. Reservation for single girl child has also been made in Kendriya Vidyalayas. Reservations of two seats per section in class I, and 2 seats per class from Class VI onwards have been made. These seats are available over and above the sanctioned class strength.

## Mahila Samakhya

This scheme was initiated by Government of India in 1989 to empower women in rural areas, particularly those from socially and economically marginalised groups. The focus of the scheme is women empowerment through education. The scheme identifies the barriers of girl education and tries to overcome these barriers. The scheme also sensitises the society for girl education. Currently the scheme is in operation in 126 districts of 10 States covering 41,622 villages of 638 educationally backward blocks.

## Beti Bachao Beti Padhao

The trend of decline in Child Sex Ratio (CSR) is alarming. There are only 918 girls per 1000 boys in the 0-6 year's age group (Census, 2011). There are multiple reasons behind this skewed sex ratio. To ensure survival, protection and empowerment of the girl child, Government of India has announced Beti Bachao Beti Padhao initiative. The scheme is in operation in 100 selected districts with low CSR. The scheme is a joint initiative of Ministry of Women and Child Development, Ministry of Health and Family Planning and Ministry of Human Resource Development. The objectives of the scheme include:

1. Prevention of gender biased sex selective elimination.
2. Ensuring survival and protection of the girl child.
3. Ensuring education and participation of the girl child.

A budgetary allocation of Rs 100 crores has been made under the budget announcement of 2015-16. This is a multi-targeted scheme. The targets related to education are:

1. Increase the girl's enrollment in secondary education from 76 per cent in 2013-14 to 79 per cent by 2017.
2. Provide girl's toilet in every school in 100 low CSR districts by 2017.

## Schemes for Higher Education

Higher education plays a pivotal role in development of the country. It provides skilled and trained manpower to various sectors of economy and provides leaders for various walks of life. The Gross Enrollment Ratio in higher education is lower than that of developed countries. The GER in higher education was 20.4 in 2011-12. All India Survey on Higher Education (2010-11 and 2011-12) shows that girls are lagging behind the boys with respect to access to higher education. This is evident from the following Table 2.

**Table 2: GER in Higher Education**

| *Session* | *2010-11* | *2011-12* |
|---|---|---|
| Male | 20.8 | 21.6 |
| Female | 17.9 | 18.9 |
| **Total** | **19.4** | **20.4** |

*Source*: All India Survey on Higher Education (2010-11 and 2011-12).

Government of India has stated various programmes for increasing access to higher education for promoting excellence with due importance to equity. Some of these initiatives are discussed in following paragraphs.

## Post Graduate Indira Gandhi Scholarship for Single Girl Child

University Grants Commission introduced this scheme with an aim to compensate direct costs of girl education at PG level especially for such girls who happen to be the only girl child in their family. The scheme also promotes the small family norm. The financial assistance is for non-professional courses. The candidate should apply for the scholarship in PG first year. The upper age limit is 30 years. The value of scholarship is Rs 2000 per month for two years. The scholarship is available for only 10 months in a year. If candidate secures less than 55 per cent marks in first year, the scholarship may get cancelled. Women pursuing PG course through distance mode are not eligible for financial assistance under this scheme.

## Construction of Women Hostels in Colleges

The University Grants Commission has launched this scheme for providing hostel and other infrastructure facilities to achieve the goal of enhancing girls' enrollments in higher education programmes. The scheme is fully financed by UGC. The residential facility helps girls of remote areas to stay in college and complete their studies.

## Post Doctoral Fellowship to Women Candidates

This scheme was initiated by University Grants Commission for those women candidates who are unemployed and hold Ph.D. Degree, with an aim to accelerate the talented instincts of the women candidates to carry out the advanced studies and research. The selected candidates can pursue advanced studies and research in science, engineering and technology, humanities and social sciences in universities and colleges recognised by UGC under Section 2(f) and 12(B) of UGC Act. The duration of fellowship is for five years and the age of candidate should not be more than 55 years. The marks at UG and PG level should not be less than 55 per cent and 60 per cent respectively. Reserved category and minority candidates have an exemption of five per cent marks and relaxation of five years in age. A fellowship of Rs 25000 per month is provided for first two years and for last three years Rs 30000 per month is provided to the selected candidates. Besides, contingency, house rent allowance, maternity leave and medical facilities are also provided. There are 100 slots of scholarships per year.

### Swami Vivekananda Single Girl Child Scholarship for Research in Social Sciences

Government of India initiated this scheme to give special benefits for families having single girl child. Swami Vivekananda always advocated for promotion of women education. To cherish this noble thought, University Grants Commission has introduced Swami Vivekananda Single Girl Child Scholarship for Research in Social Sciences. This scheme also aims to increase sex ratio in favour of women and promote small family norm in the society.

The single girl child who has taken admission in regular full-time Ph.D. programmes in social sciences in any recognised university or institute is eligible for this scholarship. The upper age limits for general and reserved category are 40 years and 45 years respectively. There are 300 slots for scholarship every year. The financial assistance of Rs 8000 per month is provided for first two years. For last three years Rs 10,000 per month is given to the beneficiary.

## Conclusions

The Central Government interventions for promoting women education have borne fruits. Yet these initiatives/programmes have many shortcomings and lacuna in their planning as well as implementation. The scholarship schemes are marred with either very low amount or the slots are inadequate in comparison to the number of needful. The paper work and formalities involved in application process are cumbersome and these are disappointing the target group. The biggest complaint with scholarship schemes is untimely release of funds. Often students get the scholarship after the conclusion of the academic year for which they have applied for. This sluggish process of release of scholarship often fails the very purpose for which it was thought of. The access to secondary education in general and higher education in particular in government-funded institutions, is very limited. The seats available in government institutions are very less in number in comparison to demands of youth for education. This demand is partly fulfilled by private institutions, which charge hefty fees and quality of education in these institutions is not beyond questions. The majority of government higher education institutions are situated in urban areas. In rural areas there is very few government or government-aided higher education institutions. The government policy of promoting self-financed institutions and self-financed courses even in government and aided institutions has aggravated the problem. There is lack of innovative and modern courses in these governmental and aided institutions. The focus of Central Government in Rashtriya Uchchatar Siksha Abhiyan (RUSA) is on access, equity and excellence but an overview of proposed activities and programmes envisaged under RUSA indicates that there is more rhetoric than truth. Not mere window dressing but overhauling of education system is need of the hour for welfare of countrymen and development of the nation. Encouraging women education should be one of the important aspects of such prospective planning and programming in education system.

## References


- Akhilesh and Singh, R. (2010). Interventions for bridging gender gap in education. *University News, 48(31),* 11-21.
- Gangal, M. and Sharma, S. (2014). Women education. *AED Journal of Educational Studies, 3(1),* 90-100.
- Government of India (1966). *Report of the education commission: Education and national development.* Ministry of Education, GoI.
- Government of India (1968). *National policy on education,* Ministry of Education, GoI.

- Government of India (1986). *National policy on education,* Ministry of Human resource Development, GoI.
- Government of India (2014). *Annual report 2013-201,* Ministry of Human Resource Development, GoI.
- Government of India (2015). Beti bachao beti padhao. Ministry of Women and Child Development, Retrieved from http://wcd.nic.in/BBBPscheme/launch/workshop/main.htm
- Government of India (2015). Census of India 2011, Retrieved from http://censusindia.gov.in
- Government of India (2015). Constitution of India, Retrieved from http: //lawmin.nic.in /olwing/ coi/coi-english/coi-indexenglish.htm.
- Government of India (2015). *India 2015: A reference annual.* Ministry of Information and Broadcasting, GoI.
- Government of India (2015). Mahila Samakhya Scheme, Retrieved from http://mhrd. gov.in/ mahila-samakhya-programme.
- Government of India (2015). National programme for education of girls at elementary level, Retrieved from http://india.gov.in/national-programme-education-girls-elementary-level.
- Government of India (2015). Rashtriya Madhyamik Shiksha Abhiyan. Retrieved from mhrd.gov, in/rmsa.
- Gupta, N. L. (2003). *Women's education through ages.* Concept Publications, New Delhi.
- Hazarika, M. (2012). Hurdles faced by women in pursuing higher education. *Research Analysis and Evaluation, 3(32),* 38-39.
- Kumar, J. and Sangeeta (2013). Status of women education in India, *Educationia Confab. 2(4),* 162-176. Retrieved from http://www.confabjournals.com/educationiaconfab.html.
- NCERT (2006). *Position paper-National focus group on gender issues in the curriculum (NCF-2005).* NCERT.
- University Grants Commission (2015). Post Doctoral Fellowship to Women Candidates. Retrived from www.ugc.ac.in/pdfw.
- University Grants Commission (2015). Post Graduate Indira Gandhi Scholarship for Single Girl Child. Retrieved from http://www.ugc.ac.in/sgc.
- University Grants Commission (2015). Swami Vivekananda single girl child scholarship for research in social sciences, Retrieved from http://www.ugc.ac.in/svsgc.

# Chapter - 11

# Educational Strategies for Girls Education

***—Ramesh Chandra Singh, Pankaj Pant and Siddhartha Lohani***

**Abstract**

*Women and girls in the developing world are often denied opportunities for education. Lack of education limits prospects, decreases family income, reduces health, puts women and girls at risk of trafficking and exploitation, and limits the economic advancement of entire countries. Despite progress in recent years, girls continue to suffer severe disadvantage and exclusion in education systems throughout their lives. An estimated 31 million girls of primary school age and 32 million girls of lower secondary school age were out of school in 2012. Girls' education is both an intrinsic right and a critical lever for reaching to the other development objectives. Providing girls with an education helps break the cycle of poverty; educated women are less likely to marry early and against their will, less likely to die during childbirth, more likely to have healthy babies and are more likely to send their children to school. When all children have access to a quality education rooted in human rights and gender equality, a ripple effect of opportunity that influences generations to come will be generated. Education empowers women to overcome discrimination. Girls and young women who are educated have greater awareness of their rights, and greater confidence and freedom to make decisions that affect their lives, improve their own and their children's health and chances of survival, and boost their work prospects. This chapter deals with the role of government, role of society, role of NGO's and role of schools in proper planning and implementation of the recommendations of various commissions who worked over time to time for the growth and development of girls 'education. The chapter focuses on the different strategies made for the improvement of girls' education targeting the weaker sections of the society.*

***Keywords:*** *Gender equality, Discrimination, Commission, Society.*

## Introduction

Gender inequality in education entails serious losses for society. Change can result from deliberate actions of state or civil society organisations and from legislative and institutional social reform. These can influence the expectations and incentives governing human behaviour including those affecting educational participation and performance. This happens implicitly via the gender roles that members of the household themselves fulfil and explicitly through the gender framework within which making education free and compulsory is the keystone of any national plan to eliminate gender disparity in education and achieve universal education. Faced with an economically driven choice between sending sons or daughters to school, poor families often send their sons. Fee exemption or financial support to families with daughters in school, as well as explaining the advantages of sending girls to school, can make a real difference. Education is the basic requirement for human development and right to education is a fundamental human right. This fact has been recognised by our Constitution, various international conventions, and declarations. Every person irrespective of their sex, caste, creed religion should be provided with opportunities to avail education so as to attain complete human development. Education is a concurrent subject and the Constitution of India contains the following provisions concerning it.

## Right to Education

It is noteworthy that India after independence had undertaken significant steps towards providing 'Education for All'. On April, 01-2010, India joined the league of over 130 countries that have made legal commitments to provide free and compulsory elementary education. The right to education Act 2009 finally made education a fundamental right of Indian children in the 6-14 year age group and entitled them to get free and compulsory elementary education. It was enshrined in the Indian constitution as a directive principle of state policy in Article 45 before the 86th amendment introduced new Article 21 (a), making the right to education of children of 6 to 14 years of age a fundamental right.

## Role of Government

The government role in this is important in three principal ways: creating an enabling environment for promoting gender equality in education through legislative and policy reforms; investing in redistribution by targeting resources for female education and introducing special measures to reduce inequities; and mitigating the burden of external shocks on girls and women such as the effect of conflict, economic crisis and HIV/AIDS. Although changes to education policy are critically important, in order to be successful actions to promote gender parity and equality in education need to be nested within a wider set of measures affecting many other aspects of economy and society.

The Constitutional amendment of 1976, which included Education in the concurrent List, was a far-reaching step with substantive financial and administrative implications requiring a new sharing of responsibility between the Union Government and the States. While the role and responsibility of the States in regard to education remained essentially unchanged, the Union Government was entrusted with increased responsibilities of reinforcing the national and integrative character of education; maintaining quality and standards; monitoring and studying the educational requirements of the country as a whole with regard to manpower for development; catering to the needs of research and advanced studies; looking after the international aspects of education, culture and Human Resource Development; and, in general, promoting excellence at all levels of the education throughout the country.

## National Policy on Education, 1986 and Programme of Action, 1992

The National Policy on Education (NPE) gave prominence to both enrollment and retention of children. As the PoA put it crisply

"Enrollment by itself is of little importance if children do not continue beyond one year, many of them are not seeing the school for more than a few days." The highlight of the NPE was that it sought to address the most difficult aspect of access, viz. access to education of millions of girls and working children who because of socio economic compulsions cannot participate in the school system. The National Policy on Education (1986) provides a broad policy framework for total eradication of illiteracy and a commitment to make primary education free and compulsory up to fifth standard, besides ensuring higher government and non-government expenditure on education that should constitute six per cent of GDP. Several schemes were launched by the Central Government to meet the needs of not only the educationally disadvantaged but also for the overall strengthening of the social infrastructure of education.

## Major Policies and Schemes Paving Way for Girl Child Education

NPE also stressed that the recruitment of at least 50 per cent of the teachers should be women so as to create conducive atmosphere for girl children in schools. This programme also had laid down the concept of minimum levels of learning according to which irrespective of caste, creed, location or sex, all children must be given access to education of a comparable standard. This strategy for improving the quality of elementary education is an attempt to combine quality with equity. It lays down learning outcomes in the form of competencies or levels of learning for each stage of elementary education. The strategy also prescribes the adoption of measures that will ensure achievement of these levels by children both in the formal schools as well as Non-Formal Education centres. The NPE also introduced the scheme Operation Black Board in 1987 to provide minimum essential facilities to all primary schools in the country.

## Elementary Education

NPE proposed to set up new primary schools according to the norms in the non-served habitations. These schools were supposed to be opened by the State Governments following the norms specified under Operation Blackboard. The norms of OBB specified that there should be at least two teachers in a primary school and one of them should be a woman teacher and each primary school should have at least two classrooms. NPE also recommended the expansion of infrastructure at the upper primary level so as to increase enrollment at this stage. The norm of providing an upper primary school within three kilometer distance has been introduced to benefit the girl child.

## Secondary Education

Access to secondary education was proposed to be widened with emphasis on enrolment of girls, SCs and STs, particularly in science, commerce and vocational streams. Boards of Secondary Education were also proposed to be reorganised and vested with autonomy so that their ability to improve the quality of secondary education is enhanced. A programme of computer literacy (CLASS) was implemented in secondary level institutions to ensure that the children are equipped with necessary computer skills to be effective in the emerging technological world. Children with special talent or aptitude were provided opportunities to proceed at a faster pace, by making good quality education available to them, irrespective of their capacity to pay for it through the Pace-setting residential schools called Navodaya Vidyalayas. Their broad aim was to serve the objective of excellence coupled with equity and social justice (with reservation for the rural areas, SCs and STs), to promote national integration by providing opportunities to talented children from different parts of the country, to live and learn together, to develop their full potential, and most importantly to become catalysts of a nation-wide programme of school improvement.

## Curriculum Framework

NPE also undertook the responsibility of raising the standard of the text book syllabi to incorporate the contemporary trends. The positive approach of the total literacy campaigns of NPE resulted in raise in demand for primary education. The awareness generated among the parents had led to better participation of the children in primary schools, which benefited especially the disadvantaged groups, the girls of SC and ST, by attending the schools. The states were advised to take up curriculum revision to incorporate proper understanding of the work ethos and of the values of a humane and composite culture. The plan of action of NPE primarily dealt with the inclusion of the institutions to develop concrete actions plans. It also suggested the setting up of monitoring units to ensure integration of gender issues into policies, programmes and actions. The annual plan of the institutions and departments were required to spell out clearly the steps taken by them to enhance women and girls access to education. It also provided for research and women studies to promote better understanding of women contribution to social process within social and technological environmental change and their struggles. The programme aimed to investigate and remove structural cultural or attitudinal causes of gender discrimination. It provided for gender sensitisation programmes for the school teachers. The NPE and its plan of action have brought out the close relationship between the education and the status of women in the society. It has rightly established the fact that the first step towards the strengthening of the position of women is to provide for proper educational facilities to empower them. The NPE can be called as a beneficial programme to the extent that it has even recognised alternative forms of training to facilitate easy access to women.

## National Programme for Education of Girls at Elementary Level (NPEGEL)

NPEGEL has been formulated for education of underprivileged/ disadvantaged girls from class I to VIII as a separate and distinct gender component plan of Sarva Shiksha Abhiyan (SSA). This was started as an amendment to the scheme of SSA for providing additional components for education of girls at elementary level. This scheme lays down a community-based approach i.e. it involves actors at all levels following a participatory approach in its implementation. This scheme targets the out of school girls, dropouts, over aged girls who have not completed elementary education, working girls, girls from marginalised social groups, girls with low attendance and girls with low levels of achievement. Model Cluster Schools for girls were opened in all selected districts/blocks where the scheme was operational. These were aimed at improving the achievement of girls, fostering an interest in education among them, and raising the importance of girls' education in the community. Existing schools having density of SC/ST/OBC/ Minority girls were identified as model cluster schools. Model cluster schools for girls have the provision of an additional classroom, supply of drinking water, electrification, and toilet for which one time grant up to a maximum of Rs 2.00 lakhs was provided. Construction of additional classrooms, residential facilities, girls' toilets, water supply, electrification and barrier free features are the components of this scheme. The scheme provides a one time grant of Rs 30,000 for teaching and learning equipment, library, sports, vocational training, etc. The schools were proposed to consist of facilities in terms of teaching and learning equipment, books, equipments, games, and facilities for learning through computers, film shows, reading material, self-defence, life skills, bicycle riding, and reading. This girl child friendly infrastructure was proposed for the use by all the schools in that cluster, by rotation. The scheme also has provision for hiring instructors for the day or on contract for imparting vocational and other training.

## Kasturba Gandhi Balika Vidyalaya (KGBV)

Kasturba Gandhi Balika Vidyalaya (KGBV) is being implemented by the Government of India by setting up upto 750 residential schools and 16 schools with boarding facilities at elementary level for girls belonging predominantly to the SC, ST, OBC and minorities in difficult areas. The scheme was proposed to be coordinated with the existing schemes of Department of Elementary Education and Literacy viz. Sarva Shiksha Abhiyan (SSA), National Programme for Education of Girls at Elementary Level (NPEGEL) and Mahila Samakhya (MS).

## The Tenth Five Year Plan - Programmes for Achieving the Universalisation of Elementary Education (UEE)

The tenth five year plan has laid out the following programmes for Universalisation of Elementary Education (UEE). These programmes are more oriented to reduce the gender disparity and bring in the dropout children especially girls back to the education system so as to achieve the goal of UEE. It can be rightfully asserted that the achievement of UEE is impossible without the inclusion of schemes for the promotion of girl child education, a fact which has been recognised by the tenth five year plan and has formed the basis for the same.

### 1. *Sarva Shiksha Abhiyaan*

Under the tenth five year plan the SSA has to provide access and motivation to those outside the school system who are mostly girls, SCs/STs children, working children, urban deprived children, disabled children and children in difficult circumstances, without compromising on the quality of education.

### 2. *Gender Specific Programmes*

The tenth five year plan has also recommended gender specific programmes to reduce gender disparity in education. To achieve the above, the plan has emphasised on the existing women centric programmes such as Mahila Samakhya and two new schemes- the Kasturba Gandhi Swantantra Vidyalaya (KGSV) and the National Programme for the Education of Girls at the Elementary Level (NPEGEL). The KGSV and NPEGEL were proposed to take the following features during the plan period:

- Focus on educationally backward areas in girls' education.
- Focus on girls from the disadvantaged sections like those belonging to SC/ST, minorities.
- Tackling gender-specific issues that prevent girls and women from having access to education.
- Providing women and adolescent girls with the necessary support structure.
- Informal learning environment to create opportunities for education.
- Creating circumstances for larger participation of women and girls in formal and non-formal education programmes and helping girls to overcome socio-cultural and economic factors that inhibit their access to elementary education.
- Improving the quality of textbooks.
- Improving the quality of infrastructural facilities like toilets for girls, equipment and support services, playgrounds, classrooms.

## Role of NGOs

Religious education providers are also long established in many parts of the world and have often been responsible for ensuring an education for otherwise excluded groups, including girls. However, they are usually conservative organisations, tending to reinforce rather than undermine local gender stereotypes. Their activities may help to attain gender parity in education but they have sometimes made equality more distant. Both private sector and community schools are also active in many countries. For maintaining a balance NGOs' activities can be a useful complement to state endeavours. But the activities of other providers have a less certain impact on equality. In most countries in the developing world, non-state providers have had a longer engagement with education service provision than the state itself. As pressures to expand have increased particularly where the adjustment has been intense, non-state providers have become an attractive option in several countries. NGOs can be major contributors and they are generally committed to ensuring that education reaches the poorest and most disadvantaged groups.

## Sufficient Financing

Many households find it difficult to send all their children to school. Their incomes are too low to afford the costs involved. This is particularly so in poor communities and where parents can expect to receive more future income from their educated sons than from similarly educated daughters. Equalising the benefits that arise from schooling is a more fundamental process, founded upon the vision of achieving a society and labour market that are free from discrimination such that the opportunities and advantages faced by all children at given levels of education and achievement are broadly equal.

## Effective and Safe Learning

Making education free and compulsory is the keystone of any national plan to eliminate gender disparity in education and achieve universal education. Faced with an economically driven choice between sending sons or daughters to school poor families often send their sons. Removing fees or offering financial support to families with daughters in school as well as explaining the advantage of sending girls to school can make a real difference.

## Promoting Health in Schools

The school-based healthy living and HIV/AIDS Prevention education programme is taught as part of the standard curriculum to children from the early grades. The programme focuses on a range of health and social issues- from HIV/AIDS to personal hygiene, from nutrition to drugs and explores them through activities designed to develop life skills such as communication cooperation and problem solving. The programme has led to dramatic success stories such as a village in a tehsil township that started using iodized salt as a result of pressure from children who had learned of its benefits in one such class.

## Special Measures for Disadvantaged Girls

Some countries and regions where people of ethnic minorities of rural areas and the poor face discrimination and exclusion, girls often suffer a multiple disadvantage because of their gender. The more disadvantaged the girl, the more essential it is that the education system should reach out to them through special measures, rather than just assuming that the disadvantaged girls will be drawn in as part of a general drive for education for all. Since the schools belong to the community they create a sense of ownership and so are better maintained and parents show more interest in education. The department of education has successfully narrowed the difference in the proportion of primary schools.

## School Environment

It involves making schools secure for girls. When schools are associated with sexual or physical gender violence, girls' access to education is negatively affected. Boys and girls are often susceptible to psychological and physical violence in different ways and adolescents in particular can find themselves especially vulnerable to violations of their safety. Lack of safety and security in the school environment may be very obvious in terms of physical danger such as beatings or rape. The abuse of girls, sexually physically, and emotionally, by teachers is a common problem. Breaking the silence about violence at school is an important step towards its diagnosis and prevention.

## References


- Biklen, 1995, Sari Knopp. School Work: Gender and the cultural construction of teaching. New York: Teachers College Press.
- Census of India 2001, Provisional Population Totals chapter – 2 of 2001 series-29.
- From Girl Child to Person, UNESCO, 1995.
- Human Development Report, 2005, UNDP.
- India Education Report, A Profile of Basic Education, NIEPA, 2002.
- Jain, M.P., "Indian Constitutional Law"; 2003.
- Jandhyala Kameswari; "Bringing Child Labor into Schools."
- Mc Ginty, Sue., Resilience, Gender and Success at School. New York: Peter Lange, 1999.
- National Policy on Education, 1986.
- Programme of Action, 1990.
- Review of Child Labour, Education and Poverty Agenda, India Country Report, 2006, International Centre on Child Labour and Education, (ICCLE); Washington.
- Report on Task Force on Education for Women's Equality; www.education.nic.in
- Sectoral Policies and Programmes - Tenth five year plan 2002-2007; Vol. II; Planning Commission, Government of India.
- Singh, A. (1997). To study the Role and Status of Boards of Secondary Education.
- Thorne, 1993, Barrie, Gender play: girls and boys in school, New Brunswick, NJ: Rutgers University Press.
- http://planningcommission.nic.in
- http://ssa.nic.in
- http://www.censusindia.net
- http://www.education.nic.in

## Chapter – 12

# Government Schemes and Initiatives to Promote Girl Education in India

***—Swadhin Shaktiprasad***

### Abstract

*The education of women in India plays a significant role in improving living standards in the country. A higher women literacy rate improves the quality of life both at home and outside home and infant mortality rate is reduced by encouraging and promoting education of children, especially female children. As an independent group, women constitute 48 per cent of the total population of India. They not only constitute valuable human resource of the country but their development in the socio-economic arena also sets pace for sustainable growth of the economy. Taking a sincere note of the abysmal condition of girls in today's society, the government is trying to create awareness so that a favourable condition can be created for the holistic development of girls. The government has also taken many important steps to support the cause of women empowerment. Education is one of the most powerful tools to empower women. Hence the role of government in this regard stands important. The chapter highlights various initiatives and flagship programmes of Government of India to promote education of girls. Some of the major schemes have been discussed in detail.*

***Keywords:*** *Government, Human resource, Women empowerment, Flagship programmes.*

### Introduction

The principle of gender equality is enshrined in the Indian Constitution in its Preamble, Fundamental Rights, Fundamental Duties and Directive Principles of State Policy. The Constitution officially grants equality to women and also empowers the State to adopt measures of positive discrimination in favour of women. However, the varied forms of discrimination that women in India are subject to are far from positive. The role of education in facilitating social and economic progress is well accepted. Access to education is critical for benefitting from emerging opportunities that are accompanied by economic growth. Keeping in view of this accepted fact, there has been a thrust on education of girls since independence in order to bridge the gender gap in education in India. Free and compulsory education up to the age of 14 is the responsibility of the State and the fulfilment of this obligation is critical for the improvement in educational condition of girls and that of gender equality and for the universalisation of elementary education. Until 1976, education was a State subject. Since its transfer to the Concurrent List by the 42nd Constitutional Amendment in 1976, a new thrust was provided to girls' education in the National Policy on Education (NPE) 1986, which provided a holistic vision for the education of women and recognised the cross-cutting issues that inhibited the realisation of this goal. The National Policy on Education (NPE), 1986, as revised in 1992, a path breaking policy document, articulates the Government of India's unequivocal commitment, that "Education will be used as an agent of basic change in the status of women. In order to neutralise the accumulated distortions of the past, there will be a well-conceived edge for women….This will be an act of faith and social engineering. That of removal of women's illiteracy and obstacles inhibiting their services, setting time targets and effective monitoring…" Hence the Government of India has shown it's sincere commitment in implementing various schemes and flagships programmes to promote girl education. Some of the schemes are discussed in detail.

## Sarva Shiksha Abhiyan (SSA)

The targeted provision for girls under SSA include:–

- Free textbooks to all girls up to class VIII.
- Separate toilets for girls.
- Back to school campus for out-of-school girls.

- Bridge courses for older girls.
- Recruitment of 50 per cent women teachers.
- Early childhood care and education centres.
- Teachers' sensitisation programmes to promote equitable learning opportunities.
- Gender-sensitive teaching-learning materials including textbooks.
- Intensive community mobilisation efforts.
- 'Innovation fund' per district for need-based interventions for ensuring girls' attendance and retention.

## Kasturba Gandhi Balika Vidyalaya (KGBV)

KGBVs are residential upper primary schools for girls hailing from SC, ST, OBC and Muslim communities. KGBVs are set up in areas of scattered habitations, where schools are at great distances and are a challenge to the security of girls which often compel girls to discontinue their education. KGBV addresses this through setting up residential schools, in the block itself.

- 3609 KGBVs sanctioned upto 2013-14.
- 3602 KGBVs are operational.
- 3.48 lakh girls enrolled in these operational KGBVs.
- Minimum 75 per cent seats reserved for girls belonging to SC/ST/OBC or Minorities and priority for remaining minimum 25 per cent seats is accorded to girls from families falling below the poverty line.

## Gender Sensitisation

Gender sensitisation of teacher educators, teachers and community member has been a major activity of all programmes. Regular annual gender sensitisation programmes have been organised with various thrusts of addressing challenges related to education and empowerment of girls from marginalised groups. The training material for teacher educators and teachers on Gender Equality and Empowerment in the light of NCF-2005 and focus group paper on gender issues in education has also been prepared. The themes of the module would help in addressing issues related to girls' education and women's empowerment. Glossary of terms regarding Gender in Education has also been prepared.

### Ensuring Gender Sensitive Learning Materials

Gender Sensitive Learning Materials for KGBVs has been developed. In this regard Bridge Courses have been prepared in Hindi, English, Maths, History, Geography and Political Life and Art and Aesthetics. The materials have been prepared in Hindi and English based on NCERT textbooks at elementary stage. These materials would help in concepts clarification and better understanding of concepts related to these disciplines.

### Special Models of Alternative Schools for Girls

Different models of alternative learning centres were designed to suit the local needs of girls. Based on community demand, these models of alternative schools show a variation and diversity of coverage. One model was for the nine years old out of school girls and another that targeted adolescent girls with sibling care responsibilities by running learning and early childhood care centres, together. Community-based centres of religious education, the madarsas and the maktabs were made learning centres for the formal curriculum, in an effort to reach out to Muslim minority girls who were otherwise not enrolling in formal schools.

Bridging strategies, one of the most successful models, were designed to provide opportunities of accelerated learning to drop out girls and the older girls who had never enrolled in a school. Depending on the girls' age and educational background, the course content has been planned over a varying length of time. The bridge courses are either residential or non-residential. Through such efforts, many girls were mainstreamed in regular schools after successful completion of the learning cycle of the bridge courses.

Incentives such as free textbooks, stationery, notebooks, scholarships, bus passes, insurance and uniforms are provided to girls to improve their enrollment and retention in schools. Award schemes are also instituted for schools and village education committees for best performance in enrollment, attendance and retention of girls in their areas. The Government of India launched a Centrally Sponsored Scheme "Incentive to Girls for Secondary Education" in 2008-09. According to the scheme, a sum of Rs 3,000 is deposited in the name of the eligible girls as fixed deposit, who are entitled to withdraw it along with interest on reaching 18 years of age and having passed 10 class examination. The scheme covers (i) all girls belonging to SC/ST communities, who pass class VIII and (ii) all girls who pass VIII examination from Kasturba Gandhi Balika Vidyalaya (irrespective of whether they belong to SC/ST) and enrol in class IX in Government, Government-aided and local body schools. The objective of the scheme is to establish an enabling environment to reduce the drop-outs and to promote the enrollment of girl child belonging mainly to SC/ST communities in schools.

### Special Coaching Classes

In order to help SC and ST girls improve their academic performance, special coaching classes are held for them after school hours. This intervention has shown very encouraging results. A study carried out on the intervention found that achievement levels of the girls had improved significantly.

### Escorts

Often girls would discontinue schooling as the school are far away from their homes or they have to pass through lonely, forest areas to reach school or were confronted by other physical barriers on the way to school. The security of girls is sometimes under threat in such conditions. To overcome such difficulties, group of girls is escorted to school by a village elder, usually a woman. She accompanies them to school and returns with them. During the day, she attends odd jobs in the school or even teaches, depending on her background. She is paid a token honorarium for her services.

### Making Girls' Education a Community Agenda

Based on the realisation that 'demand' for primary education factors participation rates in educational processes, various options were devised to mobilise communities for girls' education. Some of the noteworthy interventions are Maa-beti melas (mother-daughter fairs), Meena campaigns, Prabhat pheris, meetings with religious leaders and community-based Sammelans (meetings).

(a) At the Maa-beti melas mothers and daughters come together in large numbers. Through different activities, awareness about the importance of educating girls is created. They acquire information about the functioning of the local school, the education system in general and also about the special provisions for girls that are available. They are also exposed to talks on nutritious foods, legal issues, and films that were screened.

(b) "Prabhat pheris" are organised as awareness generation measures that entail mobilisation walks in the village, slogan and wall writings, distribution of pamphlets and posters, door to door contact etc.

(c) Dialogues with religious leaders and opinion-makers of some communities are considered critical to get their girls in to schools. Their influence on community behaviour makes it important to convince them to in turn influence popular views about educating girls and generate community commitment for girls' education. This has been a key strategy that worked in getting Muslim minority girls within the education net.

## Education Development of Women in KVs

All girls are exempted from paying tuition fee from Class I to XII. There is a provision of reservation in admission for single girl child in KVs: (i) two seats per section, in class I to class V and (ii) two seats per class, from class VI onwards. These seats are available over and above the sanctioned class strength.

## Scheme of Construction and Running of Girls Hostel for Students of Secondary and Higher Secondary Schools

This scheme was introduced so as to improve access and to retain the girl child in secondary and higher secondary classes (IX-XII) so that the girl students are not denied the opportunity to continue their study due to distance from schools, parents' financial affordability and other connected societal factors. The scheme envisages construction of a hostel with the capacity to accommodate 100 girls in each of about 3,500 Educationally Backward Blocks (EBBs) in the country. The girl students in the age group of 14-18 years studying in classes IX to XII belonging to SC, ST, OBC, Minority Community and BPL families form the target group of the Scheme. Students passing out of KGBVs are further given preference in admission in these hostels. These hostels are required to provide accommodation to at least 50 per cent of girl students hailing from SC, ST, OBC, and minority communities.

## Mahila Samakhya

Mahila Samakhya (MS) is an ongoing scheme for women's empowerment that was initiated in 1989 to translate the goals of the National Policy on Education into a concrete programme for the education and empowerment of women in rural areas, particularly those from socially and economically marginalised groups. The objectives of the MS programme is to create an environment in which education can serve the objectives of women's equality and where women can seek knowledge and information and thereby empower them to play a positive role in their own development and development of society. Currently the programme is being implemented in 126 districts of 10 States viz. Andhra Pradesh, Assam, Bihar, Chattisgarh, Jharkhand, Karnataka, Kerala, Gujarat, Uttar Pradesh and Uttarakhand. The MS programme is at present being implemented in 41,622 villages in 126 districts covering 638 Educationally Backward Blocks (EBBs) in these 10 States. The programme reaches out to about 1.4 million rural poor women and is mobilised through 50,900 village level collectives called Mahila Sanghas.

## Rashtriya Madhyamik Shiksha Abhiyan (RMSA)

The scheme was launched in March, 2009 with the objective to enhance access to secondary education and improve its quality. The schemes envisage, inter alia, the enhancement of enrolment at secondary stage by providing a secondary school with a reasonable distance of habitation, with an aim to ensure GER of 100 per cent by 2017 and universal retention by 2020. The other objectives include improving quality of education imparted at secondary level through making all secondary schools conform to prescribed norms, removing gender bias and socioeconomic and disability barriers, etc. The funding pattern under RMSA in respect of normal States is 75:25 and in case of North Eastern States it is 90:10. The scheme is being implemented by the society set up by the State government for implementation of the Scheme. With a view to ensure efficient utilisation of funds and greater coordination, other centrally sponsored schemes of Secondary Education such as ICT@ School, Inclusive Education for the Disabled at Secondary State (IEDSS), Vocational Education (VE) and Girls Hostel (GH), have been subsumed under the existing RMSA scheme. RMSA in association with NCERT, NUEPA, UKERIE etc. have taken several initiatives including school leadership development programme, national achievement survey at class X, development of framework for school standards and performance evaluation, national repository of open education resources, etc. so as to enhance quality of teaching at secondary stage.

### Higher Education

It has always been a constant endeavour of the Department of Higher Education to frame different schemes and projects so as to ensure larger participation and enrollment of women. Therefore, reducing the gender gap in higher education is a focus area. There has been a phenomenal growth in enrollment of women students in higher education in the country. The share of girls' enrollment which was less than 10 per cent of the total enrollment on the eve of independence, has been increased to 41.50 per cent in the beginning of the academic year 2010-11.

### Higher Education of Women through Open and Distance Learning (ODL) Mode

Open and Distance Learning system is a system wherein teachers and learners need not necessarily be present either at same place or same time and it is flexible with regard to modalities and timing of teaching and learning as also the admission criteria without compromising necessary quality considerations. ODL system of the country consists of State Open Universities (SOUs), Institutions and

Universities offering education and includes Correspondence Course Institutes (CCIs) in the conventional dual mode universities. This is becoming more and more significant for continuing education, skill development of in-service personnel and for imparting relevant quality education to learners located at educationally disadvantaged locations. Access to education through the open and distance learning system is expanding rapidly and status on enrollment of the women through ODL system is improving.

## Post School Diploma (Polytechnics etc.)

One more additional stream available for enrollment to the school pass out students is Post School Diploma (Polytechnics etc.), which constitute major part of the Skill Development Strategy. In order to enhance women's participation in Polytechnic education, a scheme has been launched to provide financial assistance for the construction of women hostel in the existing polytechnics.

## Interventions of Department of Higher Education at a Glance (having direct impact on the educational development of women)

- Ministry of HRD has opened 20 Central Universities, 8 IITs, 7 IIMs, 10 NITs, 3 IISE, 20 IIITs and 2 SPAs.
- Sub-Mission on Polytechnics has been launched and 287 new polytechnics have been already sanctioned for the non-served areas/districts.
- Information and Communication Technology Mission has been launched to provide broadband connectivity to all colleges/universities.
- Scheme on interest subsidy on education loan has been launched for the students belong to weaker sections.
- While there is a 50 per cent concession in fee for girl candidates for appearing in JEE (Main) for admission to Engineering courses, there is no fee for female candidates of all categories for registration of JEE (Advanced) examination for admission to IITs.

- 82,000 scholarships including 41,000 for women have been sanctioned for the students of weaker sections.
- Women Hostel Scheme in Polytechnics has been implemented.

## University Grants Commission (UGC)

The women education has been the priority area for the University Grants Commission (UGC), a premier apex body governing university education. For this purpose, the Commission has launched a number of schemes to encourage the enrollment and promotion of girls in Higher Education. Such schemes being run by UGC are briefly as under.

## Day Care Centres in Universities and Colleges

The objective of the scheme is to provide day care facility within the university system on demand basis for children of around three months to six years of age, when their parents (university/college employees/ students/ scholars) are away from home during day time and also to provide a secure place and environment during working hours for their children.

## Indira Gandhi Scholarship for Single Girl Child for Pursuing Higher and Technical Education

The purpose of the scheme is to support higher education through scholarships to such girls who happen to be the only child in their families and also to make them recognise the values of observance of small family norms. Girl students up to the age of 30 years at the time of admission of Postgraduate courses are only eligible. The number of slots for scholarships available under the scheme is 1200 p.a. The scholarship amount is @ 2,000 p.m. for 20 months.

## Construction of Women's Hostels for Colleges

The UGC has been providing hostels and other infrastructural facilities to achieve the goal of enhancing the status of women and harness the potential availability for the development of the society, as also to bring about gender equity and equal representation of women through a special scheme of construction of women's hostels. The main objective is to support all the eligible colleges for construction of hostels for women in order to provide a residential place for women students/ researchers/teachers and other staff.

## Development of Women's Studies in Universities and Colleges

The scheme envisages assistance to universities for setting up new women study centres as well as to strengthen and sustain the university women study centres which were set up as per the Plan X, by establishing them as statutory departments in the university system, as also to facilitate their own capacity to network in other constituents so that they are mutually reinforcing as well as synergising with one and another. The primary role of these centres is to enable knowledge simulation and knowledge transmission through teaching and research.

## Scheme of Capacity Building of Women Managers in Higher Education

The University Grants Commission (UGC) had introduced the scheme for the Capacity Building of Women managers in Higher Education in the Plan X. It has been revised and continued in the Plan XI. This programme is focused on women in higher education in the academic and administrative streams so as to sensitise and motivate them and, subsequently, equip them for decision-making positions in the higher education system where currently they occupy very few such positions. The purpose of this scheme is to develop a critical mass of gender sensitised women administrators so as to create a gender friendly environment and to remove the glass ceiling. The overall goal is to facilitate the constituencies of women faculty, administrators and staff within the higher education system so as to increase the participation of women in higher education management for better gender balance, sensitise the higher education system through policies and procedures which recognise women equity and diversity and involve the women capable of becoming administrators for the qualitative development of higher education.

The programme encompasses training and skills development workshops as follows:

- Sensitisation, Awareness, Motivational Workshops, Residential, Non-Residential Workshops.

- Training of Trainers/Master Trainers.
- Workshops of the duration of six days not inclusive of travel.
- Management Skill Training Workshops.
- Refresher Workshop courses for the duration of five days not inclusive of travel.

## Post-Doctoral Fellowships for Women

The scheme has been implemented for the unemployed women candidates holding Ph.D. degree in their respective subject areas with an aim to accelerate the talented instincts of the women candidates to carry out the advanced studies and research. The number of slots available under the scheme is 100 per year. The tenure of the award is five years with no provision for further extension. The upper age limit for the candidate is 55 years as on 1 July on the year of application.

## Indira Gandhi National Open University (IGNOU)

The Indira Gandhi National Open University (IGNOU) has been making conscious efforts to reach out to the Girl/Women learners especially in remote and rural areas. Setting-up a New School, School of Gender and Development Studies aims at achieving gender justice and equity through developing and launching programmes in the area of women and development studies. Gender Studies examines the existing gender gap and addresses the issue of gender disparity. Women's Studies analyses the status of women in society with the objective of strengthening individual and institutional efforts that enable women's empowerment. The activities proposed by UGC include:

(a) Designing and developing academic programmes and courses at doctoral, post graduate and undergraduate levels.

(b) Conducting research and developing appropriate research methodology; and formulating and implementing training programmes.

## All India Council for Technical Education (AICTE)

All India Council for Technical Education (AICTE) was set-up in November 1945 as a national level apex advisory body to conduct survey on the facilities on technical education and to promote development in the country in a coordinated and integrated manner. To ensure the same, as stipulated in the National Policy of Education (1986), AICTE was vested with statutory authority for planning, formulation and maintenance of norms and standards, quality assurance through accreditation, funding in priority areas, monitoring and evaluation, maintaining parity of certification and awards and ensuring coordinated and integrated development and management of technical education in the country.

In order to increase the enrollment of women in technical education, AICTE has special concessions in the regulations for setting up of new women technical institutions. These include relaxations in the norms for land availability, concession in processing fees, deposits etc. Implementation of the tuition fee waiver scheme for weaker sections has been made mandatory in all AICTE approved institutions.

## Conclusion

Undoubtedly the government has initiated some important schemes and programmes to promote educational development of girls. But they should be properly implemented. It is not possible without the participation of people. Awareness on these flagship programmes must be created, so that beneficiaries can avail the facilities. Apart from that our society as a whole should come out from the traditional set up and understand that girls are equal to boys. They are equally an indispensable part of our society and we should respect and empower them.

## References


- Annual Report, 2013-14, Ministry of Human Resource Development, Govt of India.
- Potential good practices the ICDS experience, Ministry of Women and Child development [online] available at www.wcd.nic.in
- Schemes, Ministry of Women and Child Development [online] available at www.wcd.nic.in

- Best practices for women and child development, Ministry of Women and Child Development, Govt of India [online] available at www.wcd.nic.in
- Sekhar, T.V., Self financial incentive schemes for the girl child in India, 2010 [online] available at www.unfpa.org.
- Annual Report, 2013-14, Ministry of Women and Child Development, Govt of India.
- Dash, M. Education in India: Problems and Perspectives. Atlantic Publishers and Distributers, 2000.

# Chapter – 13

# An Investigation of Gender Inequality and Government Policy Initiatives Towards Girl's Education in Rajasthan

*—Natasha Kuldeep*

## Abstract

*Gender equality is considered as a critical element in achieving social and institutional change that leads to sustainable development with equity and growth. Inequalities between men and women manifest themselves in all areas of development. Inequalities are most obvious in health, education, economic development, violence against women, participation in public life and policy making, social attitudes and gender stereotyping. Gender inequality in education is one important aspect of educational disparity. The Constitution of India provided for universal education to all children up to the age of 14 years; the goal was to be achieved by 1980. While considerable progress has been made in this regard in the decade of the 1990s, much still remains to be done for girls' education. Gender disparity has been a major issue in India's pursuit for achieving the goal of girls' education. In order to overcome the problems faced by girls, several measures have been initiated across the country. This chapter aims to review the present situation of the participation of girls in education in India, with a special focus on gender inequality. The chapter presents a comprehensive review of research studies on participation of girls in schooling. It highlights that the participation of the girl-child is affected significantly due to social attitudes towards their education and by other forms of gender and social discrimination in Indian society.*

***Key Words:*** *Gender inequality, Government Policies, DISE, Girls' Education and Literacy Rate.*

## Introduction

Gender inequality refers to biased and unfair treatment or perceptions of individuals based on their gender. It's a hard reality that women have been ill-treated in every society for ages in India. A woman is considered as inferior to man in our society. In patriarchal society the wives are expected to be modest, meek and dutiful to their husbands and other members of families. She has to live behind the veil and has to face many restrictions by their family and society. A woman has to face this discrimination not only at her home but in schools, colleges, and at their work place also. Even the employed women are not independent in real sense, they may have the liberty of movement but they are always addressed by their kinship position by others. There are gaps between men and women in terms of literacy rate, intra house distribution of food and other means, health benefits received and so on. Men and women are just like the two wheels of a chariot. They are equal in importance and they should work together in life. So, we need to ensure equal status for the girl children as citizens in their own right.

## Objectives

- To find out the current awareness of gender equality in education and the human rights in schools, especially concerning rural girls under fourteen.
- To know the current status of girls' education in the state of Rajasthan.
- To recognise the real reasons that stand against girls' education.
- To highlight the issues of gender discrimination in Rajasthan during the period of study.
- To find out the barriers to girls' education.

## Methodology

The present study is an attempt to discuss the role of the gender differences in the school education in Rajasthan. The study also focuses on the contemporary data on some key parameters of school education in Rajasthan. In this study, secondary data of Rajasthan Education Department Annual Reports has been taken into consideration while investigating on the key parameters of school education in Rajasthan.

## Importance of Girls Education

Napoleon was once asked, what the great need of France was. He answered, **"Nation's progress is impossible without trained and educated mothers. If the women of my country are not educated, about half of the people will be ignorant."** Girl's education plays a very important role in the overall development of the country. It not only helps in the development of half of the human resources, but in improving the quality of life at home and outside. Educated women not only tend to promote education of their girl children, but also can provide better guidance to all their children. Moreover, educated women can also help in the reduction of infant mortality rate and growth of the population.

## Long-term Benefits of Educating Girls

An educated girl is more impactful than an educated boy. Educating girls has a multitude of positive effects for the wider community, as well as the individual woman. Long-term benefits of educating girls are:

- ***Enhanced Economic Development***

Decades of research provide substantial evidence of the link between the expansion of basic education and economic development – and girls' education has an even more positive and productive effect. As the primary enrollment rate for girls increases, so also the gross domestic product per capita.

- ***Education for the Next Generation***

If educated girls become mothers they are much more likely to send their children to school, thereby passing on and multiplying benefits for themselves and society in a positive intergenerational effect.

- ***The Multiplier Effect***

Education has an impact on areas beyond learning, and extends a positive influence in all the areas of a child's life. For example, children who go to school stay healthy; they know how to protect themselves against diseases. Girls' education protects them from the risk of HIV/AIDS.

- ***Healthier Families***

The effect of a mother's education on her child's health and nutrition is so significant that each extra year of maternal education reduces the rate of morality for children under the age of five between five per cent and ten per cent, according to a review of extensive evidence from the developing world.

- ***Fewer Maternal Deaths***

Research has shown that maternal mortality is also reduced by better knowledge about healthcare practices such as use of health services during pregnancy and birth, improved nutrition and requisite spacing between births.

## Background of Gender Attitudes in Education in India

The Indian society is characterised by high degree of structural inequalities with reference to caste, ethnicity, gender, religion, class and various other forms of social exclusion. The inherent networks operate to a great extent and results in deprivation and discrimination. The discrimination has to be considered very seriously while dealing with deprivation or inequalities in Indian society.

Lack of knowledge is a result of denial to access it. The denial is a result of socio-cultural, political and historical processes in Indian society and its social structure, where discrimination is institutionalised through stratification and hierarchy in the form of caste, tribe and gender. When the members of the community are denied the access to knowledge that is imparted through educational institutions of the modern times, the age old socio-cultural processes perpetuated through institutions needs to be challenged. In order to tackle the menace, the Constitution of India has provided certain measures in the form of fundamental rights to promote equal representation of both the genders.

The recent Right to Education Act, is a very new measure, the effect of its inclusion has to be tested in future.

Since education is one of the most important factors for an overall development of an individual and society, it is important to see the status of school education as school education is the foundation for the rest of the education. It is important to consider the level of education while considering the enrolment. As the gender disparities continue to exist in spite of several measures being attempted to overcome the situation, it becomes essential to understand the differentials that exist regarding enrollment in schools.

## Gender Equity in Education: A Review of Trends and Factors

Increased enrollment of girls is widely attributed to the increasing number of "informal" or "non-formal" education programmes, and associated with a public sector that is considered widely to have failed in terms of delivery of quality education. If the increasing enrollment of girls is taking place in an environment of fragmented provision and poor quality public delivery, then the question of deliverance of quality education holds value for the success of current policy and programmatic interventions in relation to closing the gender gap in a sustainable way.

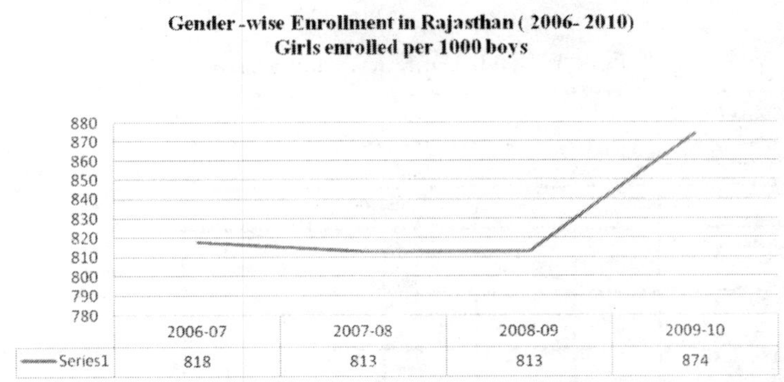


*Source*: Post enumeration survey of 5 per cent sample checking of DISE data in three districts of Churu, Dungarpur and Jhalawar in Rajasthan: 2010-11.

***Fig. 13.1: Trends in Gender-wise Enrollment in Rajasthan, DISE, 2006-10 (in girls per 1,000 boys enrolled).***

The trend in number of girls per thousand boys enrolled in the last four years from 2006-07 to 2009-10 reveals that there was a decline from 818 girls per thousand boys in 2006-07 to 813 in 2009-10, which has recently increased to 874 girls per 1,000 boys in 2009-10.

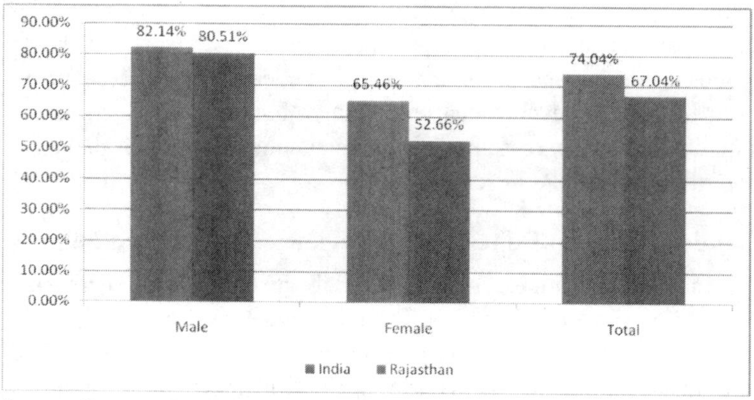


*Source*: Census of India, 2011 (Provisional).

***Fig. 13.2: Literacy Rates in India and Rajasthan by Gender, Census 2011.***

Gender-wise, there is a big gap between male and female literacy. In total literacy, Rajasthan ranks 33rd amongst the 35 states and union territories and in case of male and female literacy it ranks 27th and 35th respectively.

**Table 1: Gender Difference and Education**

| ***Respondents' family education background*** | ***Do you think that gender difference plays a role in education?*** | | | | | | |
|---|---|---|---|---|---|---|---|
| | ***Yes*** | | ***I think that*** | | ***I don't know*** | | ***No*** |
| Uneducated | 3 | 60 Per cent | 0 | 0 | 0 | 0 | 2 |
| Primary | 6 | 66.7 Per cent | 0 | 0 | 0 | 0 | 3 |
| Secondary | 17 | 94.4 Per cent | 0 | 0 | 0 | 0 | 1 |
| Graduate | 51 | 56 Per cent | 14 | 15.9 Per cent | 2 | 2.3 Per cent | 21 |
| **Total** | 77 | | **14** | | **2** | | **27** |

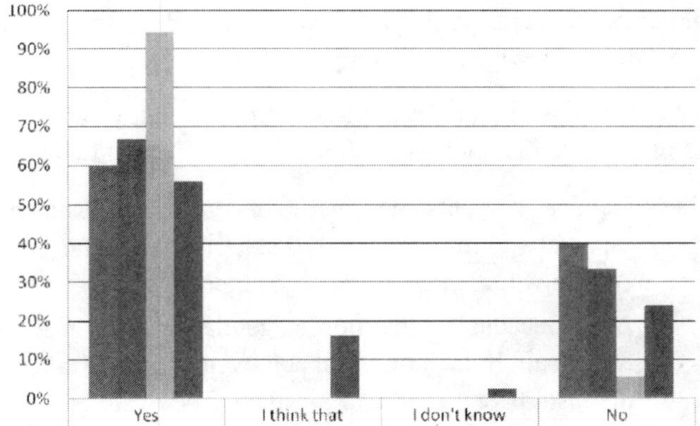


| | Yes | I think that | I don't know | No |
|---|---|---|---|---|
| Uneducated | 60% | 0 | 0 | 40% |
| Primary | 66.70% | 0 | 0 | 33.30% |
| Secondary | 94.40% | 0 | 0 | 5.60% |
| Graduate | 56% | 15.90% | 2.30% | 23.80% |

***Fig. 13.3: Teachers' Opinion on Affect of Gender Difference on Education.***

120 teachers were taken for the sample for the study, out of which five (i.e., 4.2 per cent) teachers were from uneducated family backgrounds, nine (i.e., 7.5 per cent) teachers hailed from primary educated family backgrounds, 18 (i.e., 15 per cent) teachers were from families educated up to secondary level, and 88 (i.e., 74 per cent) teachers were from graduate passed family backgrounds.

Sixty per cent teachers from uneducated family backgrounds said that gender difference plays a role in education in Rajasthan state, while 40 per cent said that gender difference plays no role in education.

Nearly 67 per cent of teachers from the primary level education family backgrounds said that gender difference plays a role in education, whereas 33 per cent found that gender difference did not play any role in education.

About 95 per cent of the teachers from secondary level educated family backgrounds said that gender difference plays a role in education in Rajasthan.

Fifty six per cent of the teachers from graduation level educated family backgrounds said that gender difference plays a role in education while 24 per cent said gender difference did not play a role in education; the rest did not have any concrete opinion.

Yet findings and general opinion suggests that gender difference does play a role in education in Rajasthan. As per findings:

- Gender difference plays a role in education in Rajasthan state especially in rural areas and is associated with the community culture values such as early girl marriages.
- After decades of attention to gender matters in the state of Rajasthan, India, important achievements have taken place in the last 10 years across Rajasthan schools and there is much greater awareness of gender equality as an educational issue than there was in the past.
- Standard economic levels has direct relation with the education level and is an obstacle factor for people to attain or provide education, parents from lower economic level backgrounds have been generally found to focus more on the education of their boys than girls, so bad economic status and high expenses of education renders girls with less chances.

## Barriers to Girl's Education

Factors responsible for the barriers to girls' education in Rajasthan can be categorised according to how one perceives and defines barriers. Some of the barriers are discussed below:

- **Poverty:** The rate of illiteracy is closely linked to poverty. Due to the poverty or low family income, if parents are not in a position to send both boys and girls to school, they usually send boys to schools and retain girls at home to do house-hold work.
- **Parental illiteracy:** The high level of parental illiteracy is also among the constraints of education of girl children. Lack of parental support and poor learning environment at home makes learning for them very difficult. The present education

system does not fit their needs, which leads to stagnation and wastage among them.

- **Number of children:** In poor families generally, there are many children. According to the priority list of the parents, girls' education is not compulsory and boys get a high chance of receiving education.
- **Child marriage:** Many girls in many districts of Rajasthan still get married at an early age, which affect their education to a great extent.
- **Customs and cultural practices:** Many customs and cultural practices hinder the higher education of girls. For example, many parents do not send their daughters to schools after they attain puberty. Purdah system is also affecting education of girls.
- **Nature of habitat:** Most of the tribes live in difficult terrain, forests and remote areas. The dearth of schools in these areas leads to absenteeism among the tribal girl children.
- **Female teachers in schools:** Girls are more interested in going to schools if female teachers are there in the schools. They feel more comfortable and more vocal with female teachers, thus they are able to actively focus and participate in the learning processes. In rural areas also, parents are interested in sending their girl children to school if female teachers are present.
- **Transport facility:** One of the barriers for girl education may be the location of schools which are far away from their homes, particularly in rural areas. Adequate transport system is needed for girls to attend the schools. It will be more convenient for them if school buses take responsibility for pick and drop facility for the girl children. In rural areas, other modes may be tried out.
- **Molestation/abuse in school:** Most of the parents feel insecure regarding the safety of their girl children as instances of abduction, rape, sexual harassment and molestation of girl dampens the enthusiasm of parents and girl students in pursuing their education beyond a certain age.

- **Inappropriate school timings:** In rural areas morning time is not suitable for girl education, as they are engaged in domestic work at homes or in farms and fields during these hours. The enrollment and retention rate may be high when educational facilities are made available during periods suitable to them when they are free from domestic chores.
- **Toilet facility:** This may be one of the reasons of lower participation rates of girls in education especially at upper primary level. The separate toilet facilities for girls must be created in the school premises. This must also cover the security aspect for girls. At the same time, toilet facility is needed for female teachers also.
- **Lack of girls' schools:** Many parents do not want to send their daughters to coeducational schools especially at upper primary level. There is an urgent need to open separate schools for girls especially at upper primary level as a powerful strategy for building a conducive girls' school environment. There must be strong provision of good quality schools for girls if demand is there.
- **Lack of hostel facilities:** One of the obstacles in girl's education is that schools are away from their homes, they cannot avail of this facility by themselves due to lack of hostel arrangements. The girls belonging to SC/ST category would continue their education particularly in rural areas, if they are provided with free or inexpensive residential facilities nearer to the schools.

## Initiatives taken by Government of Rajasthan to Improve Gender Equity in Education

In Rajasthan several major programmes have been introduced over the years to improve the formal education system, and/ or to facilitate access to education. These are:

### (1) *The Non-Formal Education Programme*

The Non-Formal Education Programme (NFE) was introduced as a flexible, low cost and manageable alternative to the formal education structure, which could not provide enough schools and teachers.

People perceived NFE as a potent alternative. A rationale as well as a concept of non-formal education was developed. According to this concept, NFE was supposed to be free from the ills of the formal system, being flexible and sensitive to the children and their needs.

Though the formal system is continuously growing and schools are available in thousands of villages, still lakhs of school age children remain out of primary education. NFE programme was started in 1975 to reach these children. In 1998-99, there were 17,600 NFE centres run directly by the Government of Rajasthan and 2,686 centres by NGOs sanctioned by the Government of India. Children who successfully complete Class Five from NFE centres are eligible for admission to Class Six in formal schools.

### (2) *The Shiksha Karmi Project*

The Shiksha Karmi Project (SKP) was started in 1987-88 after a realisation that Universalisation of Primary Education (UPE) would not be possible in 10-15 per cent of the villages in Rajasthan due to teacher absenteeism alone. The aim of the programme is to provide primary education to children living in remote, hilly and inaccessible areas. In these areas, the project aims to revitalise and expand primary education through resolving the problems of:

- Teacher absenteeism (which is as high as 50-60 per cent).
- Poor enrollment (25 per cent) and high dropout rates, particularly of girls.

The above will be achieved by actively involving the community through Village Education Committees and employing motivated and committed local people, as Para teachers also known as Shiksha Karmis. Currently the project operates in 146 Panchayat Samitis of the State, running 2600 day schools, 4829 Prehar Shalas and 97 Angan Shalas. In these schools there are 6213 teachers and 2,16,084 students.

### (3) *Lok Jumbish Pariyojana*

Programme goals are:

- Providing access to primary education to all children between 5 and 14 years of age.

- Striving to enrol children in regular schools, as far as possible, and in Sahaj Shiksha centres, wherever necessary.
- Ensuring that all enrolled children regularly attend school/ Sahaj Shiksha centres and complete primary education.
- Improving quality of education by emphasising active learning, child-centred processes and achievement of at least minimum levels of learning by all children.
- Creating necessary structures and processes to empower women, making education an instrument of women's equality.
- Ensuring equity in education to all members of the society.
- Modifying, if necessary, the content and processes of education to better relate it to the environment, people's culture as well as their living and working conditions.
- Effectively involving people in the planning and management of education.

Lok Jumbish is innovative not only in its overarching aims of empowerment and participation, but also in its attention to diverse components within the programme. Apart from school mapping and micro planning, at the community level there are women's groups, adolescent girls' forums, residential camps for both girls and boys, a school health programme and a commitment to integrating children with disabilities into mainstream education.

### (4) *Rajiv Gandhi Swarna Jayanti Pathshalas*

The main objective of this scheme is to universalise access to education with the active involvement of the community. Priority groups for this scheme includes: communities residing in remote and inaccessible locations in rough terrain and in sparsely populated areas and SC/ST girls. The Rajiv Gandhi Swarna Jayanti Pathshalas scheme has been operating in areas/habitations where there were still no primary schools. The state government has decided to open 16000 RGSJPs in the whole state, on demand from the gram sabha or the ward sabhas.

The criteria of selection of habitations for opening these schools are:

- Population of at least 200 people.

- 40 or more children in the age group of 6-11 years.
- No school in a radius of one kilometer.

**(5) *District Primary Education Programme***

The District Primary Education Programme (DPEP), launched in 1994, seeks to operationalise the objective of the World Bank Programme of Action of 1992, which envisaged district-specific projects tailored to the districts' specific needs and possibilities. Aiming to be an effective instrument in the universalisation of elementary education, it targets districts with very low female literacy rates.

**Its goals in the state are to:**

- Ensure access to primary schools (either formal or non-formal) to all children.
- Reduce to less than five per cent the existing differences in enrollment and dropout rates as well as in learning achievements between men and women and social classes.
- Reduce overall dropout rates to less than 10 per cent and raise achievement levels by at least 25 per cent.

**(6) *Mahila Samakhya***

Another externally-assisted programme with a specific focus on gender is Mahila Samakhya women's education and empowerment programme being run in rural areas particularly for women from socially and economically marginalised groups. It endeavours to create a learning environment where women can collectively affirm their potential, gain the strength to demand information and knowledge, and move forward to change and take charge of their lives. Mahila Samakhya has reached the poor and marginal women who have been able to overcome social barriers and are addressing issues such as child marriage, child labour, and violence against women. The programme is currently implemented in over 9,000 villages in 53 districts spread over 10 States.

**(7) *Mid-Day Meal Scheme***

The National Programme of Nutritional Support to Primary Education commonly known as the Mid-day Meal programme was launched in 1995. It aims to give a boost to universalisation of primary education by increasing enrollment, retention and attendance and simultaneously improving the nutritional status of students in primary classes. Under the scheme, cooked meals are served with calorie value equivalent to 100 gm of wheat or rice per student per school day.

## Conclusion

The gender differences play a major role in education in Rajasthan state. Improvement in participation of girls in education during the last 10 years, and also increase in enrollment of girls which has been more significant at the upper primary level as compared to primary level, show that progress has been made. Increase in the girls' enrollment especially in rural areas has also been observed. Whereas enrollment of girls in all areas has grown, in rural areas it increased in primary schools and upper primary schools during the same period.

While a large number of girls still face difficulties in entering school and continuing their studies. There is also a significant gender gap in educational participation in Rajasthan, the reasons behind the dropping out of girls from the schools given by parents and society in general are: incapability of the family to undertake girls education expenses, poverty, and the practice of child marriage. The socio-economic status of the families had a direct relation to the girls' education level in the family, that means economic status and culture of the family play a central role in a girl's situation.

To battle the girls' educational wastage, the government and community have to take this issue in a series way and establish the legislation to protect girls against the stereotyped community culture with the help of active programmes.

## References

- Charu Walikhanna, Report of expert committee on gender and education, national commission for women, Deen Dayal Upadhyaya Marg, New Delhi.
- Satya Venkata Siddhardha Kumar, D, Gender Differentials and Social Exclusion in School Education in India, National seminar organised by CSSEIP, on 5th January 2010, p. 2.
- Sen, Amartya. (2004). Social Exclusion Concept Application Scrutiny, New Delhi: Critical Quest.

- Tailor, R. (2007). Participation of Scheduled Castes Children of the Primary Stage in India. New Delhi: Journal of Indian Education.
- Showkeen Bilal Ahmad Gul and Dr. Zebun Nisa Khan, (2014), Assesment and Understanding of Gender Equity in Education in Jammu and Kashmir, International Refereed Research Journal, Vol. V, Issue 1(1).
- Dr. Anamika Girdhar, (2013), Gender Inequality and Sexual Harassment, Centre for Positive Philosophy and Interdisciplinary Studies (CPPIS), Milestone Education Society (Regd.), Balmiki Dharmashala.
- Anuj Bala, (2014), Identity, Society and Gender Inequalities of Women in North West India, Research Journal of English Language and Literature (RJELAL), Vol. 2, Issue 1, ISSN 2321-3108.
- Ibraheim Eldai Mohamed and Dr. Vinita Singh, (2014), The gender difference and education enrollment in Rajasthan, IOSR Journal of Humanities and Social Science (IOSR-JHSS) Volume 19, Issue 2, Ver. V, pp. 06-10 e-ISSN: 2279-0837, ISSN: 2279-0845.
- Ms. Akshay Jain and Dr. Ashok Kumar, (2013), A Survey of Government Policies to Improve the Primary Education in Rajasthan, International Journal of Education and Psychological Research (IJEPR) ISSN: 2279-0179, Volume 2, Issue 3, pp. 133-142.
- Dr. Jitendra Kumar and Ms. Sangeeta, (2013), Status of Women Education in India, Kumar, J. and Sangeeta / Educationia Confab ISSN: 2320 009X, Vol. 2, No. 4, pp. 162.
- Rachna Sharma, (2013), A Study of Socio Economic Status and Educational Problems of Adolescent Girls of Rajasthan, An International Peer Reviewed Scholarly Research Journal for Interdisciplinary Studies, ISSN: 2278-8808.

# Chapter – 14

# What the International Community can do to Ratchet up the Progress on Girls Education

*—Amitaraj Gargey, Shashi Bala Kashyap and Amit Kashyap*

**Abstract**

*Women constitute almost half of the population in the world but the hegemonic masculine ideology made them suffer a lot as they were denied equal opportunities in every field of life. The rise of feminist ideas has however led to the tremendous improvement in women's condition throughout the world in recent times. Access to education has been one of the most pressing demands of these women rights movements. Women education in India has also been a major preoccupation of both the government and civil society as educated women can play an important role in the development of the country. What can the international community can do to ratchet up the progress on girls' education? This chapter explores how investing in girls' education can spur economic development. It also looks at successful models for better educational and economic opportunities for girls and women. The chapter also provides suggestions for the way forward – with emphasis on considering local sensitivities and issues, using different methods to target different aspects of the problem, identifying strategic investments such as expanding the broadband infrastructure, working closely with all of the stakeholders and staying the course with this long-term investment in girls' lives.*

**Key Words:** *Masculine, Improvement, Models, Investment.*

## Introduction

*"If you educate a man you educate an individual, however, if you educate a woman you educate a whole family. Women empowered means mother India empowered."*

**—Pt. Jawaharlal Nehru**

Women constitute almost half of the population in the world. But the hegemonic masculine ideology made them suffer a lot as they were denied equal opportunities in different parts of the world. The rise of feminist ideas has, however, led to the tremendous improvement of women's condition throughout the world in recent times. Access to education has been one of the most pressing demands of these women's rights movements. Women education in India has also been a major preoccupation of both the government and civil society as educated women can play a very important role in the development of the country.

India is poised to emerge as one of the most developed nations by 2020, more literate, knowledgeable and economically at the forefront. No doubt, women will play a vital role in contributing to the country's development. Women power is crucial to the economic growth of any country. In India this has yet to meet the requirements despite reforms. Little has been achieved in the area of women empowerment, but for this to happen, this sector must experience a chain of reforms. Though India could well become one of the largest economies in the world, it is being hindered due to a lack of women's participation. Of the many arguments in favour of girls' education, one of the most compelling from the standpoint of economic development is that that education enables jobs - a key source of economic growth and development.

## Why Educating Girls Matters

In the past few decades, research has shown that there is a clear link between the amount of education a girl receives and her long-term ability to participate in the economy. There are several ways that educating girls leads to economic empowerment.

## Higher Per Capita Income

One way is by securing higher per capita income. The Council on Foreign Relations finds that "*One additional year of primary education alone can increase a girl's future wages by 10 to 20 per cent, while an extra year of secondary school adds another 15 to 25 per cent.*" More broadly, after looking at 100 countries, the World Bank found that "Increasing the share of women with a secondary education by one per cent boosts annual per capita income growth by 0.3 percentage points." A later report, also published by the Council on Foreign Relations adds context to this finding by saying that 0.3 percentage points "is a substantial amount considering that per capita income gains in developing countries seldom exceed three per cent a year."

Even girls who gain only basic literacy can increase a country's chances for economic growth. The World Bank claims that "No country has ever achieved economic growth without reaching a critical threshold of about 40 per cent in its adult literacy rate." In 2013, UNESCO estimated that "*Two-thirds of the 774 million illiterate people in the world are females*", so this is a serious issue. Teaching more girls to read and write does not deal with the fact that so many adult women are already illiterate, but it does have the potential to improve adult literacy in the future. For countries trying to reach the World Bank's target of 40 per cent literacy, ensuring that more girls are literate can, over time, make the goal of economic growth easier to reach.

## More Prosperous Communities

The beneficial economic impact of educating a girl continues into her adulthood in other ways, beyond her ability to earn an income. Mothers with education use the knowledge they have acquired to improve the health of their children and other family members–leading to better maternal health, reduced infant mortality rates, better nutrition for their children and increased prevention against HIV/AIDS. In fact, the World Bank finds that "Women reinvest 90 per cent of their incomes in their families and communities", for acquiring "Food, healthcare, home improvement, and schooling for themselves and their children." As ***Shashi Tharoor***, former India's minister of state for human resource development and former under-secretary-general for communications and public information of the UN, puts it, "*Scholarly studies and research projects have established what common sense might already have told us: If you educate a girl, you educate a family and benefit an entire community.*" As educated girls become women, they become capable of transforming local communities and adding even more to the world's economic prosperity. They also act as role models for other girls, so the next generation can follow their examples and offer their own contributions to economic development.

When the effect that educated women can have on their families and local communities begins to take hold, the results can be dramatic, with gross domestic product getting a noticeable boost. In a Council on Foreign Relations report, ***Barbara Herz*** and ***Gene B. Sperling*** write that "*Girls' education leads to increased income, both for individuals and for nations as a whole.*" Since girls and women represent 50 per cent of the world population, enabling them to participate in the economy helps broaden the employment pool in a given region. The World Economic Forum, in its 2013 annual report on the Global Gender Gap, states that "*Because women account for one-half of a country's potential talent base, a nation's competitiveness in the long-term depends significantly on whether and how it educates and utilises its women.*" The world needs thinkers, leaders and doers more than ever, so neglecting the minds of half the population means foregoing the beneficial ideas, contributions and actions those minds could potentially produce. In economic terms, educating girls increases the potential of human capital and makes the knowledge economy more productive.

## Better Skill Sets

In the past decade, new technologies–like smartphones, tablet computers and cloud computing–have transformed the way we live and interact, on a global scale. Looking ahead, to the rest of the twenty first century and beyond, we can be certain that technology will continue to play a defining role in all our economic futures. Educated girls, equipped with the skills needed to use today's technologies and the not-yet-invented technologies of tomorrow, are enabled to perform jobs of all kinds, including those we can't even imagine today.

Skills development is a vital part of lowering unemployment, increasing gender equality and reducing poverty. The labour market is becoming increasingly dependent on science, technology, engineering and maths (STEM) skills, and there is a growing need, worldwide, for people with information and computing technology (ICT) skills. In fact, computer networking skills will be "The global currency of twenty first century economies", according to the industry analyst IDC, but there is a significant shortage of people equipped with these skills. In Latin America, for instance, IDC predicts that by 2015 there will be a shortfall of more than 296,000 professionals with networking skills, representing a skills gap of 35 per cent.

- Globally, "85 to 95 per cent of jobs will require ICT skills by 2020", according to the European Centre for the Development of Vocational Training.
- In the United States, the Bureau of Labour Statistics estimates that "10 of the 30 fastest growing occupations are STEM occupations, including medical fields."
- In India, according to the online community Silicon India - a professional network with more than 5 million members recently published a list of the "10 Degrees That Employers Adore Most", the report showed that the top nine were all STEM-related: bio-medical engineers, biochemistry, software engineering, environmental engineering, civil engineering, geology, petroleum engineering, management information systems and applied mathematics.

Jobs in the public sector are increasingly dependent on technology too. More and more government services are now available online, in developed and developing countries alike. Women with ICT skills can help develop and deliver these services, even in places where the sexes are traditionally kept separate. In Bahrain, for instance, citizens can now renew a driver's license online. This creates a need for people who can support the online renewals, and women with programming and other computer skills can do the necessary work, either at a government office or from home.

Equipping a girl with even rudimentary ICT skills can make a difference in her productivity when she grows up, especially in developing regions. Just being able to use a smart phone or a computer with Internet access can help women increase output, even in jobs that are traditionally viewed as "low-tech." For women who produce handicrafts or textiles, knowing how to access the Internet can be an efficient way access markets–whether for selling locally, regionally or even internationally–and can offer a pathway to microloans and other banking services, especially in remote areas that may be far from bricks-and-mortar financial institutions. Similarly, women who are involved in agriculture, which continues to be a major part of rural economies throughout the developing world, can use basic ICT skills to access online resources that help them discover new techniques, anticipate weather conditions and understand crop pricing.

Take the case of One World South Asia, the South Asian Centre of One World International Foundation, which uses ICT to promote sustainable development. It has an initiative in rural India, called Life Lines, which lets farmers use mobile phones to record questions and access answers provided by agricultural experts. Participants including 150,000 farmers from 1,000 villages have reported an average 20 per cent to 30 per cent increase in productivity and income.

## Removing Barriers: Programmes that Work

To help girls become educated, we must first remove the barriers that prevent them from attending and staying in school. UNICEF has identified many of the obstacles that girls face. This section explores some of the biggest barriers that girls in the developing world encounter. It also highlights select programmes–not necessarily the most well-known ones–that are working to break down those barriers and can serve as best-practice examples for new initiatives.

## Providing Resources to the Poorest

Eliminating poverty is one of the great challenges of our time and education offers some routes to alleviating poverty. Several countries, especially in Latin America, have what are called "conditional" welfare programmes that aim to reduce poverty by giving money only to people once they have met certain behavioural criteria, generally related to education and children healthcare. The World Bank has found that conditional (and unconditional) transfer programmes can be useful–if well designed and implemented–in addressing gender inequality in education. They highlight Malawi, one of the poorest countries in the world, where a pilot programme provided cash transfers to girls who enrolled in primary schools and kept up their attendance. The two-year pilot led to a significant improvement in girls' enrollment, attendance rates and grades.

Another study, conducted by researchers at John Hopkins University, looked at conditional cash transfers (CCTs) for school attendance in 14 countries. They found that "There is strong evidence of positive effects of financial incentives on improving attendance." The Malawi programme, mentioned previously, and another programme in Guatemala were the only two in the study that specifically targeted girls and the authors are quick to point out that rewarding attendance does not, on its own, guarantee scholastic success. However, CCTs, combined with other interventions discussed in this chapter, could be a possible solution for some countries. Scholarships, which waive fees instead of giving money directly to families, are another way of encouraging families with limited means to get their girls into schools.

### A Healthier Environment

If girls are not well enough for regular attendance, they can fall behind and eventually dropout of school. The WHO indicates that "272 million school days are lost each year due to diarrhoea alone and about 400 million children in the developing world have worms that prevent them from learning." Improving health and nutrition not only increases the likelihood that a girl will attend school but also increases her chances of growing up to be a healthy adult.

The onset of puberty is a critical time to ensure that adolescent girls stay in school. UNICEF finds that "One in 10 school-age African girls do not attend school or dropout at puberty because of the lack of clean and private sanitation facilities in schools." School latrines (if they exist) may have limited privacy and poor hygienic conditions, making it difficult for adolescent girls to be in school.

Two programmes–one in Ethiopia supported by Save the Children and another in Ghana supported by the international organisation Plan International have introduced "girl-friendly" schools. These facilities give girls a private, protected and sanitary space, separated from boys. The Ghana programme uses standalone buildings, with ergonomically designed latrines and rainwater collected from the rooftop and the same schemes has been projected under "Swach Bharat Scheme" in each villages and towns by our Prime Minister Narendra Kumar Modi after coming into power in India in 2014.

## Positive Role Models

As more girls see educated women who are prominent in their careers and their communities–whether selling handmade goods online, teaching children to read, running a company or leading a nation–there is a greater incentive for them to stay in school.

Many countries have instituted quotas for women in political positions. In 1992, India amended its constitution to set aside one-third of seats, at every level of government, for women. What effect did this have on villages in West Bengal? A study by the Harvard Kennedy School of Government and the International Monetary Fund found that, with increased exposure of women in leadership roles, voters increased their approval of women as leaders. It also found that having women role models "raised the aspirations parents have for their girls and the aspirations teenage girls have for themselves." That said, that there was still a lot to do in this area. The UN reports that the global share of women in parliaments continues to rise slowly and reached 20 per cent in 2012, but this was far short of gender parity, although an increase of one percentage point was seen during 2012.

Parents can be particularly effective in ensuring that girls go to school. Programmes that help redefine gender roles and increase gender equality within the family can increase the chances that a girl will get the support she needs to pursue her education. Take the ACEV Focus on Fathers in Turkey, which uses classes and TV programmes to encourage fathers to become more involved in child-rearing. It received a favourable review in a report by the Fatherhood Institute (a UK-based think-tank devoted to issues of male parenting), which found that "although [the ACEV courses are] not delivered from an explicit gender equality perspective, fathers are encouraged to think of the developmental and educational needs of their daughters as well as those of their sons, in what is a relatively patriarchal and sex-segregated society." In this regard, they found that the courses "demonstrated positive change."

### More Schools

If the only available schools are far away, and a girl is forced to travel long distances to get to school, the family may be less likely to allow her to attend. Transportation and the cost of travel can be part of the reason, but personal safety can also be a concern. Building educational facilities that are closer to where girls live can help increase attendance. There are many organisations dedicated to building schools in impoverished or politically and socially turbulent regions, and there are various philanthropic groups and individuals who are interested in establishing schools just for girls and women. Barefoot College is one such organisation and in 2012 became the first NGO to partner with UNESCO's Global Partnership for Girls and Women' Education.

### Barefoot College in Rajasthan, Northern India

Barefoot College, founded in 1975, teaches girls and women practical skills they can share with their communities. The schools are built by and for the poor in rural areas, using local labour resources, and run on solar electricity. They offer classes at night so girls who do household chores or graze cattle, goats or sheep during the day can still go to class. At present, some 7,000 girls attend more than 150 Barefoot College night schools across rural north India. Lessons are taught by Barefoot College teachers and community members, and classes address family and community-related issues.

One programme trains adult women–many of them illiterate or semi-literate–to install and maintain solar-based lighting systems. The six-month course includes techniques on training others, so graduates are able to share their knowledge when they return home and thus serve as role models and leaders. Since 1989, the effort has brought solar electrification to villages in 52 countries. *"Some people object to women working. But if we can add income to the household, that's a good thing, isn't it?"* ***Sita Devi***, Solar Technician, India, a woman with only second grade education, attended Barefoot College to learn about solar cookers. She now has an opportunity to work outside the home and believes the benefits will extend beyond her own generation. *"My daughter must be educated,"* she says. *"She will be able to do things, to progress so much faster than I can because of going to school more."*

Another way to extend access to schools is through broadband, which has changed how we define schools. In the past, learning often took place in large, formal educational institutions. Today, educational programmes that were once reserved for the few are now available to anyone, anywhere, and at any time. Many institutions, especially at the university level, have moved quickly to establish online course work, known as massive open online courses (MOOCs), and the number of enrolled students is going up quickly. There are widely recognised MOOCs available from top-tier universities in the United States (including Harvard, Stanford, MIT and Yale) and noteworthy adult-education and vocational programmes in countries like Brazil, Guatemala, India, Indonesia, Mexico and Japan. At the secondary level, the non-profit online institution Khan Academy aims to provide "a free world-class education for anyone anywhere", and has gained support from the ***Bill*** and ***Melinda Gates Foundation***. In the United States, there are a growing number of tuition-free public online education courses that can take students from kindergarten to high-school graduation. Online courses are typically open to students of both sexes, but the model can be used to develop targeted programmes intended exclusively for girls or women. Also, because online formats can be scaled up fairly quickly, these Internet-based programmes can have a widespread impact in a relatively short amount of time.

## More Teachers

Even if a girl lives in a region with accessible schools, there may not be enough teachers to provide her with a quality education. Schools around the world are suffering from a significant lack of qualified teachers, especially at the primary level. This is partly due to population increases and a lack of funding for new teachers. It is also due to the impact of the 2005 UN Millennium Project, which identifies universal primary education as a goal for 2015 (MDG 2) and has boosted enrollment. UNESCO estimates that by 2015, 6.8 million teachers will need to be hired worldwide to meet the goal, with 60 per cent of those new positions (over four million teachers) in Sub-Saharan Africa.

Assuming adequate broadband infrastructure is available, online courses present a way of mitigating the impact of teacher shortages, given that online formats can connect teachers with students who are some distance away–even on another continent. If course content is aligned appropriately with culture and language, then Internet-based distance learning offers the potential to make more effective use of scarce teaching resources.

While the teacher shortage affects children of both sexes, girls can be particularly impacted because they may not feel as comfortable in classes taught by men. In a recent study the researchers at National Bureau of Economic Research (NBER) found that women can be effective teachers for both boys and girls, and can be particularly beneficial to girls. In some regions, teaching may be one of the few career paths that girls and women are encouraged to pursue, so the teacher shortage underscores the problem that not enough women are being trained to meet the need.

There are many organisations worldwide that train and deploy teachers in underserved regions where girls need help, as for example 'The Teachers without Borders' programme which supports the professional development of teachers on a global scale. This programme has been in operation since 2000, it provides local support for teachers worldwide. Its Certificate of Teacher Mastery (CTM) programme is designed by and for primary and secondary educators and helps teachers expand their professional knowledge, gain classroom practice and become mentors to other teachers. Programme materials are available for free, either online or off, and in several different languages. Since 2010, more than 1,900 teachers have been trained, with nearly 90 per cent of them in Africa.

Tutoring services, which offer after-hour classes in every subject, often for a fee, are growing globally and have already made an impact. Take the case of South Korea. About 60 years ago, after the Korean War, South Korea was a developing country. Today, it ranks as the 19th largest economy. A recent article in the *Wall Street Journal* (by ***Amanda Ripley***) notes that South Korea "now has a 93 per cent high-school graduation rate, compared with 77 per cent in the U.S." It highlights a for-profit online service, founded and run by long-time teacher ***Kim Kihoon***, which makes his tutoring sessions available throughout the country. The sessions are recorded as videos that are posted online, for which students pay a small fee to purchase and view. He answers student's questions online, addressing individual learners directly. The bulk of his earnings were verified at US$ 4 million in 2012 alone, come from the 150,000 students who watch his lectures online each year. A similar online tutoring system, with or without the fee structure, could be implemented anywhere that has adequate broadband access and could be targeted specifically at girls.

## Updated Content

Girls and women are more likely to attend or stay in school when they feel that the curriculum has some relevance to their own lives. In addition to basic literacy and numeracy, schools do well by teaching "life skills" that help girls face everyday challenges. A curriculum that addresses subjects like health, nutrition, HIV/AIDS, and gender equality can make girls (and women) better equipped to succeed. Class material must, of course, be presented in a culturally acceptable way, and with an appropriate level of respect for local sensitivities.

Making the curriculum relevant to present-day realities also includes helping prepare girls and young women to enter the workforce. In some countries, girls' enrollment in education has gone up, but this has not directly translated into increases in labour-force participation or productivity. Various factors, such as labour-market policies, cultural barriers, and lack of childcare facilities for working women, have an effect on this issue, but curriculum plays a role, too. It is crucial to equip girls and women with skills, including ICT that will let them be economically productive.

One initiative that does this is Intel Corporation's informal education programme called Intel Learn. Since its founding in 2004, the initiative has reached approximately 900,000 girls and young women in 16 countries worldwide. It includes more than 90 hours of curriculum that helps participants use digital skills to advance an idea, become familiar with basic concepts of business and propose solutions to community problems. In most areas, sessions are held outside the formal school settings, and the programme has consistently shown a completion rate of more than 90 per cent.

Programmes that teach adult women ICT skills can provide a path to employment, and having access to such programmes can guide girls as they finish their preliminary and secondary educations. Many of the well-established training programmes that teach high-demand ICT skills are available online or in a blended learning environment, and prepare graduates (men and women alike) for industry-recognised certifications. The Cisco Networking Academy is an example. Since its launch in 1997, it has taught ICT skills to 4.75 million students in 165 countries. The global average of female participants is 20 per cent, but in certain areas, including the Middle East, the average exceeds 35 per cent.

Bright, promising students often benefit from individual guidance, which is offered by Digital Divide Data, a digital-content company with operations in Asia and Africa. It recruits disadvantaged high-school graduates, half of them young women, from some of the poorest areas, including the slums of Kenya and rural areas of Laos, and trains them to work in digital jobs. These carefully screened young people provide digital services, such as data entry and e-Book production, to Digital Divide Data's client base worldwide. The company helps its employees learn English and obtain college degrees. Since 2001, it has hired 1,745 young people and has supported 544 university graduates. This kind of sustainable work-study programme can be used elsewhere to teach women digital skills, encourage them to pursue college degrees and help them escape poverty.

## An Effective Broadband Infrastructure

In places where girls and women have broadband access to data and services, it is easier to provide them with the opportunities necessary to expand knowledge, generate ideas and build careers. Having broadband access can also increase gender equality in education, making it possible for female students from any environment–urban or rural, rich or poor, in the classroom or at home–to obtain the same information and services as their male counterparts.

Broadband access has, in fact, become so essential to modern life that the Broadband Commission for Digital Development, a group established by UNESCO and the UN International Telecommunications Union, declared in 2011 that broadband communication "*is not just a human need–it is a human right*", similar to food, shelter and healthcare. The Commission also stated that "the benefits for broadband are profound", especially in education, where it can "[open] young minds to new horizons through educational technology."

Countries that are struggling to grow and develop are beginning to recognise that broadband access is a key enabler and accelerator for growth. Ethiopia, for example, a country ranked number 121 of 144 in the World Economic Forum's Global Competitiveness Report for 2012–2013, has established a Ministry of Communication and Information Technology, with ***Dr. Debretsion G. Michael*** as its head. In 2012, in his opening remarks to the Innovation Africa Digital Summit, he said, "Bridging ICT gap and ensuring the optimal and innovative use of ICT tools will have a decisive bearing on whether or not the implementation of development strategies is a success or a failure. In short, rapid progress for countries such as Ethiopia in this area is not a matter of choice, but of necessity." As an example of the ministry's efforts, he cited a government "school-net programme connecting all secondary and preparatory schools in Ethiopia and enabling pupils across the country to have access to quality education through ICT schools." A few years ago, one might have thought that some countries were too poor to invest in ICT, but there is a growing sense that poor countries cannot afford not to invest in ICT.

A reasonable guideline for broadband infrastructure is the ability to support download and upload rates of 100 Mbps for every 1,000 students and staff members, since this is generally the level that students and teachers need to support the audio and video content involved in digital learning and teaching. Even in developed countries, where broadband access may be commonplace in residences, commercial spaces and private institutions, the public school system may lag behind. In the United States, for example, broadband access is not always available in public education. The San Francisco-based non-profit Education Superhighway is dedicated to closing this digital divide and is working to ensure that every US K-12 public school has 100-Mbps access. Similar initiatives could be used elsewhere to increase broadband access, especially for girls.

## The Way Forward

Women can be instrumental in helping to solve the world's problems. They can help develop new technologies and can come up with better ways to use scarce resources, treat diseases, provide clean water and grow food.

Women also represent half the population. What politician who has the welfare of the population in mind would neglect such an enormous group? What corporation would hesitate to tap into such an enormous labour pool or service such an enormous market? And what community would hesitate to embrace innovative solutions that address critical social challenges?

It is essential that the international community continues to emphasise the importance of educating girls and women, especially in the most disadvantaged regions, so we can continue to pursue the goal of complete gender equality and parity and promote economic development by building on the productive capacity of women. The focus needs to be on removing the barriers that prevent girls and women from getting a quality education or from pursuing economic opportunities. The programmes mentioned in this chapter serve as examples from which we can learn and can be used as templates for new initiatives.

When considering any programme aimed at improving girls' education, especially in developing areas, there are several things to keep in mind:

- ***Consider local sensitivities and issues***

The subject of educating girls is a topic bound up with complex cultural, religious, and national sensitivities and involves issues–physical, cultural, social, technical and financial–that often overlap.

- ***Take a comprehensive approach***

These programmes often work best when they take a multi-pronged approach, deploying different methods to target different aspects of the problem. It may not be feasible to create a single programme that addresses every barrier to girls' education, but an effective programme typically pursues one or more of the following goals:

- Make education affordable for all girls, even the poorest.
- Create girl-friendly schools that are supported by the local community.
- Ensure that girls who are in school get a quality education, with reasonably sized classes taught by well-trained teachers.
- Teach a curriculum that prepares girls to participate in our technology-driven economy.
- Leverage broadband to enable greater access to knowledge and increase employment opportunities.

- ***Identify strategic investments***

Establishing and expanding the broadband infrastructure is a wise investment, since it can generate a number of positive, long-term results for girls and women. Broadband access can improve the quality of girls' education, since it enables widespread, fast access to the latest curricula, subject-matter experts, mentorships and collaborative learning opportunities for the community at large. Investing in broadband infrastructure can also improve economic outcomes for women and their communities.

- ***Work collaboratively***

Education is an evolving process, one that is ideally suited to trying out new models and seeding sustainable strategies. Public–private partnerships can create a larger pool of resources, making it easier to include leading-edge technology in the solution and broaden a programme's scope. That said, implementing this kind of partnership is a complex task given the need to manage a group that includes non-profits NGOs, government agencies, private sector businesses, educational institutions and community groups.

- ***Stay the course***

Educational programmes require a strong commitment from everyone involved (families, communities, schools, government agencies, and the girls and women themselves), especially since results can be slow to materialise–after all, completing primary and secondary education can take more than 10 years.

In every corner of the world, regardless of a country's stage of development, there are countless examples of girls and women who have the imagination, desire and energy to participate productively and inventively in the local and world economy. It is vital that we continue to be vigilant in ensuring a quality education for girls. This fosters the potential of those who will, in turn, contribute to a brighter future for us all.

## References


- See, M. Suguna, "Education and Women Empowerment in India" Zenith International Journal of Multidisciplinary Research, p.199, Vol. 1, Issue 8, December, 2011.
- Education for All Global Monitoring Report, UNESCO Institute for Statistics, 2012.
- Council on Foreign Relations, 2004.
- D. Dollar and R. Gatti, Gender Inequality, Income, and Growth: Are Good Times Good for Women?, World Bank Development Research Group, 1999.
- B. Herz and G.B. Sperling, What Works in Girls' Education, Evidence and Policies from the Developing World, Council on Foreign Relations, 2004.
- Opening Doors, Education and The World Bank, World Bank, 2002.

- "Education For All Global Monitoring Report Fact Sheet on Girls' Education", http://www.unesco.org/new/fileadmin/ MULTIMEDIA/HQ/ED/GMR/images/2011/girls-factsheet-en. pdf, October 2013.
- The Economic Power of Women, Women Investing in Women Initiative, A Project of Calvert Foundation, 2013.
- S. Tharoor, "Why We Should Invest More in the Education of Girls," Forum Blog, December 2012.
- B. Herz and G.B. Sperling, What Works in Girls' Education, Evidence and Policies from the Developing World, Council on Foreign Relations, 2004.
- The World Economic Forum's Global Gender Gap Report, World Economic Forum, Geneva: 2013.
- Networking Skills Gap in Latin America, IDC, 2013.
- Joint Research Center, European Commission, March, 2013.
- United States Bureau of Labour Statistics, Employment Projections, 2010–2020.
- Silicon India (jobs.silicon.india.com), November, 2013.
- Life Lines Program, One World South Asia, 2013. (Note: This is an initiative that is partially funded by Cisco.)
- M. Baird and B. Olzler, Designing Cost-Effective Cash Transfer Programmes to Boost Schooling Among Young Women in Sub-Saharan Africa, The World Bank, 2009.
- R. Slavin, Can Financial Incentives Enhance Educational Outcomes? Evidence from International Experiments, University of York and Johns Hopkins University, 2009.
- Raising Clean Hands: Advancing Learning, Health and Participation through WASH in schools. A Joint Call to Action, UNICEF, 2010.
- Sanitation: The Challenge, UNICEF, 2005.
- S. Lee and B. Kerner, "What Do Menstruating Girls Need in Schools?", Save the Children, A Global Village Journal, January 2013, Issue 9.
- Girl-Friendly Toilets for School girls: Helping Adolescent Girls' IRC under the SSHE, UNICEF, 2006.
- R. Pande and P. Topalva, "Women incharge", Finance and Development, June 2013, Vol. 50, No. 2
- We Can End Poverty: Millennium Development Goals and Beyond 2015 fact sheet (http://www.un.org/millenniumgoals/ pdf/Goal_3_fs.pdf).
- ACE Visa member of the World Economic Forum and this chapter was edited by the ACEV programme's chief executive officer.
- ACEV, 2013.
- F. McAllister and A. Burgess, Fatherhood: Parenting Programs and Policy, Fatherhood Institute, August 2012.

- "School in India Teaches Women to Improve Lives, Towns", PBS NewsHour, www.pbs.org/newshour, 2008.
- "One Man, One Computer, 10 Million Students: How Khan Academy is Reinventing Education", Forbes, 19 November 2013.
- "Global Teacher Shortage", UNESCO, visual.ly/global- teacher-shortage, 2012.
- K. Muralidharan and K. Sheth, "Bridging Education Gender Gaps in Developing Countries: The Role of Female Teachers", NBER Working Paper No. 19341, September 2013.
- Teachers Without Borders, 2013.
- The World Economic Forum's Global Competitiveness Report 2012–2013.
- A. Ripley, "The $4 Million Teacher", The Wall Street Journal, wsj.com, 3 August 2013.
- International Center for Research on Women, 2012.
- Cisco Systems, 2013.
- Digital Divide Data, 2013 (note: the company receives support from Cisco and Cisco Foundation).
- UN press release, www.un.org/apps/news/story. asp?Cr=broadband&NewsID=40191, 25 October 2011.
- Dr Debretsion G. Michael, "Summit Speech", Innovation Africa Digital Summit, www.mcit.gov.et, 2012.
- State Educational Technology Directors Association, www. setda.org, 2012.

# Chapter – 15

# Importance of Vocational Training for Girls' Education

*—Sujata Sinha*

**Abstract**

*Women constitute about 48 per cent of the total population of the country. But, in employment market, out of the 459.1 million employed populations in 2004-2005, women are only about 148 million. In a country like India problems like high level of poverty, early marriages, social prejudices and other discriminatory gender practices and lack of formal education including vocational training, adds to the woes of women hindering their equal participation in the human capital of the nation. Education plays a pivotal role in shaping the lives of individuals. Education enriches people's understanding. It improves the quality of their lives and leads to broad benefits for individuals and society. In order to effectively deal with the fast changing realities of globalisation and economy India needs to develop its human capital of educated and skilled people who are fully equipped to participate in the growth and development of the country. Educating girls and women is probably the single most effective investment a developing country can make. It creates a multitude of positive remunerations for families including better family health and nutrition, improved birth spacing, lower infant and child mortality, and enhanced educational attainment of children. In this chapter, based on secondary research authors have traced the importance of vocational training for girls' education, basing the case on the great success story of Shri Mahila Gram Udyog - an organisation which has paved the way for economic empowerment of women.*

**Key words:** *Vocational Training, Primary and Secondary Education, Content of education.*

## Introduction

*"The future must not belong to those who bully women. It must be shaped by girls who go to school and those who stand for a world where our daughters can live their dreams just like our sons."*

— **President Barack Obama** at the
UN General Assembly, 2 September 2012.

Women constitute about 48 per cent of the total population of the country. But, in employment market in 2004-2005, out of the 459.1 million employed populations, women constituted only about 148 million. Even of this, only about 5 million women are in organised sector while remaining 143 million are in un-organised sector. Female deprivation is particularly acute in India with high levels of poverty, early marriages, social prejudices and other discriminatory gender practices. The most dramatic and telling statistic of women's status is the sex-ratio of the country, that stood at, 908 females per 1000 males in 2012. Differential in mortality is only one of the dramatic manifestations of systematic discrimination against females; it also extends to the food habits and health-care issues amongst the families. It should come as no surprise then that, female literacy and education fall far short of male literacy and education. As per census 2011 an effective literacy rate for men was 82.14 per cent while it was only 65.45 per cent for women, the divide is even greater in rural areas where, as per census, only 58.5 per cent of women are literate as against 78.6 per cent males. Largely poverty and prejudice are to be blamed for the extent of female deprivation and considerably lower status of women in India.

## International Concerns on Gender

Gender related issues have dominated the agenda of policy formulation of governments and other development agencies at national and international levels for past many years. The increasing international concern regarding women's issues and universal primary education paved the way for it being incorporated among the eight millennium development goals. One of the most path breaking initiatives related with women's education was *World Declaration on Education for All*. The landmark declaration was adopted at the

World Conference on Education for All, which took place in Jomtien, Thailand, in 1990. The conference, which had been attended by representatives from 155 governments, 20 intergovernmental bodies, and 150 non-governmental organisations, arrived at a worldwide consensus on the importance of universal access to education and Article (3) 1 of the Declaration pertains specifically to female education.

The 1995 Fourth World Conference on Women, held in Beijing, was another landmark as it reiterated the international concern regarding some major issues such as:

- The persistent and increasing burden of poverty on women.
- Inequalities and inadequacies in, and unequal access to, education and training.

The fourth World Conference of 1995 also called upon governments, the international community and civil society, including NGOs and the private sector to develop a better plan of action pertaining to several gender issues.

This growing concern of gender issues at international level was based on various studies conducted by International bodies during the previous century, which revealed an increasing feminisation of poverty. Compared with men, the number of women living below the poverty line had not only increased between 1970 and 1980 but by 1988, an estimated 60 per cent of poor people were women.

## The Economic and Social Gains from Female Education

Education has come to play a major role in transforming the lives of people. In the current globalised society knowledge empowers people into making informed choices about the course of their lives and livelihoods and acts as the vehicle of positive change inducing growth and development. Women's access to education has an intrinsic value as it leads to greater economic gains. The most compelling argument in favour of greater education for women is that it enhances the capacity of an educated woman to contribute to the economic progress of her family as well as the society. Human capital theory and economic growth theories find a positive correlation between the levels of education and economic status of a country. Through formal academic or even informal and vocational education a proper platform can be provided to raise productivity amongst women and promote entrepreneurship and technological advances which may be driven by them. Better education can play a very crucial role in securing broad economic and social benefits for women in India and improving their income distribution.

## Social Efficiency

Educating women not only leads to greater economic benefits but larger social gains in terms of health and well being of children as well as the whole family. Female education has a powerful effect on the fertility rate (and hence on population growth), the infant mortality rate, the female disadvantage in child survival, and child health and nutrition.

Although great strides have been made by India in the last thirty years as an emerging economy, our performance on gender related issues sadly lags far behind the nearest comparable economies.

**Table 1: Women's Workforce Participation Rate**

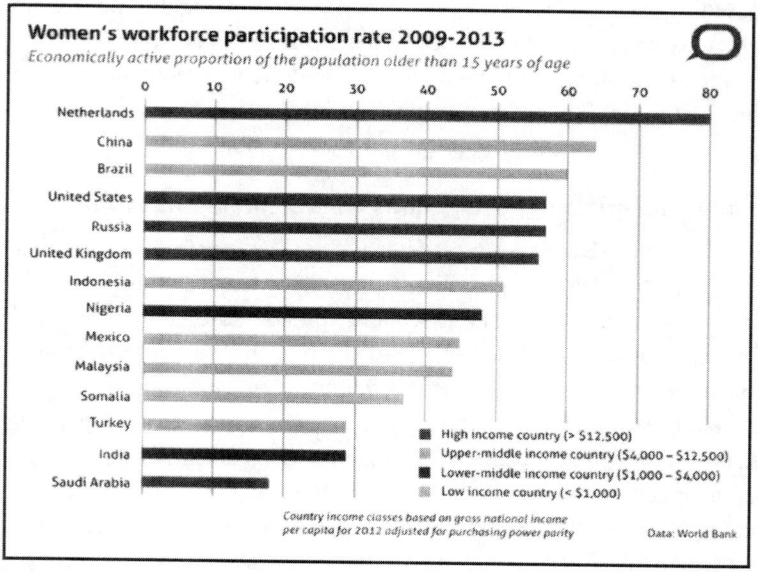


*Source:* Akshat Rathi 'Women in Informal Employment Globalising and Organising'.

As per a World Bank study conducted in 2009-13, India still was found to have the lowest women's workforce participation among the BRICS.

The figures in Table 1 show a relatively bleak picture: we find few states—including Iran, Pakistan and Saudi Arabia—do worse than India when it comes to women's participation in the workforce. Even countries like Somalia, Bahrain and Malaysia do much better. Among the BRICS (Brazil, Russia, India, China and South Africa) which are comparable emerging economies, India has the lowest female participation rate, with only 29 per cent of women over the age of 15 working. As the Table above depicts, even among the MINT countries—Mexico, Nigeria, Indonesia and Turkey—only Turkey has the same participation rate as India.

According to Sher Verick, a senior fellow at the International Labour Organisation the two main factors keeping women at home are social customs and very low education levels. Overcoming societal norms is hard for most women in India particularly with rising concern about their physical safety. In the existing social structures whatever

**Table 2: Worker's set Ratio in some Indian States**

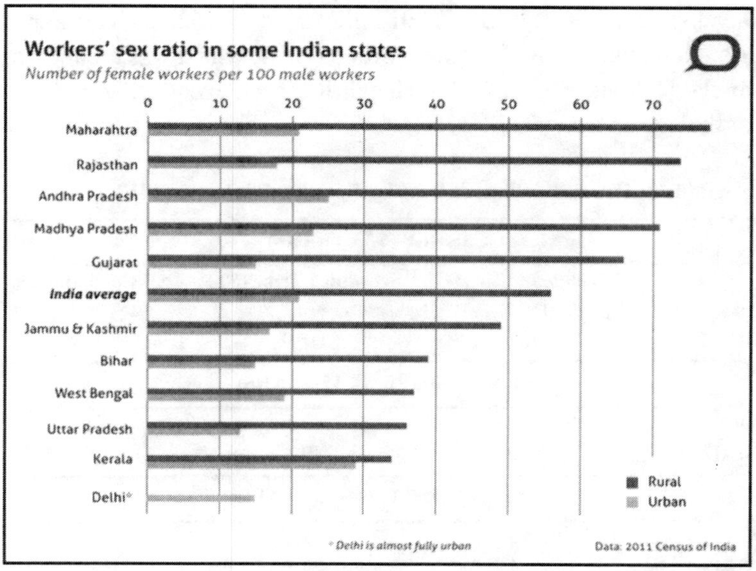


*Source:* Akshat Rathi 'Women in Informal Employment Globalising and Organising'.

work women do is out of compulsion "rather than choice." Table 2 provides a better understanding of the status of women participating in workforce in the states of India.

Table 2 reveals that there are more rural than urban women participating in the workforce in India. We also find that the highest male-female ratio in the workforce comes from the states of Maharashtra and Rajasthan. *Sher Verick* opines that there is a *U-shaped relationship* between education and participation of women in the workforce. She feels illiterates participate more out of necessity. One of the reasons for this situation can be the shortage of skills in what women can do and what is on offer. The much touted economic boom in India has seen growth in sectors like retail, manufacturing and construction which have little to offer for women as employees.

## Status of Education Level of Girls in India

A report on the status of Girls' Secondary Education in Madhya Pradesh on Demand side barriers to girls' education revealed that 'Substantive educational disparities primarily impact girls and women'. The report compiled under the aegis of Department for International Development U.K. (DFID), in 2013 illustrated the status of education through that the Gross Enrollment Rate (GER) which was around 65 for classes 9 and 10, (Table 3). The GER dipped even further to 39.3 for the higher secondary level.

**Table 3: Gross Enrollment Rate by Community, India (2010-2011)**

| | CLASS 1-8 (6-13 YEARS) | | |
|---|---|---|---|
| | **Scheduled Caste (SC)** | **Scheduled Tribe (ST)** | **All Communities** |
| **All** | 117.1 | 119.7 | 104.3 |
| **GIRLS** | 116.9 | 118.7 | 103.7 |
| | **CLASS 9 and 10 (14-15 YEARS)** | | |
| **All** | 70.9 | 53.3 | 65 |
| **GIRLS** | 67.5 | 49.1 | 60.8 |
| | **CLASS 11 and 12 (16-17 YEARS)** | | |
| **All** | 38.3 | 28.8 | 39.3 |
| **GIRLS** | 36.1 | 24.8 | 36.1 |

*Source:* Statistics of School Education 2010–2011 (as on 30 September 2010).

## Vocational Education and Training

For most of the recorded history systematic investment in education was not considered important. Expenditures on schooling, on-the-job training, and other similar forms of investment were quite small but all this began to change rapidly with the forces of globalisation and the emergence of information communication technologies. The last three decades have seen extraordinary expansion in the field of education. Education here refers to 'schooling' or at least some form of formal instruction. The increasingly competitive labour market demands ever-higher levels of education. People without formal education are at a growing disadvantage. In order to meet the challenges of the new globalised world order and the demands of the labour market Government of India lately felt the need to bridge the skills gap and the demands of the rapidly expanding economy by focusing on the development of a proper system of vocational education and training. A World Bank report in 2006 mentioned that while the economic growth had accelerated the employment growth fell during the 1990's and at the turn of millennium. India seemed to face the prospect of a 'jobless growth'. These concerns were addressed in the Eleventh Five Year Plan (2007-2012). Taking cognisance of a growing need, Government of India launched the 'National Skill Development Mission' in 2008-a three-tier institutional structure consisting of:

(i) PM's National Council

(ii) National Skill Development Coordination Board (NSDCB) and

(iii) National Skill Development Corporation (NSDC).

Vocational education and training (VET) focuses on specific trades and imparts the practical skills which allow individuals to engage in a specific occupational activity. VET programmes are aimed at creating employment opportunities and imparting suitable skills for self-employment, particularly in the rural areas and unorganised sectors. There are 17 ministries/departments which administer VET programmes; the Ministry of Human Resource Development and the Ministry of Labour and Employment (MLE) are the two major nodal ministries for strategising, planning implementing and evaluating the VET programmes.

Vocational programmes are offered at secondary and higher secondary levels. Some programmes are also offered at pre-secondary level. Vocational education is offered at school level in grades 11 and 12 in the formal schooling cycle. Vocational training includes institution-based training programmes which fall outside the formal schooling cycle, and is mainly provided through public Industrial Training Institutes (ITIs), private Industrial Training Centres (ITCs) and Polytechnics (both public and private). By 2011-12, there were about 9000 ITIs/ ITCs having a capacity of more than 1.2 million students under the MLE. Additionally there are 1244 Polytechnics with a capacity of more than 295,000 students under the Ministry of HRD (Government of India). There are various other institutes and bodies involved in providing training for the informal sector under separate ministries. Some of these are Community Polytechnics, Jan Shikshan Sansthan and National Institute of Open Schooling. Agencies like Khadi and Village Industries Commission, Entrepreneurship Development Centres, Department of Women and Child Development, and National Renewal Fund also run some training programmes.

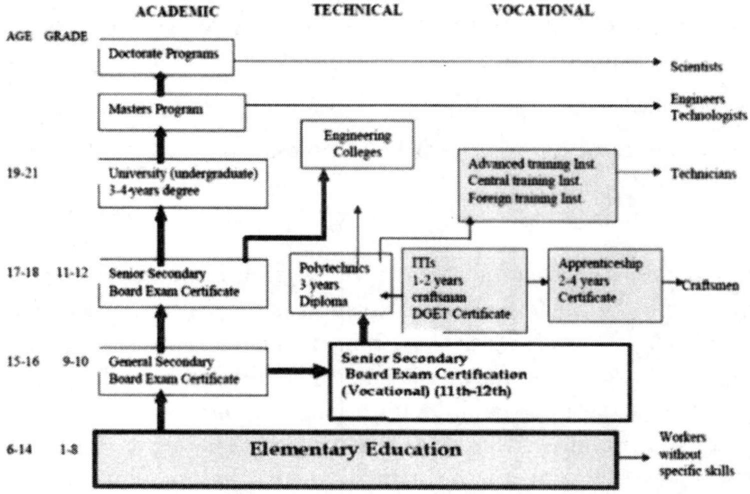


*Source:* Skill Development in India World Bank report 2006.

***Figure 15.1: Current System of Vocational Education and Training in India.***

Under the current system of vocational education is embedded the overall system of education and the two have not been totally segregated. However, with the emergence of new thoughts a lot of research is taking place in the domain of vocational education. Ms. Swati Mujumdar, Director, Symbiosis Centre for Distance Learning in her article 'Need for Vocationalisation of Education in India' has proposed the following model for vocational education. The model is proposed based on her study comparing various education models from across the world. It cuts across the general academic education

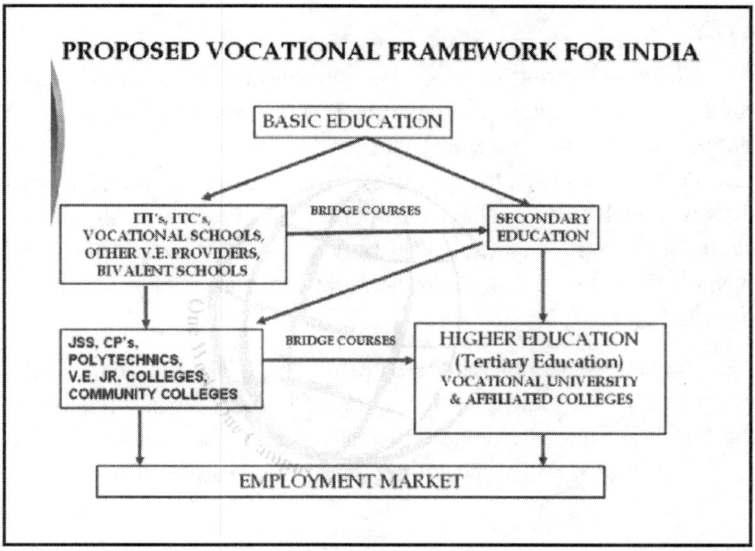


*Source:* India Education Review.

***Figure 15.2: Proposed Vocational Framework for India.***

system with bridge courses; the following model also proposes the establishment of a university.

Educating girls and women is the single most effective investment a developing country can make, whether or not women work outside the home, the socio-economic remunerations of women's education and training are multifarious and can't be ignored.

## Notable Schemes Dealing with the Vocational Training of Girls and Women

### *Jan Shikshan Sansthans (JSS)*

Jan Shikshan Sansthans are revised versions of Shramik Vidya Peeths that cater to educational and vocational training needs of adult urban slum dwellers. They offer close to 225 vocational training programmes ranging from candle and agarbatti making to computer repair. With the expansion in the field of education the base of JSS has been increased to include rural areas.

### *STEP*

With an intention to build the 'job relevant skills' among poor rural women, Ministry of Women and Child Development launched Support to Training and Employment Programme for Women (Step) in 1986-87. This programme addresses the occupational aspirations of poor women who do not have the opportunity of formal skill training. Training and skill enhancement is provided to poor and marginalised women above the age of 16, in the traditional trades largely from the informal sector.

The revised guidelines for STEP in 2014, aims to enhance the reach of the programme by including new trades. Assistance under the STEP scheme is available in many sectors for imparting skills related to employability and entrepreneurship, mostly in the following trades:

(a) Agriculture, Horticulture, Food Processing.
(b) Handlooms, Tailoring, Stitching, Embroidery, Zari, Handicrafts etc.
(c) Computer and IT enabled services along with soft skills.
(d) Skills for the work place such as spoken English.
(e) Gems and Jewellery.
(f) Travel and Tourism.
(g) Hospitality.

## Women's Vocational Training Programme under Directorate General of Employment and Training (DGET)

DGET was designed and launched in1977 for increasing the participation of women in workforce and to mainstream them. The programme which falls under Ministry of Labour and Employment also runs women's vocational training programmes. The vocational training programmes attempt to promote the women employment in industry (mainly in organised sector) as semi-skilled/ skilled and highly skilled workers by increasing their participation in skill training facilities under Craftsmen Training Scheme and Craft Instructors Training Scheme. Programme also offers higher skill training for the Instructors of various skill training organisations. To achieve this objective exclusive Institutes for women have been set up. Apart from conducting trainings DGET also works towards identifying newer areas for vocational training and creating sensitisation campaigns. Taking into account the needs, viewpoints and interests of women, National Vocational Training Institute located at NOIDA, and other Regional Vocational Training Institutes - located at Thiruvananthapuram, Kolkata, Vadodara, Allahabad, Bangalore, Panipat, Jaipur, Mumbai - conduct regular short-term and long-term courses. Some of the regular training programmes being offered at NVTI/RVTIs are :-

- Dress Making
- Embroidery and Needle Work
- Fruit and Vegetables Preservation
- Secretarial Practice (English)
- Hair and Skin Care
- Instrument Mechanic
- Electronics_Mechanic
- Computer Operator and Programming Assistant
- Architectural Draughtsmanship
- Desk Top Publishing

Apart from this the Ministry of Agriculture's Krishi Vigyan Kendra's (KVK) impart training to farmers, women, rural youth and grass roots level extension workers in broad based agricultural production systems.

## Conclusion

There is a constant endeavour from the government and other agencies such as NGO's, SHG's and other local organisations to overcome the obstacles in the Technical and Vocational Education and Training TVET and create a workforce empowered with improved skills, knowledge and internationally recognised qualifications so as to enable them to gain access to decent employment and ensure India's competitiveness in the dynamic Global Labour market. Government of India has set an ambitious plan of training 500 million individuals by 2022 which comes to roughly training of 42 million people an year for bridging the gap between the demand and supply of the labour market. National Skill Development Corporation and several international agencies like World Bank, United States Agency for International Development (USAID), and the Department for International Development (DFID), UK are increasingly considering vocational training to be the launch pad for improving the Human Capital of India by providing a know-how on employment avenues and entrepreneurship.

Every change must be attended with a word of caution and though it is felt that there should be no gender stereotyping in education yet it is equally important to remain contextual to the social milieu of India while designing the content of these vocational education programmes, because many times the desired outcomes from a well meant drive are not delivered. So while opening new avenues for girls in vocational education their social roles and social acceptability must also be kept in mind. It is important to introduce those trades and avenues in vocational education for girls which are not in direct conflict with the socially accepted roles for women.

A pertinent example to back the argument is that of Shri Mahila Griha Udyog (Lijjat Papad) which is today a multi-million dollar entity. It's a sterling story of uneducated women who only knew how to make papad in terms of skills, which they upgraded and established a business model worth emulating. It's a cooperative run totally by women and works on Gandhian principles of simplicity and currently employs about 43,000 women. We need look no further for women's empowerment.

## References


- The role of education in economic development: a theoretical perspective ilhan ozturk Journal of Rural Development and Administration, Volume XXXIII, No. 1, Winter 2001, pp. 39-47.
- http://womentraining.gov.in/general/moreaboutus.htm Extracted on 5 Feb 2015
- SRS Report 2012 . Registrar General and Census Commissioner, Ministry of Home Affairs, Government of India. 19 April 2014. Extracted on 7 Feb 2015.
- http://wiego.org/news/india-has-lowest-workforce-participation-rate-women-among-bricshttp Extracted on 10 Feb 2015
- UN. 1995. Critical areas of concern. In Report of the Fourth World Conference on Women, Beijing, 4-15 September 1995, Extracted on 10 Feb 2015.
- http://r4d.dfid.gov.uk/pdf/outputs/ORIE/W0704_Demand-Side-Barriers-Girls-Secondary-Education.pdf Extracted on 12 Feb 2015
- http://www.ncert.nic.in/oth_anoun/npe86.pdfExtracted on Feb15/2015
- http://www.indiaeducationreview.com/article/need-vocationalisation-education-india (Extracted on Feb15/2015)
- http://www.ideasforindia.in/article. 21/Feb/2015
- http://www.apjce.org/files/APJCE_14_1_15_26.pdf
- http://12thplan.gov.in/12fyp_docs/9.pdf
- http://www.wcd.nic.in/REVISEDSTEPGUIDELINES2014.pdfExtracted on 21/Feb/2015

# Chapter – 16

# Various Government Schemes to Promote Girl Education in India

—*Rajni Bala*

**Abstract**

*According to the Indian Constitution, education is responsibility of Centre and State Government. Women constitute 48 per cent of the total population of India. They can contribute to economic prosperity and national development. But the statistics indicates gender gap in education of girls. Government of India formulated many policies to reduce gender gap in girls' education. This chapter deals with the various schemes and policies formulated and implemented by Government of India to promote girl education.*

***Key Words:*** *Constitution, Prosperity, Development, Gender gap, Schemes.*

## Introduction

Education is considered as an important instrument for the development of a nation. Education is the key to the task of nation building as well as to provide requisite knowledge and skills required for sustained growth of the economy and to ensure overall progress (Kumar, 2012). Only education can reduce women inequalities in society and can improve their status within nation. The principle of gender equality is enshrined in the Indian Constitution in its Preamble, Fundamental Rights, Fundamental Duties and Directive Principles of State Policy. Free and Compulsory education up to the age of 14 is the responsibility of the State and the fulfilment of this responsibility is an important step for the improvements in girls' education and that of gender equality in universalisation of elementary education.

Since independence women education has been a matter of special concern for the government. India's first attempt towards women education was made in 1958 by appointing a national committee under the leadership of Durgabai Deshmukh, which recognised that women's education posed a special problem that required bold and determined efforts to close the gender gap in education. In the first three Five Year Plans, girls' education was shown as a special component with earmarked allocations but was discontinued subsequently. Policy documents like National Policy of Education (1986) and its Plan of Action (1992) emphasised on women education to overcome inequalities and disparities. The chapter titled 'Education for Women's Equality' states:

Education will be used as an agent of basic change in the status of women. In order to neutralise the accumulated distortions of the past, there will be a well-conceived edge in favour of women. The national education system will play a positive, interventionist role in the empowerment of women. It will foster the development of new values through redesigned curricula, textbooks, the training and orientation of teachers, decision-makers and administrators, and the active involvement of educational institutions. This will be an act of faith and social engineering... The removal of women's illiteracy and obstacles inhibiting their access to, and retention in, elementary education will receive overriding priority through provision of special support services, setting of time targets, and effective monitoring.... (GOI, 1986, 1992).

GOI initiated many programmes and schemes like Mahila Samakhya Programme (1989), Sarva Shiksha Abhiyan (2000-01), Sakshar Bharat Mission for Female Literacy (2002), National Programme for Education of Girls at Elementary Level (2003), Kasturba Gandhi Balika Vidyalaya Scheme (2004), The Right of Children to Free and Compulsory Education (Right to Education Act, 2009), so to bring gender equality in education. As per Census 2011, the final population of India is 1210.57 million comprising 587.45 million (48.5 per cent) females with 65.46 per cent literacy rate which shows that all policies have contributed towards the female literacy rate in India

**Table 1: Literacy Rates in India**
**(Figures as Percentages)**

| *Census Year* | *Persons* | *Males* | *Females* | *Male-Female gap in literacy rate* |
|---|---|---|---|---|
| 1951 | 18.33 | 27.16 | 8.86 | 18.30 |
| 1961 | 28.30 | 40.40 | 15.35 | 25.05 |
| 1971 | 34.45 | 45.96 | 21.97 | 23.98 |
| 1981 | 43.57 | 56.38 | 29.76 | 26.62 |
| 1991 | 52.21 | 64.13 | 39.29 | 24.84 |
| 2001 | 64.84 | 75.26 | 53.67 | 21.59 |
| 2011 | 74.04 | 82.14 | 65.46 | 16.68 |

*Source*: Census of India.

The Table 1 indicates that female literacy rate has increased from census year 1951 to 2011. As per Census 1951, the female literacy was only 8.86 per cent, it increased in every census year and in census 2011 it was 65.46 per cent. The 2011 Census has shown that male literacy rate increased by 6.86 per cent, from 75.26 per cent in 2001 to 82.14 per cent in 2011; the female literacy rate increased by 11.79 per cent from 53.67 to 65.46 per cent during the same period. The gender gap which was 21.59 per cent points in 2001 has receded to 16.68. Yet the gender gap still remains much above the targeted 10 per cent. The close look on male-female gap in literacy rate reveals that the literacy gap (16.68) was least in census 2011. But still a lot of attention needs to be paid towards female education so as to overcome the existing literacy gap.

## Mahila Samakhya Programme (1989)

Mahila Samakhya is a scheme for women's empowerment that was launched in 1989 as a result of the new Education Policy (1968). It was created for the empowerment of women in rural areas especially for the socially and economically marginalised groups. The main objective of this programme is to create an environment in which education can serve the objectives of women's equality, where women can seek knowledge and information and thereby empower themselves to play a positive role in their own development and development of society. At present the programme is being implemented in 126 districts of ten States viz. Andhra Pradesh, Assam, Bihar, Chhattisgarh, Jharkhand, Karnataka, Kerala, Gujarat, Uttar Pradesh and Uttarakhand. The Mahila Samakhya programme is currently being implemented in 41,622 villages in 126 districts covering 638 Educationally Backward Blocks (EBBs) in these 10 States. The programme reaches out to close to 1.4 million rural poor women, mobilised into 50,900 village level collectives called Mahila Sangha.

**Sarva Shiksha Abhiyan (2000-01)**

Sarva Shiksha Abhiyan was an importance step of GOI towards achieving the goal of Universalisation of Elementary Education (UEE) by providing elementary education to all children in the age group of 6-14. It also focuses on girl education by providing following provisions:

- Free textbooks to all girls up to class VIII.
- Separate toilets for girls.
- Back to school camps for out-of-school girls.
- Bridge courses for older girls.
- Recruitment of 50 per cent women teachers.
- Early childhood care and education centres in/near schools.
- Convergence with ICDS programme.
- Teachers' sensitisation programmes to promote equitable learning opportunities.
- Gender-sensitive teaching-learning materials including textbooks.
- Intensive community mobilisation efforts.
- Innovative fund per district for need based interventions for ensuring girls' attendance and retention.

## Saakshar Bharat Mission for Female Literacy (2002)

National Literacy Mission launched in 1988 for adult education was in operation till 31.3.2012. By the end of 10th Five Year Plan (2002-2007), 127.45 million people had become literate, of which 60 per cent were females. Saakshar Bharat is the new variant of the National Literacy Mission. Now Saakshar Bharat Programme has been included in the XIIth Five Year Plan (2012-17). Saakshar Bharat is the world's largest adult education programme which aims to make 70 million adults literate by 2017. The main focus of the programme is on women, SCs, STs, minorities and other disadvantaged groups. The Mission has four main objectives:

(i) Impart functional literacy and numeracy to non-literate and non-numerate adults.

(ii) Enable the neo-literate adults to continue their learning beyond basic literacy and acquire equivalency to formal educational system.

(iii) Impart non and neo-literates relevant skill development programmes to improve their earning and living conditions.

(iv) Promote a learning society by providing opportunities to neo-literate adults for continuing education.

## National Programme for Education of Girls at Elementary Level (2003)

It is an important step of Government of India, to reach the "Hardest to Reach" girls, especially those not in schools. It is part of Sarva Shiksha Abhiyan. The scheme focuses on developing a "model school" in every cluster with more intense community mobilisation and supervision of girls' enrollment in schools. Under this scheme model cluster schools should be equipped with additional infrastructure facilities like:

- Additional class rooms
- Drinking water facilities
- Toilet facilities
- Electrification
- Child friendly elements

The National Programme for Education of Girls at Elementary Level (NPEGEL) needs to be focused on blocks with Rural Female Literacy Rate (RFLR) below 30 per cent as per 2001 Census as well as the existing criteria of the scheme, (i.e. educationally backward blocks or EBBs) where the level of rural female literacy is less than the national average and the gender gap is above the national average; in blocks of districts which are not covered under EBBs but are having at least five per cent SC/ST population and where SC/ST female literacy is below 10 per cent; and also in select urban slums. NPEGEL was implemented in 61 Educationally Backward Blocks (45 during 2003-04 and 16 during 2005-06) of 17 districts and four urban slums of four districts where the gender gap is more than the national average of 21.59 per cent and rural female literacy rate is less than 46.13 per cent. Gender sensitisation of teachers, development of gender-sensitive learning materials and provision of need-based incentives like escorts, stationery, workbooks, sports and uniforms are some of the endeavours under this programme. Up to June 2012 under NPEGEL around 41,779 model cluster schools have been developed in 3,353 blocks of 42 districts covering about 41.2 million girls through different strategies. Around 2065 ECCE centres are operational to relieve girls from sibling care and facilitate in attending the school.

## Kasturba Gandhi Balika Vidyalaya (2004)

The KGBV scheme was launched by Ministry of Human Resource Development (MHRD) in July 2004 for setting up residential schools at upper primary level for girls belonging to Scheduled Caste (SC), Scheduled Tribe (ST), Other Backward Caste (OBC) and Minorities in Educationally Backward Blocks (EBBs). KGBVs can be opened in Educationally Backward Blocks (EBBs), previously defined on a composite criteria of blocks with a rural female literacy rate below the national average (46.13 per cent: Census 2001) and gender gap in literacy higher than the national average (21.59 per cent: Census 2001). The criterion of eligible blocks was revised with effect from 1st April, 2008 to include the following:

- EBBs with rural female literacy below 30 per cent; and
- Towns/cities having minority concentration (as per the list identified by Ministry of Minority Affairs) with female literacy rate below the national average (53.67 per cent, Census 2001).

In view of the targeted nature of the scheme, 75 per cent girls from SC, ST, OBC or minority communities would be accorded priority for enrollment in such residential schools and only thereafter, 25 per cent girls from families below poverty line.

Initially it ran as a separate scheme, but was merged with the SSA programme with effect from 1st April, 2007. With the RTE Act, 2009 coming into force with effect from 1st April 2010, and the SSA Framework of Implementation being revised to correspond to the RTE Act, the KGBV component of SSA would also be implemented in the overall context of child rights and child entitlements and in harmony with the spirit and stipulations of the Act.

**Table 2: Category-wise Girls Enrollment in KGBVs**

| | ***Status of KGBV*** | ***Status per cent wise*** |
|---|---|---|
| Total KGBV Sanctioned | 3609 | - |
| Total KGBV Operational | 3602 | 99.81 per cent |
| KGBV yet to be Operate | 7 | 7 0.19 per cent Gap |
| **Enrolment Category wise:** | | |
| SC Girls Enrollment | 105934 | 30.46 per cent |
| ST Girls Enrollment | 85793 | 24.67 per cent |
| OBC Girls Enrollment | 108807 | 31.29 per cent |
| Minority Girls Enrollment | 24244 | 6.97 per cent |
| BPL Girls Enrollment | 22947 | 6.60 per cent |
| **Total Girls enrolled** | **347725** | **93.9 per cent** |

*Source*: Annual Report, 2013-14 Ministry of Human Resource Development.

The Table 2 reveals that total 3609 KGBVs have been sanctioned, out of which 3569 are operational. Total 93.9 per cent girls are enrolled in KGBVs. The enrollment percentage of girls belongs to other backward classes is highest i.e. 31.29 per cent, followed by Schedule Caste girls with 30.46 per cent and Schedule Tribe girls with 24.67 percentage. 6.97 per cent minority girls and 6.60 per cent girls are enrolled in KGBVs who are below poverty line.

## National Scheme of Incentive to Girls for Secondary Education (2008)

The Centrally Sponsored Scheme "National Scheme of Incentive to Girls for Secondary Education" was launched in May 2008. The main objective of this scheme is to establish an enabling environment to reduce the drop-outs and to promote the enrollment of girl children belonging mainly to SC/ST communities in secondary schools. The scheme covers:

(i) All girls belonging to SC/ST communities, who pass VIII and

(ii) All girls who pass VIII examination from Kasturba Gandhi Balika Vidyalaya (irrespective of whether they belong to SC/ST) and enroll in class IX in Government, Government-aided and local body schools.

According to the scheme, a sum of Rs 3000 is deposited in the name of the unmarried eligible girls as fixed deposit, who are entitled to withdraw it along with interest after attaining 18 years of age and passing X class examination. Canara bank is the implementing agency for the scheme. During the period from 1st January, 2013 to 31st March, 2014 an amount of 99.02 crores have been sanctioned covering 3,30,076 girl students.

There are many initiatives taken by Government of India to ensure participation of girl students in higher secondary and higher education. In order to reduce gender gap in higher education following schemes have been started by the Government of India:

## Indira Gandhi Scholarship for Single Girl Child for Pursuing Higher and Technical Education

The main purpose of this scheme is to support higher education of girls who are the single child of their parents. Girl students up to age of 30 years at the time of admission of postgraduate courses are eligible for the scholarship of Rs 2000 per month for 20 months.

## Scheme of Construction and Running of Girls Hostel for Students of Secondary and Higher Secondary Schools

The focus of this scheme are girl students in the age group of

14-18 of class IX-XII belonging to Schedule Caste (SC), Schedule Tribe (ST), Other Backwards Classes (OBC) and minority communities and BPL families. The scheme promotes secondary and higher secondary education of those girls who left the school due to long distances from school, parents' financial problem and other connected societal factors. The main objective of this scheme is construction of a hostel with capacity of 100 girls in each of about 3500 educationally backward blocks in country. Girls passing out of KGBVs are given preference in admission in these hostels. At least 50 per cent of girls' students should be from SC, ST, OBC and Minority Communities.

### Post-Doctoral Fellowships for Women

This scheme is implemented by UGC for unemployed women candidates holding Ph.D. degree in their respective subjects who want to do advance research. Under this scheme 100 slots per year are available. The tenure of this fellowship is five years. The upper age limit for candidate is 55 years as on 1 July on the year of application.

### Conclusion

Education as a universal human right is recognised by every country. Its important role in facilitating social and economic progress of a nation is highly recognised. In pursuance of the provisions contained in the National Policy on Education, 1986 and the Programme of Action, 1992, several schemes were adopted to promote education of girls. In order to bridge gender gap, Government of India has provided various incentives like free education, free books, dress, hostel facilities and various scholarships etc., under these schemes. Education is the only strong weapon which can reduce gender and social inequalities significantly.

## References


- 10th Joint Review Mission of Sarva Shiksha Abhiyan, 20th to 31st July, 2009, MHRD, Government of India, New Delhi.
- Annual Report, Department of School Literacy and Education, 2011-12, MHRD, Government of India, New Delhi.
- Annual Report, Department of School Literacy and Education, 2012-13, MHRD, Government of India, New Delhi.

- Chapter on Elementary Education (SSA and Girls' Education) for the XIth Plan Working Group Report, Department of School Education and Literacy, MHRD, Government of India, New Delhi.
- Kumar, D.S. (2012). Recent reforms in education in India – Achievements and unfinished tasks. International Journal of Social Science and Interdisciplinary Research, 1 (8), 82-95.National Evaluation of KGBV Programme, 2013, Government of India, New Delhi.
- National Policy on Education and Programme of Action, 1986 and 1992, Department of Education, MHRD, Government of India, New Delhi.
- Ramachandran,V. (1998). Girls' and Women Education Policies and Implementation Mechanism, Case Study: India, Planning and Sector Analysis Bangkok: UNESCO Principal Regional Office for Asia and the Pacific.
- Ramachandran, V. (2003). Paper commissioned for the EFA Global Monitoring Report 2003/4, The Leap to Equality.
- Report on Adult Literacy and Education in India by Karla Kevin.
- Report to People on Education, 2011-12, MHRD, Government of India, New Delhi.
- Swain, P.K., and Tripathy, S.N. (2006). Unequal treatment to women and gender-bias. Sonali Publications, New Delhi.
- The Streering Committee on Elementary Education and Literacy For the Eleventh Five Year Plan, 2007-12, Planning Commission, Government of India, New Delhi.
- Working Group Report of the Development of Education of SC/ST/ Minorities/Girls and other Disadvantages Group for 11th Five Year Plan, 2007-2012, Planning Commission, Government of India, New Delhi.

# Index